AF422113

MASCULINE

MASCULINE

Stories from Bad Clown Books

L. Christopher • Daniela Clemens
T. E. Cole • Parker Durrance
Brock Eldon • Silvia Fonseca
Bob Graham • Nate Hanrahan
LaTesha Harris • R. A. Hinkle
E. L. Jacobs • Simon Johnson
A. A. Kostas • Clifton Joseph Lee
J. T. Morel • Spencer Oakes
Peyton Popp • Antoine Robertson
Rasmus Rosenkrantz • J. M. Son

Bad Clown Books
badclownbooks.com

Copyright © Bad Clown Books, Limited Co. 2026

Each story belongs to their writer. Used by permission. All rights reserved.

Epigraph comes from "In Response to Mr. Frost" and "Boys Again" in *Dust* (2023) by E. L. Jacobs. Used by permission. All Rights Reserved.

Edited by Christian Ham and R. A. Hinkle
Cover design by Matt Crenshaw
Bad Clown Books colophon by Carson French

Cataloguing-in-publication data
Paperback ISBN: 979-8-9-922149-4-9
E-book ISBN: 979-8-9922149-5-6

Bad Clown Books is happy to offer great discounts for bulk purchases by prisons, schools, and various nonprofits, book clubs, etc. Please contact us at: badclownbooks@gmail.com

This is a collection of fiction. Names, characters, places, and situations are either the product of a contributor's imagination or used fictitiously.

First Printing Edition (2026)

Contents:

Letter from the Publisher

For the purpose of this book, the masculine is understood as an energy related but not bound to gender. Everyone encounters the masculine outside of and within themselves.

Twenty stories were selected for this collection. Of the submissions we received, we chose the stories based on their ability to display a kernel of the masculine experience in a way both original and precise. Ultimately, this resulted in a book that features less violence, machismo, and assertion than you may expect.

The stories in this book are special. Some of them are written in the style of a feel-good story but with more darkness and complexity—see our opening story *The Stainless Steel Hubcap Principle* by J.M. Son. Others bear the flaws of the masculine open wide—often not without also giving hope for repair. (See: *I Never Liked Men* by Silvia Fonseca.) Boys become men, men and sons deal with the consequences of their unchecked power, a father looks at his daughter and sees himself, friends feel feelings for one another they've never known in romance, priests drink beers, romantics fix machines—and they ride them.

Responsibility is evaded. Death and grief are faced. As Spencer Oakes introduces his story, *Machete Man*, so too with the whole of this book: *The style of [these stories] is not that of a romance. The love story, however, is inescapable.* Ultimately, this is not a book about the masculine but a great attempt to capture the whole of human experience.

Much credit is due to the writers of the stories. They put up with our many requests for edits, random emails, sometimes even video calls. We are a new press, and we often behave that way, but these writers responded to our inexperience with patience and excellence.

Perhaps the most exciting thing about this book is the fact that this will be the first time many of the writers' work will appear in print. Even more exciting, and we are proud to say, they deserve it. This book is for them and now it is for you. We gave a lot of thought to the order of these stories but read them in any order you like. We doubt you will be disappointed.

There are stories of violence, of course, but there are stories of tenderness, too. Stories of fathers and sons (and daughters) trying to relate to one another and find themselves. Stories of love (and motorcycles). Stories of labor, of identity, and of place.

Each story within this collection holds its own ability to challenge, to encourage, to lament, to revere those traits which are categorized within the masculine identity.

Matt, Christian, and Trey
March 2026

Let there be peace, in the pines of the east.
Come to me Eden, don't sink to your grief.

Gold are the flowers, emerald the earth,
violent the sunlight that grapples for worth.

Conjure your storm clouds, rise like a gale,
darkness takes turn, and the gold rays prevail.

***

Like boys again, we climbed the tree,
in the midst of father's farm.
Blood no longer crowned our knees,
there're layers to the harm.

...

MASCULINE

The Stainless Steel Hubcap Principle

J. M. Son

They're up to highway speed, heading east through Bohemia on Route 454, when the boy spots a chip of light winking in a weedy field across from MacArthur Airport. He half-stands in his seat, craning forward for a better look. The junk man eases off the accelerator, waiting, a Chesterfield King hanging from his lip. After so many miles scrounging for scrap, they speak body English.

As they near the field, the boy knows what it is.

Hubcap! he says, with a level tablespoon of enthusiasm—hopefully enough to avoid The Look for not respecting the stainless steel hubcap principle: A hubcap might be worth only a buck or two, but that's how you make a living as a junk picker. Even with the higher prices because of the Ayatollah's bullshit in Iran, you could get a couple gallons of gas out of the deal or a few packs of cigarettes.

Even so, it seems nuts—slowing down suddenly enough to snap your neck, and for what? There's already a loaded dumpster waiting down the road behind Advanced Avionics that could hold a jackpot: the real goodies, like aluminum, copper, and brass from the aircraft gizmos they make at the factory.

Hang on, the junk man says.

He lifts his foot off the gas pedal and downshifts to engine brake—hard. The V8 in the wide, boxy International Harvester step van growls like a junkyard dog as it soaks up momentum through the drivetrain. The engine turns into a massive air pump fighting to breathe, hammering pressure waves down into the exhaust system: *Brrrrr,* like the biggest fart from the biggest dinosaur ever. That's what the boy thinks when they engine brake, and it always makes him smirk. He and the junk man both pitch forward in their seats as the van slows down.

"Inertia! Newton's First Law," the boy says in his head to an imaginary interviewer from *Analog Science Fiction and Fact,* who frequently taps him for his gift at explaining physics to the layman. "A body in motion tends to stay in motion unless an external force is applied. Force equals mass times acceleration. Do you understand now?"

Newton fills his head like steam in a pressure cooker. Since tearing through a book called *Einstein's Universe* the previous three nights, he sees physics everywhere. It is truly the most amazing shit he's ever learned. Like he can't wait to tell someone about it and release the steam.

Sonofabitch! the junk man says loudly.

They've overshot the point on the shoulder nearest the hubcap. The junk man pulls over, half on, half off the road, slips the tranny into reverse, and backs up slowly. A tractor-trailer blasts its horn as it passes, so close the side mirror shudders in its slipstream.

Aw, suck my cock! the junk man shouts, flipping the driver the bird.

The boy hears *weeohhh* as the truck passes, rising in pitch as it approaches, then falling as it recedes and the sound waves stretch out again. Doppler Effect! He remembers from the book that the *ohhh* part is like the redshift in light from galaxies speeding away from Earth at a million miles an hour, carried by the expansion of space itself, which is so cool he can hardly believe it.

The International lurches to a stop, and the junk man nods toward the boy, lasers him with his eyes: it's The Look.

Hey, sonny boy! Stop daydreaming and get your ass in gear.

The boy buttons up his coat, grabs his canvas work gloves off the dash, and reaches for the latch on the cab door.

But he hesitates. The van still juts into the road. What if the trucker hadn't swerved in time and sheared off the whole goddamn left side? Splattered his old man in his seat? Then what?

Shouldn't we be more on the shoulder? he asks the junk man.

What? Oh Jesus. You worry about everything. You're like a woman. He flicks his eyes toward the field. *Make sure you reconnoiter that other pile out there.*

Reconnoiter—one of the junk man's World War Two words, picked up in New Guinea where he unloaded cargo ships. He was always saying "reconnoiter" this, "reconnoiter" that.

The boy rolls back the heavy steel door, hops off the step well, and jogs into the weeds. He can feel his father's eyes on him. Watching for that "pep in his step." Checking if he's "hitting it with a grand enthusiasm." Making sure he's not being "lackadaisical" about "making a buck." All that shit he always says.

The boy grabs the hubcap and heads for the nearby pile. He rifles through scraps of plywood roofing, 2-by-4 cutoffs, and other worthless crap they can't sell. On the way back to the truck, a flash of canary yellow catches his eye—a Hot Wheels Camaro in the weeds, missing its driver's side door. Without breaking stride, he bends to snatch it and slips it into his coat pocket before his father can see.

As he climbs into the van, the boy frisbees the hubcap into the back and drops into his seat. *Just the hubcap,* he reports, eyes forward, back straight, expecting to hear something like, "Good man."

A second later, he realizes what he's done—but it's already too late. The junk man palms the gearshift knob, starts to slot it into first, then stops.

What do you mean, just a hubcap?

What do I mean? the boy says.

You said just a hubcap.

He wants to say, no, he didn't say just "a" hubcap. He said just "the" hubcap. Meaning there was nothing else in the field worth a dime, but the words are stuck in his throat. Eyes locked on the tops of his boots, he starts the counting. Wiggles his left ear once, right ear once—twos are no good. Wiggles the left again, making three. Threes are good, though five would be better. He's on his way to seven when the junk man interrupts.

If you were walking down the street and saw a nickel on the sidewalk, would you pick it up?

Oh Jesus, here we go again. Yeah, he'd pick it up. Why not? Does the old man think he's an idiot or something?

Yeah, sure I'd pick it up.

That's the spirit, the junk man says, and the boy sits up a little straighter and lights a cigarette.

Alright, enough of this bullshit, the junk man says. *Let's get to that dumpster tout suite. And knock off the daydreaming, you hear me?*

Yeah, I hear you.

***

The industrial park isn't far up the road, and soon they're turning into the paved alley behind Advanced Avionics, where the dumpster fills the space between two big bay loading doors. The junk man pulls alongside, leaving enough room for the boy to toss out any goodies he finds without hitting the van. It's usually a random mix of unrecyclable junk and some salable scrap, with the occasional jackpot.

The boy hops out and takes a deep lungful of the moist, cold air. The sky is uniformly gray, and he feels a flake of snow land on his forehead.

The dumpster is a 40-yard roll-off, so the boy takes a running start, launches himself up the side like a long jumper, and perches on a side rib to look over the top. One glance down, and the knot in his gut says it's too late.

Some other sonofabitch got there first.

Below, the junk man adjusts his cap and hikes one leg of his faded work blues—the uniform that the fuel oil company issued to him when he drove for them last winter—up on the front bumper of the van. He fishes a Chesterfield out of his breast pocket and lights it.

Well?

Hold on, the boy says, stalling. He drops into the dumpster and rummages through cardboard boxes and pieces of wooden shipping containers. Relieved, he finds a banged-up 100-amp breaker box and some odds and ends of galvanized pipe with electrical cable still inside, which he drops over the lip of the dumpster.

Jesus Christ, is that it? the junk man asks.

There's nothing else here, the boy says.

Oh for Christ's sake. The junk man turns away from the boy, his gaze caught by something at the end of the alley. Beyond a tall chain-link gate, a smaller dumpster sits on the asphalt. New. Freshly painted orange. The gate is cocked open.

Go reconnoiter, the junk man says, gesturing with his head.

What's wrong with him? Can't he see that the other dumpster is inside the gated area? PRIVATE: ADVANCED AVIONICS PERSONNEL ONLY.

Okay, the boy says. He climbs down off the dumpster and heads for the gate, snowflakes ticking against his face. He starts counting them, but stops. Don't be lackadaisical. Don't be afraid. Don't be a womanly worrier.

He glances left and right like a TV-show burglar, slips through the gate, and spots the white lettering on the dumpster's end door: Sullivan Metal Recovery. How will he tell his father?

The junk man calls Sullivan *that thieving Irish sonofabitch.* He's been cutting deals all over Long Island. Places like Advanced Avionics set aside their metal recyclables in exchange for a cut of the final weigh-and-pay.

The boy jumps up and braces on the lip of the dumpster with both hands, gymnast-style, and looks down.

Holy shit, he says, drops to the ground, and gestures *come here* to the junk man, who quickly drives the van over.

Circuit boxes, like that other time, the boy tells him.

What? the junk man asks. *What did you say?*

Cast aluminum boxes. For circuit boards. Hundreds. Wiring harnesses—

No shit? Okay, quick, quick, let's go!

But the boy just stands there next to the dumpster.

Did you hear me? the junk man says.

It's one of Sullivan's.

The junk man gives him The Look. The *you-are-an-idiot* look.

So what?

The boy's eyes stay fixed on his boot tops.

What if Sullivan calls the cops?

He won't.

What if he calls the guys at the scrap yard?

He won't say anything. Those greedy bastards will make a lot more than we will.

The boy hesitates. Tears start to pool as he speaks, but he keeps his head down.

What happens to me if you get arrested? the boy says.

Enough already! the junk man shouts, and the boy flinches. *I'm your father. Do what I tell you!*

He turns his back on the boy and swings open the big rear loading doors of the International. The boy follows suit, unlatching the heavy end door to Sullivan's pot of gold.

Then he works like a robot: carries out armload after armload of aluminum circuit boxes, which they will strip clean of steel screws and connectors to get the best price. Bunches of wiring harnesses they'll burn, then shake off the fine ash until only a dense fistful of copper wire remains.

Then it's done. The boy closes and latches the dumpster as the junk man swings up into the driver's seat and fires up the engine. The boy joins him.

Let's get to the Chinese place and eat, the junk man says, not looking at the boy. He flips on the wipers and sits for a moment.

The boy stares at the tops of his shoes.

I won't get arrested, sonny boy, he hears the junk man say. *We're just taking back what Sullivan took from us. Do you understand?*

Yeah, I get it.

***

The Jade Palace is a cheap takeout place that gives good portions. They'd had Hungry Man roasted turkey TV dinners the previous day for Thanksgiving, but the Chinese food is the junk man's real treat. For him, takeout food is not a sometimes—it's an almost never.

There's only two cockeyed tables in the back on either side of a leaky emergency exit. The boy peeps out of one of the big gaps and feels the cold air blow across his face. He leaves his coat on and hugs himself in his chair, like one of those pill bugs from freshman Bio that curl into little balls.

What do you want? the junk man says flatly. The boy isn't sure if he's still in trouble.

Wonton soup and an egg roll, he says, eyes already under the table.

That's it?

Yeah. It comes with white rice too.

The tired, pretty Chinese lady who's always there takes the order. The junk man reaches over to the other table, grabs a worn copy of *Long Island Newsday*, lays it flat, and starts flipping pages.

A flicker of brown under the table catches the boy's eye. It's a mouse with a flake of fortune cookie in its choppers, perched on the toe of the junk man's boot, looking straight at him. The boy taps his foot to scare it off before his father sees, because if he does, that's going to be an ex-mouse.

The junk man freezes mid-flip at a two-page booze ad. It says "Happy Days" across the top and "Pre-Thanksgiving Discounts to Lift Your Holiday Spirits." Rivers of scotch, vodka, and gin spill from bottles, with little icebergs floating in them. Bottles of wine and cans of beer tumble from a horn of plenty, and Santa's sleigh is loaded with Blue Nun and Bailey's Original Irish Cream.

A Star of Bethlehem hovers over the scene, which makes the boy think of the supernovas in *Einstein's Universe* that give birth to neutron stars so dense a sugar cube of one would weigh a billion tons.

He opens his mouth to speak, wanting to release some of the pressure in his head by telling his father about the spinning neutron stars that give off gravity waves that travel at the speed of light, but hesitates when he sees the way the junk man's eyes are flicking among the bottles and brands like it's the Jade Palace's trifold menu.

He flips forward a page, then back to the ad, and exhales slowly through his nose.

Huh, he says, shaking his head, flinging the paper aside.

Is he angry? Did the boy say something wrong when they ordered?

Okay, listen, sonny boy. Your old man's sorry about before.

It's alright.

You know we're in a fight for survival out here.

I know.

You don't know.

The junk man grabs the *Newsday* again and drops it in front of the boy, tapping the date on the front page twice with his index finger. The boy reads the date, looks up, shrugs.

There, the junk man says, tapping. *You see that?*

Then the boy gets it: The newspaper is from the day before Thanksgiving. The day, a year ago, they released his father from Pilgrim State Psychiatric Hospital.

It was still summer when the boy and his little brother biked up to visit the junk man. He told them about a guy who walked three steps forward and two steps back all day, and about the other ones who shit in the bushes.

I'll blow my brains out before I go back to that miserable fucking nut house, the junk man says. *We can't be lackadaisical about chasing the almighty dollar.*

The boy doesn't think he is. He hops out of the truck with a pep in his step. He hits it with a grand enthusiasm. He helps to get the goodies before the other sonsabitches do. He pulls his weight for a 15-year-old. Why can't he think about the stars, too?

Listen, sonny boy, hey, look at me, the junk man says. *When I see you hop up into a dumpster and dig down to get the goodies, it makes your old man proud. You hear me?*

Alright. Yeah.

Okay, enough about this.

The lady brings the food and they start wolfing it down. Something about the smell of the goopy chicken-and-vegetable chop suey the junk man ordered sparks the boy's memory. It reminds him of the sour ammonia smell coming from the junk man's room at the halfway house. He remembers the row of one-gallon plastic milk jugs full of urine and the empty whiskey bottles next to the bed where the junk man nearly drank himself to death until the boys called 911 and they took him to the nut house.

Soon, the food is gone and the junk man has paid. They zip up their jackets and head out.

They pull out onto Jericho Turnpike. The snow has stopped, and there's no traffic ahead except for a beat-to-shit old Pontiac. As the junk man slips in behind the Pontiac, the boy spots a massive pothole filled with water ahead of the car.

Whoa, watch out! he says—which is stupid, since there's no way the driver could hear him—and a second later the Pontiac's right front tire slams into the crater with a loud *whump.*

Something round and silvery flies off and clatters into a parking lot along the road.

The boy vaults to his feet.

Hubcap!

J.M. Son *teaches people in the United States and other countries to speak and understand English. He hopes to complete his first novel by the time he applies for Social Security or dies, whichever comes first. He writes, "In* The Stainless Steel Hubcap Principle, *I explore the relationships between the fathers and sons I grew up around as a blue-collar boy on Long Island."*

Las Cenizas

LaTesha Harris

The police find the body when the snow melts. Washed up on the ravine bank, sniffed out by K-9s the next town over. News of the discovery is spreading in discreet whispers when Marcel sends me to the senator's office. There, he gestures for me to sit down—a wave of his hand that reads more politician than parent—before inquiring whether I still dabble in hard drugs.

"No."

Technically true.

"This isn't about the campaign."

"Sure."

"They've located the missing Northview student." My stomach turns. I force a smile. Can't hold it long, so my eyes return to the floor. "She overdosed." Sweat dampens my palms. He's quiet. I scratch the skin behind my ear until liquid spills, raging copper, down my fingers. "Stick with grass."

I nod. I don't know if he's worried about me or the campaign.

"Look at me." Our eyes, identical shades of moss bed on forest floor, meet for the first time in months. "This is the big one. Toe the line."

My heart's beating so loud I pop an oxy and crawl under my bed. After it quiets—probably an hour or a day when I resurface and wipe my nose clean of dried snot—I sit down to write the letter.

***

The missing person's report wasn't filed until February twenty-seventh, but her parents arrived at the police department on the twenty-sixth. She didn't call that Sunday. They must've taken the first flight out 'cause Argentina is ten hours away from town; an insignificant dot on the map, one of millions tucked away in Blue Ridge.

Mr. and Mrs. Delgado. Papá y Ma. Exactly how I imagined them: speechless if not delivering pained requests for God's mercy. They walked up and down Main Street, putting up MISSING posters, hand-in-hand, clutched tight as if they'd vanish without an anchor. Ignoring Commissioner Miller's advice, they gave their speech in Spanish, then English. They said she was a perfect daughter, devout Catholic, ideal student. She always rang home after mass.

We shared the stage. I stood between my mother and father; beside the president of Northview; behind Mr. and Mrs. Delgado.

I flinched every time a camera flashed. My father dug his nails into my shoulder and created small indentations—purple half-circles that later scarred. I was flying high, but the decent thing seemed stepping off stage when Mrs. Delgado asked if the kidnapper wouldn't mind bringing her daughter home. Behind a curtain, I emptied the contents of my stomach into a trash can. Marcel handed me a handkerchief. Reporters started to ask questions.

The letter's pathetic, so I stuff it in the bud tin hiding at the back of my closet.

I stop sleeping in Horton. I must be too high to ride my bike 'cause Marcel insists on driving me out of the cul-de-sac, through town square where everyone waves and I have to wave back, over the bridge, and onto campus for class.

"You'll have to stay in your dorm tonight; your father's having the mayor for dinner." Marcel pauses, waiting on a smile. He frowns when he doesn't get it. Loyal, he offers instead, "We can pull an all-nighter in the Quad."

I scowl as Marcel slides me a cocktail of uppers. I don't ask what they are. I pop 'em for a dry swallow.

The Delgados stop by to tell my father they're taking her home. They truly appreciate his dedication and care and respect. She always thought he had such character. She loved Northview, too, too much. They're not holding hands.

***

Her name was Celeste.

Celeste Evangeline Delgado. It's the most beautiful name I've ever heard.

She was the president of Northview's Lambda Theta Alpha chapter, secretary of Northview-International Student Association, and went to every volleyball game without fail. Graduation was months away, and she had already accepted a paralegal position at a law firm in Chicago.

It's one thing to be well-known, and it's another thing to be well-liked. Celeste was both.

She deserved to be both. But I think people liked her look more than anything. Don't misunderstand me. It's just that I'm the only person who got her.

The Delgados leave for Buenos Aires the next day. They're going to spread her ashes at her favorite beach.

Badges come to the house again. They ask to speak to Stewart. Not Rodriguez or Johnson. It's not even Miller. They're from out of town.

My father, myself, and my mother sit on the love seat and trade pleasantries with the detectives. In the hallway, shadows flicker across Marcel's angular face. I must be shivering 'cause a fuss gets made over all the open windows.

After my father encourages the detectives to vote Barton for Governor, they turn on me.

"You told local authorities you never met Celeste Delgado." The blonde says this. Detective Foreman. Stray rays of sun drift in and transform Foreman's irises to glinting emeralds. I have to look away.

"We were in one course together junior year."

Technically true. I only just started planning my schedule around Celeste's. The whole truth is we had five classes together in the last four years. Foreman could check the records, but I could just as easy claim I never noticed. Ain't like we ever sat together.

"Yours or hers?"

I smile. Grandma's voice, raspy from years of abusing tobacco, is loud in my head. *That gal's got gumbo on the stove.*

"Mine."

"Why did you lie to officers before?"

Detective Zheng doesn't appreciate bullshit. Even though she's accusing me of obstructing justice, I want to be closer to her. Her eyes are matronly and warm and the laugh lines around her mouth are deep.

"I didn't think sitting in a three-hundred-person lecture meant I knew her, ma'am."

Zheng frowns. "Based on notes we received from the precinct, you're one of a handful of people who didn't know her. There's even quite a few locals who have a slew of nice things to say."

That's 'cause she volunteered at Northview elementary on Thursday mornings. Every parent in town adores her. My cheeks flush. The warmth turns my neck scarlet. A window is opened without comment.

"My son's a bit of a loner," my mother chirps, "not too many people know him on campus, especially since he didn't graduate with his class last year." She's got on her campaign-winning smile: bright red lips spread from ear to ear. I wish I trusted her.

"You seem to be quite a celebrity in town." This is Foreman again, undeterred.

I scratch my head, dandruff falling in a snowstorm. I laugh, dry and low. I should tell 'em how tomorrow is the one-year anniversary of my baptism. The question of my being eternally damned always meant a lot to her. First warm day of the year, Celeste christened me 'Stewie "globo de nieve" Barton'. We both agree it sounds better in English.

"This is our home," my father says suddenly. He sounds sincere. I don't dare look at him. "It takes a village to raise a child. Stewart is this town's child. Just like I was."

I'm grateful my parents speak for me. The uppers wear off, and I need to cry.

***

Celeste studied in my dorm.

She rented a tiny studio from Mr. Morano to save money but said her schedule made a mid-day bridge crossing impossible. Studying in the library was equally impossible 'cause, reportedly, too many people interrupted to chat. Always wondered who had enough balls to speak to her in public.

One day, I found her at my desk after an exam. Ernesto Sabado left forgotten in her lap, she watched a tornado of rust and spice, falling leaves outside the window.

"Hi globo," Celeste said before cackling in her obnoxious way. "We'll have winter early. How was the exam?"

I couldn't focus. Spent the entire time considering my father and his campaign and how mad he'd get if I spent another year as a super senior. I answered one question.

The thought of disappointing Celeste turned my stomach. All I wanted was a bowl and some sleep. I crawled underneath the covers and mumbled. "It was fine."

Wasn't a minute to ask if she minded leaving me alone before Celeste slipped into bed. Her arms wrapped around my chest like I was the only thing in the world that mattered.

That got me started. Real, earth-ending shakes, and just about the worst wailing. Celeste always saw through me. It should've made me uncomfortable. I grabbed her hand.

"Mor, everything is alright. Just breathe."

My mother can't look at me when the detectives leave. Marcel slides a pills into my hand. My father decides he's going to see the detectives get to their hotel just fine. I don't know if he's worried about me or the campaign.

I take an oxy and crawl under my bed.

Wish I had something of hers.

***

We weren't too fond of each other at first.

I should be honest—I hated her. At most, she was indifferent. This made me hate her more.

First semester of sophomore year, her freshman, she showed up at People Watcher's club. On paper, it was an official organization with registration, campus funding, faculty mentorship and all that, but I spent the meetings getting stoned in the Quad and writing bad poetry. No one ever came. As president, her interruption irritated me.

"Is this the People Watcher's club?"

"Yes?"

"You're Stewart Barton, right?"

"Yes."

I hated that she knew my name. My eyes fell on the thin gold cross resting at the bottom of her throat, and I hated her.

"I thought more people would be here." Wind blew. She hugged herself. Several charms hung off a gold bracelet around her wrist—when they clanged against each other, the air filled with the sound of small bells. "Eleven is a weird time for a club meeting."

"You can see people better at night."

She frowned and sniffed the air. "Are you smoking marijuana?"

"No." Despite my best efforts to imitate the senator, Celeste didn't even flinch.

"I won't tell anyone," she said, quiet, before kneeling to sit. She smoothed out her skirt. "You should reconsider. Marijuana destroys brain cells."

I was too high to remember if I scowled.

Even though I repeatedly told her I would never incorporate any of her marketing ideas or restructure our leadership, Celeste kept showing up to People Watcher's club. Marcel reminded me to be hospitable, so I brought appetizers. I said they were from Food Lion even though I spent days experimenting on them.

I didn't notice she was nice to be around until the end of the year. It was the first time she laughed.

Until that moment, she'd only smiled, polite and civil-like, so I jumped when she suddenly started to cackle. Fast as it came, Celeste covered her mouth. She seemed embarrassed.

"Oh my gosh. Stewart," she gasped, wiping away a tear, "you're really funny."

I said something about Goldman Sachs when a tall guy in a suit ran past us. My face flamed as I thanked her. It was probably the dumbest thing I've ever said, and the thought of being a moron around this powerhouse of intelligence devastated me. Whispers of jasmine drifted through the wind when she dropped a hand on my knee.

"Do you mind if I ask you something?" I nodded. For the first time, I noticed a small mole underneath her left eye. Honestly, she left me a little starstruck. "Why don't people like you?"

"The chef in Horton does," I said, dumbfounded. Celeste lacked the art of being subtle. I really like that about her.

The corner of her lip twitched. "I love our club, but I've heard some bad things. Pretty bad, actually."

"I don't talk a lot. Tends to make folk uncomfortable, I figure."

"My friend told me you sell drugs," she said. She said this with zero delicacy, straight-forward, like relaying the weather forecast. Her eyes never strayed from mine. "Hard things, like cocaine and meth."

I blinked. I was offended, but not enough to defend myself. Technically, at that very moment even, I usually had enough on my person to be charged with intent to sell, but Rodriguez and Johnson wouldn't dare. "I try those, sometimes, but I don't sell 'em."

Celeste's face fell. Stiff, she withdrew her hand. Relief and disappointment infected my blood in equal part harmony.

"Good night," she said.

"I would never do heroin," I said lamely, lying. She was long gone anyway.

I stayed there an hour, fiddling with blades of grass, trying to ignore the growing pit in my stomach.

I called Marcel and he arrived in five minutes.

We drove to the city for ingredients and returned to an empty house. I dropped a tab of acid before grabbing my apron. Marcel sat at the island with a crossword.

A beam of orange light, this beautiful peach-apricot shade, brightened the kitchen as I finished. I laid a blanket over Marcel, asleep on the loveseat, and left. Even though my backpack was heavy with tupperware, I managed to bike to Lewis, Celeste's residence hall at the time, before the first chime of birdsong.

Two hours, I waited in the lobby 'til she walked in with her friend Jackie, both of 'em drenched with sweat. Celeste's cheeks were flushed; soft red like tulips in early bloom. I cleared my throat, searching for confidence, I guess, before standing to attention. Expertly, Celeste avoided looking at me—Jackie glared—as they walked past.

I let it happen. She was nearly at the side door when I called her. It was a whisper, really, and she used my cowardice as an excuse to keep trucking on. I trailed behind. I called her name again, louder.

"Hello! Can I help you?" Her smile stretched from ear to ear and didn't quite reach her eyes.

"Brought you something," I told the floor.

"You know Stewart Barton?" Jackie asked.

"No." She laughed, nervous, before amending, "I mean, we're in Patel's race and law. She partnered us up."

"Yeah," I said, regretting a lie for the first time in my whole life, "Brought your notes."

"Thanks. You know, we should chat about the presentation while you're here." She grabbed my arm and began to retreat. "Nice run, Jackie!" Celeste led me downstairs and into the basement. Suddenly, it dawned on me I didn't quite think this one through. "What are you doing here?"

"I was thinking about what you said the other day. When you said you missed home."

Silent, she stared into my backpack. Asado con chimichurri, mollejas, locro, pastel con dulce de leche, and, obviously, empanadas. She had explained how to make all this stuff only about a hundred times that spring.

Her voice wavered when she finally spoke. "These aren't from Food Lion."

"They could be."

Her eyes glistened. "Thank you."

"Don't mention it."

I turned to leave. Her hand fell into mine. "My parents sacrificed a lot for me to come to the United States. I can't ... I can't mess up. They'd be so disappointed if something bad happened. It's our big chance, you get me?"

I did get her. Of all the things Celeste had to explain to me, reputation wasn't one of them. I told her as much and said to be safe in Texas and remember to find some time to have fun at her internship.

She kissed my cheek.

That surprised me, but not as much as when she showed up to People Watcher's club in the fall.

***

"You understand this is serious, right?" Detective Zheng asks. She's cornered me outside of Horton. The senator has made it clear I won't be speaking to anyone without an attorney present, but also refuses to make the call 'cause we have nothing to hide. I feel this makes me look guilty, so I offer Zheng a cigarette and play my part. "She was an international student. Domestic authorities aren't running the show anymore."

20

"I'm not sure how I can help."

Zheng wraps her lips around the cigarette. Her eyes catch fire, two burning embers in her skull. I blink it away; the cocktail Marcel gave me earlier might've been strong. She blows smoke out the side of her mouth.

"We got a call from Jacqueline Muñoz yesterday. A sorority sister of Celeste's, she graduated last year." Not a question, so I stare blankly. Zheng's irritated with me. "Any reason she would tell us to look into you?"

"No. I don't know any Jacquelines."

Technically true.

"You know anyone on campus, Barton?"

I smile. "I'm good friends with the head chef in my building."

Zheng says she'll see me around. I go cross-eyed staring at the trunk of her sedan. The urge to vomit overwhelms me. I extinguish my cigarette, using my wrist as an ashtray. Marcel pulls up.

He's been watching.

My skin gets to damn near blistering as I slither into the front seat. Marcel's silent, knuckles white against his steering wheel. We pass Mr. Morano's. I don't gotta look to know there's fresh marigolds on the ofrenda. Even after all this time, she is truly the best part of this forgotten wasteland.

"What did the detective say?"

"She got a call from Jackie."

"That doesn't sound good."

It's not.

On one of my birthdays, Celeste said I was selfish. She wasn't too good with important dates and stuff like that, so I don't hold it against her.

I was researching how to make pecan cream cheese when her key turned the lock. She held a bag of takeout in one hand and her phone to her ear with the other.

"Ya lo hice," Celeste said. Annoyance deepened her brow. "Ma, okay. Okay. Okay."

Without ceremony, Celeste handed me the Chinese before collapsing in my beanbag chair. The sight should've been funny—the swollen red cloth all but swallowed her petite frame—but something had her distressed. Panic ebbed and flowed in her voice, reaching heights I'd never heard. The storm eventually cleared. She returned to monosyllabic words.

Later, I would realize it wasn't Sunday. It must've been something urgent for her parents to accept an unscheduled, expensive long-distance call.

Celeste's eyes were misty when she hung up. My stomach fell. She wasn't real big on crying. I put my lo mein aside and reached for her hand. "What's wrong?"

"I'm mad at you, I think," she said. Her hand laid limp in mine, so I let go.

I blinked. "Care to elaborate?"

"I met your dad at elementary today." Again, my stomach turned. "He asked how long I'd been working there. He thought I was a janitor."

"I'm sorry," I said. I breathed, relieved. Honestly, I didn't see what that had to do with me. I have never tried to sugar-coat the senator for her.

Celeste sighed. She moved to the edge of my bed. A curl escaped her bun, cascading down her shoulder. Sunset stole in through the window and turned her gold.

"My dad lost his job. My parents hid it from me as long as they could, but we can't afford to stay."

"Shit. Are you serious?" She nodded. "I'm sorry," I said. I thought on it a second. "You want some money?"

Celeste grimaced. "I don't need your money."

"You just said—"

"I'm not a charity case, Stewart."

"I know, I just—"

"It's the principle." She was on the verge of tears. "You have so much money. Your father has so much money. You can do anything you want and be anything you want and learn anything in the whole world, and you decide to be addicted to drugs. It's selfish, damn you. You get me?"

"That's..." What could I say—unfair? uncalled for? really not how I want the most important person in my life to see me?—She didn't get it. Can't see how any of the transplants could. I never blamed her, really, but where I'm from, I'm one of the lucky ones, which has everything to do with the senator. I've managed to mostly stay out of the crank. Can't say the same about the kids I used to know.

"I would kill to have your life."

"You don't want this, babe."

Celeste sighed before reaching over to grab her food. She inhaled a piece of orange chicken, leaving a smear of glaze on her cheek. Eventually, she apologized: "You do it better."

She stayed away nearly two weeks that time. I thought it might get permanent until I started finding armies of gummy bears scattered around the dorm. Small offerings.

I found her on my bed, angrily chewing on a cashew curry I had been thinking about all day.

She asked how much power my father had in this town. The financial aid office sent a letter.

"I'm apparently a recipient of the M.R. Cel merit scholarship. It covers tuition, room, board, and a carte blanche travel stipend until I graduate. Even during summer. I've never heard of that. I certainly didn't apply." Her sweet face, round like a full moon, had become all harsh lines. Serious to the point I knew womanhood would treat her kindly. Her voice, steady as ever, rang tender. Grandma would've loved her.

I hummed, absent, before brushing a thick curl behind her ear. "I've never heard of it either. Congratulations, though. We should celebrate. You like that curry?"

"I love it." Celeste inspected me. I held my breath. She let me pass with a raise of her eyebrows. "I guess I should write a thank you letter."

In a rare ten minutes of sobriety, I send the letter off in a large manila envelope addressed to Mr. and Mrs. Delgado. I return to my dorm.

The police are at my door in the morning.

***

We spent the entire day together.

I'd been sober four months and hadn't experienced any withdrawals going on two weeks. In the middle of February, she thought it'd be nice to celebrate at the shore. Perfect temperature, perfect waves, and the whole beach to ourselves. Look how right she was. I said she was the only person alive hard-headed enough to make weather bend to her will. We were living in high cotton.

The longer we huddled inside our sand-made igloo, the more I started to anticipate missing the moment. She was gonna graduate soon, and we had carefully avoided what that meant a whole year. I was decent enough to keep this to myself, but I got the feeling I could die fast in a world where I'd never see Celeste again.

Finishing the handle, Celeste gazed at the waves. Her curls, dark from the ocean, were slick against her face.

"I'm proud of you, globo," Celeste said.

"I'm really proud of you, Cel," I said. She grinned, revealing two deep dimples and a crooked canine tooth.

In a flash, she clamored to her knees and started rifling through the sand. Celeste brought a handful to her nose and pretended to breathe. My heart swelled.

"The wine in my home country has a much better flavor. Deeper, more rich."

"I'd hope most things from Argentina taste better than sand."

She pouted. "How dare you! I'm a proud Sicilian!" Celeste learned English on *Golden Girls* reruns. She stayed away a month after revealing that fun fact.

I snorted. "Is that supposed to be an Italian accent?"

She persisted. "Picture it, Sicily, 1842! Why you laughing, you hussy?"

"That's terrible!"

Celeste broke her mound of sand over my head. I doubled over with all my laughter. I rolled and rolled, hysterical, until tears spilled down my cheeks, onto my chest. The nice moment ended with me crying in Celeste's arms.

Once I got a handle on breathing, Celeste dug in her purse. I stared at her bracelet. I hadn't noticed the new charm yet. Nestled between the moon and ceibo tree was a small snow globe. She handed my phone over.

With a whisper of luck, Celeste's lips brushed my ear. I dialed my father. Five times, straight to voicemail. Marcel called. Over static, rambunctious chatter reminded me I was supposed to be at a campaign fundraiser.

"What's up, kid?"

"Can you get him on the phone?"

"Tied up at the moment. You need me to come?"

"I really gotta talk to him."

Marcel sighed. Rustling. A click—the phone disconnected. I moved farther away from Celeste. Was the sound of waves lapping sand always so ominous? The phone rang.

The senator sounded tired. "What?"

A ways away, Celeste was standing tip-toe, trying to line our sand sculpture with twigs and rocks and seashells. "I'm leaving Northview."

He managed a snort. "To do what?"

That was a curveball. "I don't know."

Radio silence. Celeste tripped over a trail of seaweed and brought half the igloo down. The itch came. The one that vibrates your bones and infects your bloodstream. When my father finally spoke, there was no senator, no governor to blame.

"You ever get tired of being a fucking disappointment? Lord, tell me, what evil did I do to deserve such a loser, piece-of-shit son? You got the whole damn world handed to you on a silver fucking platter and you can't sit down and just play your fucking part. It's not a big one, you hear me? We're in the middle of the most important campaign of my career and you want to drop out. My mother, God rest her soul, can't even be dead in peace, 'cause her only grandchild ain't got what it takes to be a fucking man. Go on, Stewart. Go on and piss your life away. Promise you what, you leave Northview, you're on your own."

Eventually, Celeste found me lying in the backseat. We drove home in silence–four whole hours to brainstorm how I would hide my relapse. When we arrived, I told her I needed to be alone.

I searched all over.

Back of the closet: two oxys covered in dust at the bottom of a shoebox. I wiped them on my shorts. I debated whether to send it on both of 'em.

Her key turned the lock.

She stepped inside and frowned. Her voice was thread thin. "I brought some Cokes. What did he say?"

"Nothing important. Can you leave, please?"

"Don't lie, Stewie."

"Cel, I really don't feel like fussin'. Just go. Please."

Her eyes watered. "You don't have to take those."

"I do."

"Why? Talk to me, and we can come up with something."

"'Cause, Cel. Go before they start checking IDs."

"I don't want to go. Why do you need those? You don't. We don't. We've been so good."

Something snapped. "The hell you care for, Celeste? Still won't be seen with me in public. You think I'm pathetic too, just like him."

"No, I don't."

"Get out."

I had never yelled at her. It scared her more than my possible relapse, I knew. She stepped closer and wrapped her hands around mine. "I'll drive us to the clinic."

"I don't need the clinic."

My resolve weakened. I didn't even want the fucking pills anymore. But there she was again, testing me. Pulling a puppet off the shelf and dusting off its strings. The one time in my life I choose to get stuck on principle.

"Whatever you do, I do, remember? If you take one, I have to take the other."

That sweet face, her wide smile. I couldn't see past my father.

Time slowed. I placed an oxy on my tongue. Her eyes widened as I dropped the other in her hand.

Eventually, she slipped in bed behind me. She ran her fingers through my hair. I started fading real quick, the distance between me and her leaping in bounds while she explained how she designed her entire life path when she was ten. Her future never involved loving a Yankee drug addict.

I'll always wonder if she said more than that. Don't blame her if she didn't.

My hair was soaked when I woke up. I gagged, an instinctual reaction to a vile stench that had infected the air. My heart stopped. I turned. "Oh, baby."

Her forehead felt like ice.

She started throwing up. She was throwing up and I wasn't fucking awake to make sure she stayed on her side. So, she choked. She rolled on her back, choked, and her tongue, dripping with neon-orange vomit, lolled out of her mouth. She died with her eyes open.

I scrambled for my phone. I tried for an ambulance, but Marcel answered. He arrived in five minutes. I followed his instructions. We cleared my dorm, erasing all evidence that my miserable existence had ever crossed paths with hers. Everything was fine. Then, Marcel said we had to burn the body.

"What?" I turned to him, in the woods, under cover of night. He repeated himself. "Fuck you talking about? What the hell is wrong with you? We're not doing that." Marcel grabbed me by the shoulders. Tears streamed down my face. "Get the fuck off!" Hysteria crept up on me.

"Listen, kid. You have fucked up a million times. I always had your back, right?"

"I didn't do anything."

"I had your back, right? Right. It's your turn to have my back now."

"I didn't, I didn't do this. You know that!"

"Don't matter what you did or didn't do, kid. Only matters what it looks like."

"You can't burn her."

I pushed to the car, past Marcel. We traded throwing each other against the trunk of his sedan where my best friend was dead, wrapped in stained sheets of a fucking twin mattress. He shattered my nose. I fell to my knees, throwing up.

We threw the body in the ravine. Snow fell and never stopped.

I don't know if I was worried about myself or my father's campaign.

***

Start out calm. Respond to their questions with short, monotonous phrases. Campaign voice. An overdose isn't homicide, detective. I've never spoken to her, like I said. They request an alibi for the nights of the twenty-fourth and the twenty-fifth. I was at home. No, not my dorm, the senator's house. My parents' house. Don't know where my car is. I stutter. They slap on handcuffs. They say they've found DNA under her fingernails. I yell. Get your hands off me. Get your fucking filthy hands off me, bitch. Do you know who the fuck I am? They slam my head against the doorframe. I cry. It was an accident. I didn't know. Swear to God, I didn't know. I loved her, I loved her. They force me out the dorm, down the stairs, through the lobby, out the building, right past my father and his constituents.

LaTesha Harris *is a server from Round Rock, Texas. In her free time, she roleplays a smelly halfling and coaches people through the learning of self-expression. Her writing has appeared in* NPR *and* Adi Magazine. *Tap in to more of LaTesha's work at* Mercurial Surplus, *a newsletter on Substack. (@mercurialsurplus). Of* Las Cenizas, *she shares, "I wrote this story as a microcosm of the human condition and hope it highlights the myriad of ways in which women of color are unconsciously and consciously harmed by the worlds they inhabit."*

I Never Liked Men
Silvia Fonseca

She had never liked men. Not out of anger, nor from any great wound, but with the same inevitability one dislikes a climate in which one cannot breathe. They entered spaces like weather fronts: gathering, swelling, louder than thunder. And when they passed, a film remained on every surface, a residue that altered the air itself.

She had never thought of herself as a lesbian either. The word had always felt like a key cut for another door; one she could not claim as her own. Desire, for her, had never fit the binaries offered. So, she refused it. Her world was orderly, almost ascetic. Books rose in tall, mute partitions, companions that demanded nothing and gave her silence in return. The mirrors, turned toward the wall, erased the possibility of seeing herself through the eyes of others. What she had built was a life sealed against the noise of men, a sovereignty of one.

She believed she knew the architecture of masculinity the way a city-dweller knows the route of a bus never taken through the certainty of its trajectory. Its roaring arrival, its authoritarian doors, its relentless schedule. Always the same performance, repeated until mistaken for nature. Masculinity, as she had received it, was choreography transmuted into essence: shoulders squared into proclamation, laughter stretched into conquest, touch calculated to claim. To enter a room under its spell was to move through a field of directives, each gesture a command. She learned to adapt by erasure, by thinning herself into the margins, by avoiding the center of the page.

Refusal became her defense and her dwelling. Over time it hardened into habitat, a structure whose ivy softened its severity while hiding its walls. Years drifted past like narrow boats, indistinguishable in their cargo of tasks and days. In daylight, she moved with precision, each duty finished with a private nod that carried no witness. In the long hours after, she turned to books letting her hand scrawl small thoughts in the margins, as if her life could remain safely secondary, a commentary to an unread text. Distance became her discipline. She trained herself to prize it as clarity, to believe that composure was best preserved at the cost of intimacy. The world of men she kept in her sight and purposefully out of focus: silhouettes blurred on the horizon, observable and never permitted detail, so that their sharpness could not cut into hers.

Yet one morning, with the subtlety of a hinge turning in a familiar door, the frame of the world shifted. Nothing in the room announced a rupture. A lamp could have been moved; a current of air could have learned a new path from window to window. Still, she felt the shift: an arrival without spectacle, a presence without claim.

Presence, she noticed, not man. The difference mattered, though she could not say why at first. Presence was a field, not a figure. Where she had expected noise, she encountered a clarifying stillness. Where she had expected the choreography, she felt the steps disperse into un-patterned awareness. The world around this presence did not dim for lack of command, it only brightened, as if light had been redirected away from the stage and toward the objects themselves.

Suspicion rose with the discipline of a long-trained muscle. She lifted the phenomenon with intellectual tweezers and carried it under the lamp of analysis. Where, exactly, was the mechanism of conquest hidden? She inventoried the gestures with careful notation, as if she were cataloging a new genus of motion. Hands that knew their weight and so did not demand to be heavier than necessary. Speech that emerged only to measure the room's capacity to hold silence. A posture whose geometry said: I exist, but not *instead of* you.

She waited for the reveal the way a patient waits for pain that usually follows rain. It did not arrive. Days accumulated, ordinary and exact. Nothing was asked of her except what the day itself already asked. And yet within that simplicity she began to perceive a difference. The quiet respect in how space was left unclaimed, the care in how objects were handled without requests, the silence that did not press to be filled. What once seemed like mere routine began to feel like a new language of presence, spoken in gestures too small to dominate, yet large enough to change the air around her.

Surprise is not an emotion one trusts instantly. She distrusted hers. Self-doubt returned, that careful custodian of earlier protections. Had she misunderstood herself all along, translating a fear of injury into an identity that spared her the experiment of proximity? Or had she misunderstood masculinity, confusing one dialect for the grammar, one choreography for the ontology? The questions multiplied like windows in a building that grows translucent at sunset. She found herself walking the corridors of her refusals, touching the walls with her fingertips, listening for hollowness. Somewhere, she thought, there must be a door disguised as a wall, a seam where a planned impossibility turns out to be a hinge.

It was in that imagined hinge that the question lodged itself: *what is masculinity, stripped of conquest?* Not the mask she had always known, not the fortress of noise. Something else. Something bare, still waiting to be named. The thought resisted like a stone set in a river, altering the current even as the water smoothed its surface. Could masculinity be more than assertion, less fortress, more riverbank, holding form not by domination but by consent to be shaped, grain by patient grain? If not spectacle, then stewardship, a mode of care that tends without owning. If not domination, then restraint. Not the clenching of teeth against desire, but the knowledge of one's own force in space, and the choice to use it to preserve rather than consume the contours of the other.

Her refusal had always been epistemic as much as ethical. She had never believed other architectures existed. Now she began to see them everywhere in negative, the way a muscle aches after being named. A father who prepares an apology before an argument begins, not to disarm, just to remain porous to correction. A boy in a subway who allows a woman's flinch to complete itself without demanding absolution for the flinch he did not "cause." A scholar who recognizes the territory of his certainty as a province, not an empire, and marks its borders with provisional flags. These were faint diagrams, insufficient in themselves, yet cumulative enough to suggest a grammar.

With the diagrams came dreams. In sleep she walked the Museum of Masculinities, a building that existed only at the hour when the city turns itself inside out and shows the lace of its systems. Gallery A displayed the heavy reliquary of familiar artifacts: the laughter that takes the room hostage; the handshake engineered for narrative; the apology that argues its own innocence. The vitrines were perfectly lit; the labels wore their centuries in immaculate fonts. She moved through them without disgust, but also without reverence.

In Gallery B the light thinned into something like winter truth. Here the artifacts were less legible: a chair pulled back without flourish; a sentence ending before it could turn triumphant; a mug washed because it was there. There were no plaques, no dates, only the hum of a different order. She stood with her hands folded behind her back like a student in a room of minor miracles. The guards, if there were guards, slept.

In Gallery C there were mirrors that reflected pairs without devouring either outline. In the corner a small table displayed sketches of rooms where women's voices maintained their timbre even when spoken near men. The architect of these rooms, unsigned, had drawn the walls in pencil so the lines could be erased and redrawn each season to accommodate changes in weather and will.

She woke with the residue of graphite on her hands, though there was no graphite, only the conviction that the design was possible. Conviction frightened her more than doubt. Doubt had kept her safe by keeping her still. Conviction asked her to move with delicacy across a new floor.

And then there was the body. The body learned without proclamations. It recognized pressure that did not trespass, attention that did not extract. It learned the difference between a touch that measured itself against an ethic and a touch that measured itself against a story it wished to tell about power. It learned to breathe where previously it had braced. It discovered that consent is not only permission given but permission received. The humility of hearing *no* as a form of knowledge, the grace of hearing *yes* without translating it into inevitability.

Desire came like clarity after fog, not as a sudden blaze but as a sharpening of edges: a railing under the hand, a staircase where each step revealed itself just in time for the foot to trust it. She startled herself not because she felt but because she could feel without reducing herself to an audience for someone else's myth. She found she could assent without surrender, approach without contraction.

Still, suspicion visited like weather. On some days it rained in her thoughts until the gutters sang. She allowed it to pass through, not as an enemy to be defeated but as a custodian to be respected. Suspicion cleaned the museum, dusted its vitrines and tested the doors. Its labor did not cancel the rooms; it preserved them by refusing to let them congeal into fantasy.

She tried to write a thesis, and then tried not to, because theses prefer straight lines and the experience required curves. What emerged instead were meditations. Masculinity emerges as a language, not fixed in commandments, carried instead through gestures, errors, and repetitions, where exceptions hold fragile meanings that rules cannot contain. It appears as an ethic of restraint, a patient awareness of moments when force clarifies or corrodes, when power steadies or unravels. It lives also as stewardship, the quiet tending of a shared field of attention so each voice breathes without straining to be heard. And it unfolds as withness, the art of moving alongside others, allowing coexistence to deepen without turning presence into spectacle.

The presence remained unnamed, which was not coyness. Names have a tendency to claim; claim has a tendency to calcify into story; story, once ossified, recruits the body into its own exaggerations. Unnamed, the presence could remain a set of practices rather than an emblem. Unnamed, it could be no more than a relay rather, a way of handling weight, a way of arranging words, a way of being near.

The world, faithful to its older scripts, still proposed the statue in the square. She did not topple it. She walked past it as one walks past a retiree of history taking sunlight on a bench. She recognized what it had been asked to do. She recognized what it had done. She recognized that her own muscles tired at the thought of repeating its posture. She preferred, now, to enter buildings with windows.

In those buildings she witnessed the experiments of coexistence that are too modest to make headlines. An argument that slowed itself at the edge of escalation. A correction offered with precision rather than humiliation. A task done without audience. An expertise articulated with tentativeness that did not dissolve into abdication. None of these were fireworks. All of them were infrastructure: the kind that fails only when you neglect it, the kind that, when cared for, lets a city breathe in different weathers without collapsing.

Her earlier life did not become false in retrospect. It remained part of the record, instructive in its brusqueness. She did not betray the girl who learned to be narrow in order to pass unseen, she admired her. She did not betray the women whose harms had taught her the dimensions of danger, she carried those dimensions like a carpenter carries a rule, sliding it out to check a span before laying a beam. Caution, discipline, refusal: these remained tools. What changed was their exclusivity.

If there was a revelation, it arrived without trumpets: *masculinity is not abolished by being questioned, but it is certainly altered by being practiced differently*. To practice it differently is not to feminize it, as if gentleness were a garment borrowed from the other side of the closet. It is to understand strength as a material that requires shaping. Unshaped, strength is debris. Shaped, it becomes structure.

Often, in the blue hour between lamp and dark, she returned to the sentence she had written so many years by implication and only recently in ink: *I never liked men.* She would hold it up to the light and see that the ink contained other colors: grief for what had been unavoidable, gratitude for what had protected her, fidelity to the versions of herself that held the line. Then she placed beside it a second sentence, written with the same hand: *But I have since learned that masculinity is not only noise, that it can breathe in other forms.*

The presence slept sometimes beside her like a coastline. She watched the way the breath altered the geography, how the ribs made small weather, how the hand learned in sleep what it had learned awake: to remain its own weight. She did not narrate this to herself as heterosexuality acquired at last, as conversion, as capitulation. She narrated it as the success of a different grammar: two pronouns refusing to become a single subject, two trajectories sharing a field without requiring merger. The body, literate now in another script, did not forget the old one. It carried both, as a biographer carries two accounts of the same morning, each incomplete, each necessary for truth.

Outside, the city rehearsed its ancient methods: cranes craned; sirens revised the idea of straight lines; statues remained where statutes had placed them. Inside, the daily practice continued. On some days it failed. Fatigue shortened the radius of patience and inherited reflexes sprang up like old pipes knocking when the heat rose. Failure revealed where reinforcement belonged. Repair followed. An apology as blueprint, a plan attached to a word, a window added where there had been only wall.

Years did their ordinary work. The museum kept opening at the hour when the city inverted itself. New artifacts entered the rooms: tools used without fanfare and boundaries learned without effort. She visited less often, not from boredom but because the exhibits had leached into the street. The museum had been a metaphor because she had needed one. Now it was no longer needed.

She did not revise her public labels. If anyone asked, she let the question dissolve into air. Not because the answer was secret, but because the answer was a room, not a word. Rooms cannot be handed over like coins and flipped at will. They must be walked, occupied. If pressed, she would say only that she had expanded, and that expansion had not required surrender.

On a winter morning dry as paper she stood by a river and read its lesson again: water moves by yielding; banks hold by being shaped, not by resisting shape. The lesson felt embarrassingly simple, like advice one should have absorbed in childhood but missed because the teacher's voice was drowned by an older chorus. She laughed once, not at herself but at the longevity of myths. The air took the laugh and wore it as a brief scarf of warmth.

By then the interior had changed in ways that resist inventory. The mirrors, once faced to the wall, had been lifted, not to demand performance but to return perspective. The books had shifted from barricade to bridge. The furniture learned the sound of being moved by two pairs of hands that had learned to anticipate each other's lift without rehearsal.

She understood, finally, that liking or not liking men had never been the point. It was imagination: what forms were available, what forms were foreclosed. Where forms narrow, ethics starve; where they multiply, new virtues become legible. Gentleness, once dismissed as a secondary characteristic, revealed itself as the art that allows strength to exist without harm. Restraint, once mistaken for inhibition, revealed itself as the intelligence of forces. Attention, once feminized into service, revealed itself as a democratic distribution of presence.

There remained statues. There remained squares. There remained days when the city insisted on old legends and demanded the choreography. She kept her border tools sharp. But she also kept the new instruments oiled. Between defense and assent, a life traced its tensile line. The line did not snap. It learned to hum.

In the end, though there was no end, only days, she wrote one more sentence, a small one that required no audience: *Masculinity could be otherwise, and so could I.* She placed the sentence in the spine of a book and forgot which it was. This pleased her. Let it travel privately, like a seed caught in the hem of a coat. Let it fall elsewhere, root where conditions allow, fail where they do not, try again. The work was not to prove the seed's greatness. The work was to keep a landscape in which multiple plants could live without strangling one another.

She closed the notebook. The hinge gave its modest music. Somewhere in the city a bus announced itself and took a corner with immodest faith. The statue collected light from a sky it did not own. The river practiced the democracy of movement. In a room whose windows were open, two presences kept the air breathable by noticing it. And breath, unremarkable and thus supreme, continued.

Silvia Fonseca *is a communications specialist from the coast of Brazil who shares her time between the tiny island of Vitória and New York. In her free time, she reads obsessively, studies languages, and spends time on the jiu-jitsu mats. Her work has appeared in* Dark Mountain. *You can find her writing on Substack (@silbss) at* The Red Sweater. *Of* I Never Liked Men, *she writes, "I wrote this story after surprising myself by discovering forms of masculinity I had never been taught to imagine, and noticing that something in me quietly welcomed them."*

Black Coffee

T. E. Cole

For Don
rest high
among the Little White Clouds

I woke up this morning, I know I had, though I don't remember. The morning was always a blur. No one wakes me up and makes my breakfast these days. I don't remember driving to the coffee shop, but here I am. One drip coffee, black. No, just black. Yeah, no cream, no sugar. Yeah, thanks.

Everything is so tiresome. There was a time where I would have found humor in that exchange, I think. Not so much anymore. I feel like I've lost something.

You know that feeling of walking into a room and forgetting what you were looking for. I have that feeling all the time, I think. Of the few things I can remember, that's one of them. I like my coffee black, and I've lost something and I don't know what. "Here's your coffee, sir." 'Sir.' It reverberates in my brain. I wish she would have said my name. That would have helped me remember. Is that what I've lost? My name? No, that can't be it.

I grasp the cup with both hands to warm them. I take notice of them. Wrinkled and spotted. Bruised. Thin-skinned. When did I get so old. Maybe that's what I've lost. Time. That makes more sense than a name. I don't remember how old I am. I must be pretty old to have hands like these.

I sit down and take the lid off of my coffee so it will cool faster. I take a sip. Strong and black, just like I like my women. I've always loved to say that about my coffee. It is usually met with a laugh or two. Or maybe it isn't. Not sure who I would even say it to. I look around the well-lit coffee shop. No familiar faces. Take another sip. Strong and black. I smile to myself. Maybe I haven't lost my sense of humor.

Now that my coffee is at a drinkable temperature, I put the lid back on. I should go for a walk. Maybe then I'll find what I've lost. I try to stand up from my seat and fail. There's one thing I know I've lost, strength. I don't think it should be this hard to stand up. I brace myself on the table and my chair and with great effort I rise to my feet. I walk out of the coffee shop and turn right. The sun is shining. There are a few little white clouds dotting the otherwise clear blue sky. I hear birds singing over the sound of the traffic to my left. As I walk this city sidewalk, I wonder about what I've lost. Still can't put my finger on it, but I'm glad to have such a beautiful day to look for it.

I must have lost track of time. I don't hear the birds or the traffic anymore. There's no sidewalk, just grass. I look around and all I can see is illuminated by moonlight. I'm surrounded by trees. I decide I should go back the way I came, but I can't remember which direction that was. Every direction looks the same. Just trees. My legs are pretty tired anyway. I'll just sit down here and rest while I try to remember how I got here.

I am startled awake by the sound of dogs barking. I look in the direction of the noise and I see a flashlight shining through the woods. I want to get up and run but there is no way I could make that happen. All I can do is wait. A flashlight blinds me. "Mr. Roberts? David Roberts? Is that your name, sir?" It does sound familiar. Maybe I used to know someone by that name. "Mr. Roberts, my name is Deputy Lee and I'm with the Sheriff's office. Why don't we get you back home." The man extends his hand to me. I think that this Deputy Lee is my best bet to get out of these woods. Though I am confused, I let him help me up.

He walks me out of the woods to a parking lot where there are multiple police cars. Deputy Lee helps me into the back of one.

As the deputy drives us back into the city he asks, "Mr. Roberts, why did you wander off today?"

"I've lost something," I tell him.

"What is it that you've lost?"

"I wish I knew."

We arrive at an unfamiliar house. The deputy helps me out of the car and walks me up to the door. He knocks and an unfamiliar woman flings the door open. "Oh!" The woman hugs me tightly. "Thank you so much officer, thank you, thank you!" She hugs the deputy as well. The woman grabs my arm. "Come inside, let's get you warmed up." I'm still confused, but I am also cold so I welcome the invitation. The nice woman helps me sit down by the fireplace and covers me with a warm blanket.

I look around the room I am in. One thing catches my eye. On the mantle above the fireplace next to a small vase is a photo of a beautiful woman. My heart wants to leap out of my chest at the sight of her!

"You can't wander off like that. I've been worried sick about you all day!" I return my attention to the nice woman. I don't know her, but she definitely knows me. Should I know her?

"I'm sorry I worried you," I say. As I watch her build a fire in the fireplace I wonder about who she is. Maybe she does look a little familiar. She looks like someone I knew. Someone I know? I look back at the photo on the mantel. They favor one another.

I watch her as she becomes familiar. It all comes flooding back. It overwhelms me. I try and fail to hold back tears.

"Oh it's ok, Dad, I'm just glad you're ok." But I'm not okay, because now I remember what I've lost.

I lost my wife.

My high school sweetheart. We were married as soon as we graduated. I was in my second year of college when she got pregnant. I left school and took a job at the local firehouse to support us. I never held it against her. I preferred it, actually. I loved our little family and would have given anything up to have it. I worked 35 years at the fire department along with other odd jobs to help pay the bills and make sure the kids never went without.

We had three kids. Luke, Daniel, and Jennifer, who was in front of me now, building a fire. We had built our own home on our own land. I made sure she never had to work. She had enough work, taking care of our three kids. If you asked her she would say she was taking care of four kids, including me, but she wouldn't have it any other way.

She loved my sense of humor.

Any time I had her frustrated all I had to do was get her to laugh. I could always make her laugh. She loved to sing. She was always filling our home with her angelic voice. Filling my life with her song. I think if we had not gotten pregnant so young she would have tried to become a famous singer. Anytime I asked her about it she would say "the only audience I care to sing for lives inside these walls." Once all our kids grew up and moved out we rekindled our love. We had more time for one another than ever before.

When I retired, we did what all retirees do. We sold our house and moved south. She loved that old song by Otis Redding so much she insisted we buy a house on a bay somewhere. We ended up on an island off the Florida coast, on the bay side of course. We enjoyed that simple, retired lifestyle for years. Mostly me fishing while she hummed that tune on our dock of the bay.

All good things must come to an end.

I had always been forgetful, losing my keys or misplacing my wallet, but it had gotten much worse. I was forgetting things she had just said to me or forgetting how to get to places I had been going to for years. She insisted I see a doctor. I remember sitting in that cold office with her. She cried so much.

There was nothing they could do. I would only get worse.

As it progressed I began to wander. I would forget myself and leave and not remember how to get back. She didn't sleep much after that, always having to keep an eye on me.

I know it was hard on her. The worst part was forgetting her. Right now I can see the hurt in her eyes when I didn't know her face. She was so strong through it all, but I knew it was over when she stopped singing. The stress was too much. It was my fault. Having to take care of me is what killed her.

I sold our house on the bay. The doctors recommended I live somewhere I was familiar with so I moved into a nursing home in the town we had raised our family in. Jenny was the only one of our children who still lived there. She came to see me often.

She had taken me out today to get some fresh air. We went to my favorite coffee shop. I went in ahead of her while she took a phone call in the car and I wandered off before she had finished. I hated being such a burden, but I knew I would soon forget.

Jenny got the fire started and joined me on the couch. "Why don't you sleep here tonight, Dad." "I would like that," I croaked through my tears.

I woke up this morning, I know I had, though I don't remember. The morning is always a blur these days. I am in a cafeteria surrounded by old people, most of whom are in gowns.

"That's weird," I muttered to myself. I spotted a coffee maker on a counter to my left. With great effort I stood up from my chair; I don't remember that being so hard. I walked over to it and poured myself a cup. After I sat back down and my coffee had a chance to cool, I took a sip. I looked to my right where a young woman in scrubs smiled at me.

"Strong and black, just like I like my women." She blushed. We both chuckled.

T.E. Cole *is a firefighter in Middle Tennessee. In his free time, he is typically renovating his fixer-upper and preparing for his firstborn son.* Black Coffee *is his first published work. Of* Black Coffee, *he says, "I write to process emotions that I find difficult to express, so I wrote this story to work through the difficulty of having loved ones with dementia."*

Barbed Wire Fence Blues

Bob Graham

I walked into the shop first thing Monday morning and Jim gave me my job list. He was blowing steam from his coffee mug. He always insisted on using a diner mug instead of a go mug. The shop was cavernous. He told me I had to go up to the north quarter, string the fence back up that he had instructed me to dismantle the previous Friday.

"Why?" I said.

"Some neighbour said they can't drive their cattle that way anymore. Complained to the county, said they have 'right of way' or an 'easement' or some shit and that adjoining property owners are obligated to keep fences up in order to facilitate the uninhibited movement of livestock," Jim said.

"Fuck that. Thompson's took their fence out last spring, county didn't make them put it back up."

"Property with the last remaining standing fence carries the responsibility, they said. Guess the county will back them up on that."

So, I groaned and cussed and stormed out of there. I loaded up all my shit and muttered in the truck as my breath filled the cab and the heater blew frantically. As it whirred, weighed down by years and years of dust, along with the rumbling on gravel, I felt myself ease back down. At least we hadn't yanked the posts out yet. That'd be the real bitch.

After I parked, I laid out all my tools on the bed of the truck and I anchored the top wire to the brace post, wrapped it around twice and clipped off the tail once it was secure. I spooled the roll of wire back out the length of the quarter section. It was much easier with the wire reel this time, mounted into the hitch of the half-ton. Once it was strung out, I clamped the wire into the wire stretcher and started to ratchet up the tension. The wire slowly lifted out of the grass with each pull of the lever like a lazily levitating corpse. As the tension grew and grew and it became more and more difficult to ratchet any further, it sent wild pulsating rhythms shooting down the half-mile of barbed wire. The frantic energy seemed to reverberate in sharp metallic overtones, like a concert pianist forced to improv at gunpoint. Veins bulged from my forearms, and I grunted as I pulled the lever one notch further and the wire clanged tight against the fence posts and things began to return to how they had been.

I first started working on Jim Daly's farm right after seeding wrapped up and there was a natural lull about the place. My timing was pretty good, because there was no way a stressed out, sleep-deprived farmer would have put up with my incompetent ass for the month or so it took for seeding from start to finish - give or take a couple rain days, or grenade days, as they were known around the farm. Grenade days were when everything shut down cause some important piece of machinery *grenaded*, as Jim liked to put it.

I'm not so much incompetent as I am just generally mechanically useless, which is a poor trait to possess on a farm. That's why I tried like hell my whole working life to get anything but a farm job. But, growing up in the middle of buttfuck nowhere leaves a guy's job prospects mighty thin otherwise.

My working life hasn't been particularly long anyhow; only been at it six or so years. Well, those first couple years only involved weekends and summers. But full-time from seventeen till now. At fourteen, dad started to let me use a shitty old quad to drive up and down the gravel roads, where I would mow old folk's lawns for them, pull weeds, general clean up type stuff. I'd shovel their walks in the wintertime. That's how I made money for the first while. Got a good reputation about the area 'cause of it too, which didn't take much 'cause most the other kids my age were already figuring out how to drive drunk and how to not itch their crotch too much after they'd been in town for the weekend.

When I was seventeen I bought a decent little Pontiac Sunfire off of Barb Delroy who lived on an old dairy. She had a son, Adam, die a year or so before I started taking care of her yard. Adam was only a year ahead of me in school. We became friends pretty quick in my first year of high school after realizing that we were the only two boys in the whole county who didn't give a shit about sports or trucks or fighting. She was one of the only yard customers I had that wasn't old as hell. The Sunfire had been Adam's; he hadn't had it for terribly long before he died, but she couldn't bear to get rid of it until after he'd been gone for a whole year. She told me that he would've wanted me to have it, and she tried to just gift it to me, but I wouldn't have it. Gave her the money to make the deal proper. Her husband was the dairy man, so they were doing well when everybody was still alive and kicking, but he died, too, only a few months after Adam. Supposedly, he fell asleep at the wheel of his truck driving on a bridge in the city, but everybody quietly knew that he just couldn't take it anymore. Gotta hand it to the guy though; he made it look like an accident enough that life insurance paid out, so between that and Barb selling off the dairy quota and the whole cow herd, she'd never have to work again.

That Sunfire ensured that I could get a job in town and never have to step foot on a farm if I had anything to do about it. That worked for a while, Dairy Queen, stockboy, cashier at the Sev. I did all sorts of shit, but I finally lost my job not long after I started working in the lumber yard at Timbr-Mart. I came in early for my shift one morning and I guess my hoodie smelled like weed, so my douchebag manager shitcanned me.

I'd been bouncing around a little while, and it was starting to get pretty methy in town, so I figured fuck it. Might as well try a fuckin' farm. Every other asshole ends up on one at some point. That's when I called up Jim. He and my dad are buddies, drink in Jim's shop every Friday night.

Jim's a good dude, but he knows who I am. When I asked him for the job he said, "You sure? No really, you're for sure?" When I told him, yes, I was absolutely for sure, he said, "Ok, but you gotta know you're only gonna be getting the grunt jobs to start."

Yes, I knew that.

So, that's how I ended up in an old half-ton, with a couple pair of fencing pliers, couple five-gallon buckets, shit load of work gloves, and this galloot in the passenger seat named Gary.

Gary and I were the new guys, though he had about twenty-five years on me. This was his first week and I had a couple months on the job. We got tasked with taking apart a barbed wire fence, then rolling up the wire by hand. Goddamn wire reel was broke, or so Jim told us. I figured it was just an unsanctioned probationary test. Gary had been working up north on the rigs but had gotten sent back down after he got too many DUIs and hit with a possession charge, which is kind of like getting kicked out of a breakfast buffet for eating too many scrambled eggs and sausage patties.

It was a June morning, eight o'clock. Still cold enough that I had the heater turned on to keep the fog from building up on the windshield. I like only hearing the blower fan and the gravel first thing in the morning.

"Jesus kid, what's wrong with you? I guess you kids probably don't even know what radio is anymore." Gary chuckled stupidly to himself and reached his arm to the radio to turn up the volume. There was a four on the floor kick drum and simple synthesizer melody with a young sounding woman singing about only living for tonight.

Gary violently turned the radio dial, waded through the static ocean, and grumbled. "Fuckin' music today sucks. Bunch of retards with computers, that's all music is anymore." He stopped turning the dial when he landed on a song that I always heard the losers at the lumber yard play. It was all overproduced drums, wanky, dumb guitars, and a man singing about only living for tonight.

"Hell ya, now here's some real music!" Gary yelled. I winced. He turned the volume up louder and I turned it back down as he tried to head bang and play air guitar, but his neck was too fat and he was too uncoordinated, so he looked more like he was about to have a seizure in slow motion.

"What the fuck kid! This song got too much balls for you?" He sneered.

"No, I just think it sucks." I said.

"Well what kind of music do you like then? Probably some new gay shit."

"Ya, I guess that's probably right."

He snickered, "Are you gay? All you kids are fuckin' gay now. I listened to this podcast that said like ninety percent of all kids born after the year 2000 think they're gay. If you are, it's not a problem, I knew all kinds of queers up north."

I sighed. "No, I'm not. But it really sounds like you would have a problem with it."

He waved his hand in front of him and pulled on a vape with the other. "You kids are all so fuckin' sensitive now. Can't say anything anymore. Bunch of pansies, all of you."

I couldn't think of anything worth saying so we drove silently for the next few minutes until we got to an approach and I pulled into the pivot corner.

"Jim said this is where we should start. We'll start working north on this fence all the way up to those grain bins at the start of the next quarter." I said.

"Look at you, hot shit. Didn't you ever hear anything about seniority on the job site?" Gary said.

"Uhhh ya, but I think that refers to your time spent working for that specific company, not - you know - actual seniority."

"Smart ass. Whatever, I'll show you how things are done anyhow. I haven't rolled up wire since I was a greenhorn, but I bet I'll beat the shit out of you at it."

I muttered under my breath while I stared out long to the horizon. I counted how many quarter sections I could see and squinted my eyes until I couldn't count any more. I figured the boundary line for the county was twelve miles out, on the other side of the river. Twelve miles. That's twenty-four quarter sections, three-thousand eight-hundred forty acres. That's just what one line covers straight from me to there. All this empty space around us, unseeded ground, pasture, air, and the biggest sky you've ever seen; all this space and here I was, stuck. Trapped. Waiting for the shop coffee to kick in, wishin' I were deaf or unemployed.

I put the work gloves on and tossed a set of fencing pliers in with each five-gallon bucket.

Gary almost gasped, "Gloves?! You're wearing gloves?!"

I looked far on the horizon and squinted my eyes. "Yes, Gary. I'm going to wear gloves so I can roll up barbed wire and not stab my hands a million fucking times. You're not?"

"Pfffft," he said, and waved his hand in front of him again. "Gloves are for pussies. If you're a real working man your hands should be tough enough that you don't need no gloves. Them barbs are just tiny little things anyhow."

Gary approached the fence and cut each of the four wires at the brace post and then promptly pulled the staples from the top wire on each of the first four posts in a row, tossing the bent old staples into his bucket. He then returned to the start of the wire. "Watch this," he said.

He wrapped the wire around in a loop, a little bigger than a manhole cover. I watched him carefully place his hands between each set of barbs on the smooth sections. Once he had made the first loop and began to slowly spool up the wire as he walked, the smooth sections inevitably became intertwined with new barbs, unavoidable for his naked hands. He grimaced and whispered curses and I smiled. I let him continue on for a while.

I started behind him on the next wire down and didn't say anything when he went back to the truck for gloves of his own. By the time he got back to his roll, I was pretty well caught up and he started up again.

"So you're a young kid. You must be getting all sorts of pussy in town, huh?"

"Ummm I don't know, man."

"What do you mean you don't know? You either are or you aren't!"

I just stared at him. I wondered if Gary had ever drunk his own bath water.

He laughed, "Guess you're not getting any then." He ripped from his vape again and dropped the roll of wire into the grass. "Don't know what the hell is wrong with you. When I was your age, I was gettin' all sorts of snatch. Anywhere I went. Chicks love a hard-workin' man, so I guess that's half your problem." He continued laughing. "Sure you're not gay, kid? Better be careful, don't want to end up like Barb's boy."

I dropped my roll and it clanged like a rattling cage. I stepped toward him and stomped down the hesitation in my gut. I hoped to God he was sober. "What'd you say?"

"Ah, never mind. Sensitive. Way too goddamn sensitive."

"No, fuck that. You don't get to bring up something like that and then just walk away from it. What about Adam?"

Gary sheepishly looked at the ground and kicked at the grass till dirt sprang up. He looked like a bloated, defective toddler.

"Well everybody knows he offed himself 'cause he was the way that he was. That's all." He hauled off his vape and refused to meet my eye. I could see the graying stubble on his chin.

"What the hell would you know about why he did what he did? Can't be anything other than a rigger or a farmer in a shithole like this without everybody and their dog talking shit until you break down into the mold." I said.

"Well I wasn't even around when he was coming up…" Gary trailed off while muttering feebly.

"Exactly," I said. "If you weren't around then how would you know anything about him?"

"My grandpa," he said. "After I moved back in, he filled me in with all the goings on. That's what he told me."

I scoffed. "You're living with your grandparents?"

He spit, and expanded like a bullfrog, "Ya, figure they're gonna go out to pasture sooner rather than later, so might as well get moved in now. That house is gonna be mine anyhow, no other family left to take it."

I continued with my wire and he with his until we reached the end of the quarter section - half a mile. Not long after our exchange, I had passed Gary. My anger made me move with more intention. I pulled the staples out of the weather worn fence posts like toothpicks from a marshmallow. When I reached the brace post at the end, I cut all four wires and then started my new roll as I headed back. Gary had been wheezing worse than a bronchitis ridden sow and had a hypnotically shimmering lather of canola oil sweat gliding about his skin-tagged and mole-peppered face. As I passed by him, I refused to acknowledge him, but couldn't help but stare as his body strained to perspire the last of the northern coke remnants from his lardy pores.

When we were back where we started, I tossed a roll of wire in the box of the truck. I saw Gary's back as he craned his neck and spoke in a hushed voice into his phone.

"A roast sounds great, Grandma. Okay. Okay. I…Okay - I love you. Okay, bye."

He hung up and continued to stare downwards for a moment. Before he turned, and before I could say anything, I felt it.

You always feel the rumble of tires on a gravel road before your body registers it in any other way. I felt it and then I heard it and then I saw the dust shooting everywhere before I saw Barb Delroy's brand-new white Tahoe rolling up to us. She rolled the slightly tinted window down as her passenger side tires came to a peaceful rest in the partly greening grass in the ditch, wet with the last lingering lamentations of winter. She leaned across the center console and smiled her great big smile at me.

"Hiya honey! How are ya?" Her long brown hair swayed easily, and her skin was a tan two months ahead of the sun.

My heart beat fast and I knocked my five-gallon pail onto its side as I hurried to straighten my posture. The bent and rusted staples rattled inside. "I'm good, Mrs. Delroy. Just workin'." I forgot how to smile for a moment and forced one out. Her eyes were bright in mine.

"I'm sorry to bother you at work, but I seen your work truck go by earlier and figured you'd be down this road somewhere. I didn't want to bother Jim, but some of his bulls got out of the pasture and are in my yard again. I don't suppose you could get them back in?"

"Of course. I'm just finishing up here. I can go do that right now!" I said, a little too eagerly.

"I don't mind them in the yard, you know. I'd just hate to see them get out on the road and hit by some poor person."

I inhaled sharply and Gary trudged up to my side - I could smell the dank body odour swirling about him. He spoke too loudly, "There's no fuckin' bull too mean to be corralled by me, darlin'! We'll get them pricks put back away proper!" He winked at her and her face turned to cold stone. The sun had slipped behind a gray cloud and the age in her face revealed itself in dark caverns.

She applied a pained smile to me without making eye contact with him. "I'm sure you can handle this by yourself, honey." She rolled the window up and took off faster than she had slowed.

I remembered one time after school, on a Friday, Adam asked me if I wanted to spend the weekend at his house. I said sure, and he drove us home in his Sunfire. We listened to the top forty station on the radio real loud, and we didn't say a word. It was winter, the gravel roads were bare, and the ditches were full with snow and it was white out as far as our eyes would let us see. When we got home, we parked in the driveway by the house, and he turned the music down low. The car kept running and the vents blew hot air over the dash and down at our toes. I watched the snowflakes disappear the moment they hit the windshield. He looked over at me, but I can't remember exactly what he said. It was something like, 'what are you gonna do after high school'? So I said something like, 'shit, I don't know. What is there to do? Get outta here, I guess'. And we both just watched the snowflakes drop down and keep melting over and over again on the windshield. I asked him the same thing, and he just smiled his tiny little tight-lipped smile, looking forward. He shut the car off and I got out and looked over the roof to meet his eyes, but he hadn't gotten out yet. I saw Barb instead, standing in the kitchen window with her arms crossed, smiling down at us both.

Gary scoffed and looked at me.

"What got up her ass? She looks like she needs a real man in her life—show her what a real bull looks lik-,"

I watched his mouth finish moving, but only registered him as another article of the landscape, like the wind blowing through swaying brown native grasses all around us. I sensed the threat he posed only after I felt a sharp crack shoot up my elbow and I heard the old man grunt like a beast when I realized that I'd punched him square in the jaw. I shook my hand out and saw the flash of red scrapes on my knuckles. He staggered back and did not drop, instead stepping forward. He tugged at my shirt collar briefly before I grabbed my bucket of warbled staples and swung it roundhouse to the other side of his outlandishly large skull. He stumbled backwards and took a wild but fruitless swing at me before losing his balance. His back foot dropped over the lip of the ditch, and he toppled over like a half-empty beer can in a windstorm. Rolling and tumbling down into the bottom, still wet from collected snowmelt and insulated with long dead leaves no longer crunching. He shouted hateful and pitifully as I walked back to the work truck.

When I pulled into Barb's driveway, familiar tears reflexively lathered my eyes. I hadn't been in the yard since I bought the car, but it still felt empty knowing he wasn't at home. Though Barb had told me on the day of his funeral to "not be a stranger," I thought that was just something that people said at things like that. Only bumped into her on occasion about town in the years after I stopped her yard work, and I've felt more of a stranger to her than anyone else I'd never met.

There looked to be only a half dozen head out in her yard, leaving great gaping imprints of their hooves in the perfectly manicured lawn. There was a gate at the back of the property, and the bulls moved calmly as I eased them back towards it.

After I chained the gate shut, I walked back through the yard towards the truck and saw Barb standing on the back porch observing me. Her eyes were glassy like mine, and she held her arms outstretched towards me, the two of us the only ones who could know how the other felt.

Folks with jobs in the city like to talk about the modern era as some bastion for progressive labour policies and the absolute pinnacle of radical new ideas, but for most of us, things are the same as ever, never to change or update. Folks can have all manner of different jobs, and they can experience the properly scheduled arrival of legally required wages, holiday pay, overtime pay, time-off, and health plans - those people have never worked on no goddamn farm. So, when Jim invited me to the shop for beers at the end of that day, which happened to be a Friday, I knew that I had gotten through the probationary period that didn't exist in work codes or manuals.

I was handed a can that was claimed by Saskatchewaners to be their own, but I had yet to hear anyone admit that it was owned by just another conglomerate out of Toronto, so whatever they thought was brewed by their own was the same bullshit some suit was sipping on Yonge Street.

Jim saddled up next to me and clasped his hand on my shoulder. He looked at my dad with misplaced pride. "So Doug, you heard what your boy did today?"

Dad shot a quizzical look at me. He'd never known me to do much of anything.

"Took exception to this ex-rigger I hired on last week. Gave him two shots in the jaw, toppled his ass over into the ditch." Jim burst out laughing and clapped my back. "God you shoulda seen him, leaves in his hair and mud stains all over those stupid reflective coveralls. He was just cussin' up a storm when he came back into the yard."

Dad looked at me wide-eyed, "No shit. What got into you?"

I drank deeply from my can while the white LED lights illuminated the concrete floor smooth and clear. Years-old oil stains masqueraded as shadows.

"Didn't clean up his mouth around Barb." I said.

"Oh right, I heard through the grapevine that them bulls got out," Jim said, "did you get that sorted out?"

"Yep," I said.

"So where is this guy?" Dad asked.

I looked at Jim.

"Dunno, fired him at the end of the day." Jim said.

"No shit?" I said.

"Yep," Jim said.

"How come?"

"If it wasn't you, it would have been someone else. Someone who could actually land a punch."

I felt the stiffness of the day from so many rolls of wire. I drank from my beer and rubbed my hand; I was sure it was broken.

With all four strands of barbed wire anchored at either end, I grabbed my bucket full of brand-new staples and started pounding them around the wire and into the fence posts. It was methodical and I did not have to be present for it. With each swing of the blunt end of the fencing pliers, I could feel the tenderness of my broken hand. Each swing sent lightning up my arm. I thought of who might have put this fence up in the first place. Jim's dad, or maybe his grandpa. Maybe Jim's grandpa was an asshole too. Maybe he wasn't. I thought of what they all thought of this place back when they were my age. I wondered if they belonged. I wondered if anybody ever belongs. I imagined I was them. I saw the shop lights on Friday night illuminating a shining Peterbilt backed perfectly into its bay. I smiled at the red-faced men drinking from cans who didn't know what they were smiling at. I kept pounding staples for all the leaves and mud and ditches and jaws and fists and melted snow. I thought of grandmas who made their grandbabies roast dinners no matter how old either of them had gotten or what mistakes they had made. I stood before this fence that couldn't seem to go away, and I kept swinging and swinging and the wires kept rattling and I thought of corralled bulls and women with pretty hair and complicated skin who bring beautiful boys into the world.

Bob Graham *is a cattle feeder from Southern Alberta. In his free time, he likes to walk through the prairie and look at the sky. His fiction has appeared in* BRUISER *and* SUM FLUX*. You can find more of his work on Substack @bobgraham, where he writes* Uncle Bob Is Ruminating. *Of* Barbed Wire Fence Blues *he says, "Man does not require a fence to be corralled, but they do help."*

Death in the Gulley

E. L. Jacobs

In the evening, under orange haze, the boys walked over a pine log which spanned across a trickling creek bed. The sun was low and shy behind spring's canopy but cast harsh fragments of light through coming dark. It was almost summer. The woods were chirpy and jaunty. Nearing virility.

Isaac stopped abruptly.

Joss ran into him and grabbed him so they wouldn't go rolling down. Hosea ran into Joss. Zeke ran into Hosea.

"What is it, Iz?" Hosea asked.

"Look." He pointed down into the little valley where a raccoon sat on a rock.

"Big deal," Joss said. He offered the creature a brief glance. "Let's keep going."

"No, look closer."

"Damn…" Zeke said. The boys were experimenting with new forms of expression, Zeke leading the charge. He had 11 years. The oldest by two months.

"Rabies?" Hosea asked.

"Gotta be…" Zeke said. "We ought to keep moving."

"Is it suffering?" Isaac asked. "Joss, you know about this stuff."

"Yeah, Dad says they suffer pretty bad. But it could kill us—if we got bit. So leave it be. Like Zeke said." He tried his best to sound firm, but it came out more suggestive and timid.

"But shouldn't we take it out of its misery?" Isaac's eyes were urgent.

"I wish we could, but we shouldn't risk our skin for it."

"Yeah, it ain't worth all that," Hosea said.

"Keep walking," Zeke said.

They fell silent. Zeke pushed Hosea who pushed Joss who pushed Isaac. He took a step, then stopped. Looking down in the gulley again, he saw the raccoon walking in circles and foaming violently. It was fuzzy like his dog, but ragged and unruly. And it was little. Not just small, but little, like his dog when it was a puppy. Big tail, tucked low. Its eyes held life, but were not vibrant. Not playful. Barely seeing.

"Guys, we've gotta kill it," Isaac whispered. "We'll go get a gun."

"My .22 is miles away," Joss said. They'd walked to the woods from Hosea's house, who lived in town. They were spending the night there. He looked at Hosea and said, "Do you have one?"

"A rifle? No. Dad does. But he wouldn't let us carry it through town to get here. He don't even know how far we walk…" Hosea looked off in a brief dread, scratching his face thoughtfully.

"But if we just asked him," Isaac started.

"We can't ask him," Hosea cut him off. "Do y'all want to get in trouble?"

"Let's just go back to Hosea's and play Call of Duty," Zeke said like an adult.

"But this is more important, this is real-world shit," Isaac said. Hosea stumbled and Zeke dropped the crooked stick he'd been walking with. Iz was the youngest of them, the purest.

Another cold silence. It resonated with the gentle ring of cicadas. It was one of the quieter years for cicadas.

"Why are you so set on this?" Joss asked.

"Not sure. Just a feeling."

"Well, Iz. There's no way to get a gun out here without causing a scene."

"Yeah," Zeke said, "no need to be a hero. Not like it's a dog or anything. That would be different."

"But what about the dogs? The ones in town?"

"What are you talking about, Iz?" Zeke was becoming annoyed. He ran his long skinny fingers through his short brown hair.

"The dogs," he repeated. "People's dogs. They could get rabies. Like, it could spread through town." His eyes were wide and his head was cocked as if this evidence was completely obvious.

"We're a long way from town," Hosea said. His feet felt the distance.

"Dogs travel a long way from home."

"Dude, give it a rest," Zeke said. He wiped sweat from his head using the belly of his white t-shirt.

"Think about Trixie," Isaac said. "What if this coon made it to y'all's yard?"

"Then dad would shoot it," Hosea said. "He might even let me."

"What if y'all didn't know?"

"Well let's tell him just to be safe. We can say it was nearby."

"I meant hypothetical…" he stammered, "but look. What if it never got that far? If we just handled it out here?"

"Hero complex," Zeke muttered. "Where's the girl you're trying to impress?" He looked around theatrically.

"Look," Joss interjected. "I'm with you. I get it. The raccoon needs to die. And yeah, that would help the whole town. But we just ain't armed for it." He gestured toward the path, in vain.

"You've always got your knife. I bet all three of you do."

"Who's getting close enough for that?" Joss scoffed. His heart jumped in pace and he bit his lips to keep a level face.

"Not you," Zeke said to Isaac directly, "you've never stabbed anything anyway."

"Gotta be different than shooting it," Hosea said, "I can't imagine."

"Yeah, but better than letting it suffer."

"You're not getting that close," Joss said, "sorry Iz." Isaac was to be protected at all costs.

"Then sharpen me a stick," the boy said.

Silence. Loud, heavy silence. The raccoon stumbled on beneath the pine tree. The boys sat down on the log and watched. The sun was setting. Their sneakers kicked back and forth gently over-head of the raccoon. They gripped the bark with sweaty fingers.

"That ain't a bad idea…" Joss muttered.

"What?" Hosea snapped.

"We could use a spear. Death is mercy." Joss looked at his friends hoping for validation. Isaac smiled but the others stared blankly.

Isaac stood and walked from the log to the woods, west of the creek bed. The minutes he was gone felt like hours. Zeke kept an eye on the beast, to protect Isaac upon his return. The boy came back with a pencil-straight shaft of a fallen oak branch. A rarity, and as long as he was tall. He'd broken off all the twigs and crooks. Isaac held it aloft like Excalibur. Then he held it out towards the others. Joss grabbed it and started shaving the tip sharp with his pocket knife.

"Wait," Isaac whispered, as if the coon might hear, "where is it?"

"Up there," Zeke said, "thing's moving fast."

"See," he responded vigorously, "it could make town easy!"

Hosea started to kick his feet in a fidgety fashion.

"It could not," Zeke said. "This is silly."

"I dunno man," Hosea said. "Look how far it's gone."

"Not you, too."

"Look man, I gotta think of Trixie!" Hosea stood up on the pine. He was in.

Joss nodded, his white forehead glinting in the early moonlight beneath the parting of his red hair. He sharpened fervently.

"This is silly, guys. That thing will die before it makes Elkinsford."

"Death is still mercy," Joss said. "Look at the poor thing."

"And just in case," Hosea said, "for the dogs."

"The dogs, the dogs," Zeke said, "I think they can take care of themselves! It's just a little raccoon."

"They don't know what rabies is, ain't you seen Old Yeller?" Isaac growled.

"I've seen it…"

"We're just doing our job," Isaac said. "Stewards of God's earth. Ya know."

"You're 10 years old," Zeke said.

Isaac didn't answer.

"Death is mercy," Joss whispered, still working.

"Death is mercy," Hosea echoed.

"You guys sound like a cult."

It was nice and sharp now. Isaac led them across the log, where they climbed some wet roots to get down into the gulley. The raccoon was still foaming. It walked towards them at first, then got upset and stumbled backwards a little. Its eyes were cold and dark. But they still held a certain sadness. The juxtaposition was new and ugly. Real-world shit.

"Hand it here," Isaac said.

"No sir," Joss said. "You're too young."

"We're one year apart," Isaac began to argue.

"No," Hosea interrupted, "you aren't doing it."

So they all stood, looking at the spear. Joss held it, but didn't want to.

Zeke stood tall over the others, shaking his head. Joss and Hosea looked upon the beast together. Isaac stood apart, by himself, looking at the moon in the trees.

"Well, you were the first one to agree to this," Zeke said.

"I know, I just…"

"Let me do it," Isaac said, chest out.

"No," Hosea said, pushing him back a little.

"I'll do it, alright?" Joss said. "Just give me a minute."

He walked forward with the stick.

He thought of all the squirrels and rabbits he'd shot, and felt brave for a second, but dammit do they die fast and easy when they're shot. This was bound to be slow, he knew. This was bound to hurt. But, you know, death is mercy.

Joss raised his stick. His spear. Long and nervous in the moonlight. He was stone, staring for a few good mississippis. When he couldn't take any more of the pitiful hissing and stumbling, he struck.

The beast made a terrible noise, and the boys shuddered as Joss pulled the spear from its shoulder.

"Do it again, quick," Hosea said, voice high.

This time the spear hit the chest, but too low. The beast rolled and squirmed, screaming and foaming.

"Dammit…" Joss said.

"You've gotta hit it again, it's suffering worse," Isaac cried.

Joss looked up, gathered himself, and struck again. The neck. The spear was sharp enough to puncture, and it finally started bleeding. But the beast kept moving. It wouldn't die. He struck again. The tip of the spear glanced off the skull and hit the neck again, lodging deeper this time. The beast squirmed and hissed.

"Y'all…" Joss muttered. His eyes couldn't be more open.

"Give me a turn, man, it's okay," Hosea said, taking the spear.

He struck harder than Joss, but less accurately, and it dug into the beast's back.

"I dunno y'all," he said, "maybe we shouldn't have…"

"I can try," Isaac said, more question than declaration. The heroic glimmer in his eye was long gone and his hands were shaking.

"You're the smallest," Hosea said, without breaking eye contact with the beast, "there's no use."

"Try it again," Joss said louder, "I can't take seeing this anymore."

The worst noise the kids had ever heard came from the beast's punctured throat. A scream, but weak. More of a squeak. A groan. Foam covered the dry rocks and was spattered with blood.

"It wasn't supposed to go like this," Isaac said. He held his head in his hands.

"You meant well," Joss said. "We know you did. It's just…"

"We gotta keep trying," Hosea said, handing Joss the spear and dusting the dry bark from his fingers.

Some rustling in the leaves behind them made him hesitate. Zeke emerged between them with a big rock.

He looked down on the raccoon. "Damn. This is rough."

They all nodded. Then Zeke lifted the rock, struggling a little, breathed in a quick breath, and squeezed the rock like it was keeping him alive. He threw it. Straight down into the earth. Into the beast itself. Between the rock and the flat stones of the creek bed, the raccoon was released from her torment.

Blood splattered Zeke's white t-shirt and Joss' grey hoodie. The latter dropped the spear on the ground. The stick. It fell into shallow red water.

"It's done," Hosea finally said, the first good breath he'd taken in minutes.

"Yep." Joss wiped a tear from his eye, pretending to scratch his nose.

Zeke turned away from the defiled creature and stepped away. Isaac only stared at its lifeless form.

"Hey, come on," Hosea said, pulling Isaac by the arm. He had to pull hard. Joss grabbed Zeke's arm in the same manner, and pulled him on. Their sneakers became saturated with cool water, as they followed the stars and moon that shone between red clay banks and protruding roots.

"Shame we don't have a shovel," Joss said.

They stopped then, and looked back at the creature. It was dead. Surely dead. Not just dead, but mutilated. And the trickling creek was marbled with red life.

"This was the right thing to do," Isaac reassured himself.

They nodded at him, but didn't speak.

Side by side, arms around each other's shoulders, they marched through the spring woods. The stars were bright and the frogs sang and the boys were silent.

***

The walk home was long. The night air felt fresh and unfamiliar.

E. L. Jacobs *is a woodworker from Concord, Ga. In his free time, he enjoys adventures in the outdoors. He is the author of* Dust, *a collection of romantic and southern gothic poetry. Currently, he is working on a historical novel set in the Pre-American South. Of* Death in the Gulley, *he says, "Growing up is a hell of a thing. I wanted to explore the logic of boys as they try to be heroes."*

Somewhere in the Woods

Clifton Joseph Lee

It was getting dark—lingering somewhere in the raspberry haze between day and night, and it took all the willpower contained in my five-year-old body not to burst into tears.

"Wait, you said this was a dream?" Evelyn interrupted me, which was odd—as she was one of the few friends I had made in my time in the city that wasn't riddled with a muddle of different neuroses like I was, and was an exceptional listener. I gave her the benefit of remembering that I had been a whirlwind of emotions and scattered thoughts when we met at our usual Sunday coffee and brunch place on the corner of Magnolia and 10th street, and she was probably as confused as I was.

"No—well, I mean, yes—it was a dream. But it was like I had dreamed a memory—one long buried. I've not thought about that day since—well, since a very long time ago." There was a certain slice of well-hidden grief in my voice that even I heard, and I knew, as perceptive as she was, that Evelyn had heard it too. But if she did, she did not show it, leaning back into the canvas couch. I looked out as the sweet-gum leaves fell in a small blizzard of oranges and yellows in the increasingly cold breeze.

"Please, continue," she said, and so I returned to a world that felt so strangely far and excruciatingly close.

We were in the woods—it was sometime in that middle-place of fall where the trees hadn't quite given up hope in warm days again and clung to their browning leaves. I was with my father and my brother—we'd spent the entire day at the hunting camp surrounded by the rest of the club. It was the first day of hunting season—at least it could have been. Since that night, I had never felt the need to know the exact day except as a point of safe conversation between random older folk and myself back home.

We were tracking a deer, the gods of the woods, as I had begun to see them, for they were the things my kin sought and worshipped in their own way. A buck was many things: elusive, quiet, beautiful, a ghost—yet we counted on their rutting and their hormone-driven craze to drive them into the range of our guns. There was something so unendingly maddening about hearing the men around me speak with such awe and reverence about something they would inevitably and violently end. I could not understand what about me was different that I could not measure up—what part of me wasn't violent enough to cheer at the death of a god? I felt alien, sitting there among my kin and family friends, as they cleaned their guns and made crass jokes. I was the belle of a pageant of despair and death. The whole day was a blur, most of it was spent sitting on the ground as I was too afraid of heights to get into a tree-stand. I remember praying with a conflicted heart that a buck would walk out into the clearing and the whole thing would be over with in one explosive moment, and simultaneously that the deer would be spared the wrath of fire and man.

"Don't get lost in it, Jay." Evelyn took my hand, and I was grateful for it. She was Virgil, reminding me of where and who I was as I delved into a Hell I hadn't traversed in so long. I was living in the city, with friends and other Queer folk like myself. I had a partner now; I was in the final stages of writing my novel. Against the odds, I was happier now than I had ever been in the whole of my life before. I adjusted my dress, thanked her, and continued.

Both of my prayers were answered—but not in the way I had expected. Daddy and I hadn't seen a thing—a few crows eyed us suspiciously and called out their trepidations to the woods, but as the sun began to set, we sat together in utter peace. I could sense my father's frustration in the silence, but for the sake of his soul, and in some ways, mine, I was glad. The echoing crack of gunfire, however, ended any brief gladness I felt.

My father took out his phone and flipped it open to answer the call. My brother had shot a massive buck. I walked like a dead man behind my father and brother, as we embarked on our search for the buck, who had taken off towards the creek after being shot.

The day stretched itself to aid our hunt, something that felt like an utterly cruel betrayal to a child who sometimes feels like their only ally in life is the warm and playful embrace of the daylight, and what had likely been only a few hours felt like the tiring stretch of eternity. The roads we took through the tall pines all began to look the same until we abandoned them entirely, instead trekking through game trails in the underbrush. What had begun as a tempered trot behind my father had turned into a stumbling, desperate attempt to keep up. Thorny limbs grasped at my clothes and caught me on the cheeks, spider webs barred me entry to branched gateways, and creek-mud sucked at my little boots—weighing down each step and making my legs feel leaden. I remember thinking that this place, the woods that had always sheltered me and played setting for all my endless imaginary worlds and stories filled with dragons and unicorns and mythical elves, had also betrayed me. It had been twisted by something I couldn't name at the time; some force compelled it from a place of awe and beauty into a tribulation of worthiness. There was some kind of innocence taken in that moment—something beautiful lost from the world.

The thought lingered at the tip of my mind when Evelyn got up to get our coffees. As I watched her walk away towards the counter, I wondered about all the things that I had seemingly lost in one moment in time. My faith—something I'd once held so closely in fear and the trembling of the soul—had slowly been released into a quiet sea of acceptance. My family, my community—all these things were changed and could only now be accessed through the misty realm of memory—but all were lost in a final turning of the heart, or of time. I followed Evelyn's footsteps out of my thoughts and back into the coffee shop.

"So, did you ever find the buck?" Her searching eye shone brightly in the morning light, searching for answers and meaning.

"Well, yes, and no. I suppose the real answer is that I don't remember. I have a memory, but I have no way to tell whether or not it's fabricated. And besides, I'm no longer convinced the point of the story is whether or not we ever found the buck." I took a sip of coffee. It momentarily satisfied an anxious itch in my chest as I swallowed.

"You are equally frustrating and fascinating, Jay." She looked at me and grinned like some art expert, noticing a new detail in a painting that they had stared at for years. I returned her smile and took another sip. This one preceded a strange jumble of dread and understanding as I realized we truly had come to the zenith of the story, and I was increasingly sure of why this memory had returned.

"Do you want to take these to go?" I asked, suddenly feeling like the walls of the coffee shop had grown inward and were threatening me.

Evelyn fixed me in her knowing gaze, one that said *I know why, but it's not really constructive to say anything,* and we walked out into the street together. I took a refreshing sigh of the crisp October air, and felt the weight in my chest release, inch by inch, and by the time we had turned the corner onto Oriole Street, I had taken enough air and could continue the story.

The sun was low beyond the tree line, and the world had given over to the soft liminality of twilight. The sky, too large and too full to be contained by the horizon, cast its raspberry-lavender color onto the tall grass we were trudging through. We had passed beyond any semblance of my familiarity of the woods—we had gone so far out of our usual hunting grounds that the woods took on a strangeness that could only be described as alien. The ground beneath us was swampy and soft. The grass that grew out of it came to my brother's chest and my father's shoulders, which meant they felt as tall as the swaying pines to me. Interlaced with the grass were cat-claw briars, and it was nearly impossible for me to keep up. My brother had hoisted me onto his shoulders—I must have either complained enough to warrant this small act of mercy, or had been too slow and too much of a hinderance that it was the only logical option to carry me; regardless of the reason, I was grateful. From my higher vantage point, the world was transformed into a roiling sea of grass—the cold wind whipped it into waves that lapped at my legs and feet.

My father and brother were discussing how they might mount the buck and the logistics of skinning and cleaning it. It was bitter conversation, and I was once again plagued by that dissonance I felt among the men of my kin from earlier in the day. It washed over me and left me queasy. Something was wrong, but my young mind could not name it.

As the sense of unease came and went from my stomach, another sensation barged its way into my consciousness. The grass had gotten taller, and the briars curled up into the air. With each step my brother took, the briars gouged into my legs, leaving long tears that leaked droplets of bright red blood. I cried out, and my brother stopped to check my legs.

"Daddy, please! I want to go home!" I cried and clutched at the marks that were beginning to leak red streaks down to my ankles.

"Jay, you'll be alright! Just man up!" came my father's reply, and in that moment, something clicked in my brain. If this was what it meant to be a man, then I did not know if I wanted to be a man. I could not bear it any longer—manhood had become nothing but pain inflicted on me and others—innocence taken and lives snuffed out. It was violent. It was cruel. It was callous. It was ugly. It was everything that did not fit within me. I felt the hot tears roll down my cheek and fall, watched them mix with the blood on my legs, and swallowed the protests of my soul. We walked on, and I stifled a cry each time a new thorn tore into me; a reminder, over and over again, that I would never be "man" enough.

The wind brushed through my hair as we walked along the rickety boards of the riverwalk. It cooled the single tear that welled up in my eye and I blinked it back.

"Christ, what a way to come out to yourself. And you were so young," Evelyn said, shaking her head as she walked alongside me.

"Things were so much simpler then," I said, "but yes, I was so young. And I didn't have the words for it, but I knew I would never be a man in the way my father, and brother, and all the world would want me to be."

I shifted my weight onto the railing. The wind blew again, tossing my hair back from my shoulders, and I watched the river water crest in white-capped waves.

"I got a text from Mom last week. I'd been avoiding answering her about coming home for Thanksgiving. I probably will—it's the first one since Daddy passed, but being there, being home, just feels..." My words trailed off as I felt the mist whip my face.

"You don't have to have words for how it feels, you know?" Evelyn placed a gentle hand on my arm, "And you don't even have to go if you don't want to."

"I know," I said after a moment, "I have never felt like I belonged, and that is a lonely way to live. An exile in my own land—I'll always be from here; from the South—from this place along the river. And I'll always be my Momma's son and my Daddy's boy, but I'll never be a man, nor will I ever be what they want from me. And I've walked in that twilight my whole life. Some part of me always will—even when I am dead and gone to be with the saints of old, I suppose."

I chuckled a little and Evelyn smiled. We walked to the end of the riverwalk, where it ends in a rickety pier under moss-draped live oak branches. We sat quietly on a nearby bench and watched the minnows dart back and forth in the shallow edge of the river.

"You know, you gave me a cryptic-ass answer about the deer, Jay," Evelyn finally said. I laughed; a real and grateful laugh for a friend who knows just the right moment to talk after a long silence.

"Yeah, I suppose I did."

After we left the grass, just at the edge of the clearing, my brother stopped to catch his wind. The sky was still a hazy blue—night was just a breath's width away, and the world seemed to finally go quiet and still. I looked back through bleary eyes and caught the slightest glimpse of movement. A vision of a deer: a buck, with antlers that seemed to reach high into the trees, crowning him with majesty and splendor, limped towards the woods at the other end of the clearing. I gasped slightly, and he turned.

For a single, infinite moment, our eyes met. I saw something in them, galaxies of life and death and the wholeness of kindness and rage. In him I saw the miracle of life and our last common ancestor—I bore witness to the millions of years that attempted to separate us but only succeeded in teaching us how alike we are. I saw myself—or at least I saw something I could have been. I saw a man; a sacrificial god given over to crueler hands. I saw a life I'd never have— and one I was being given, without knowing who it was that offered it.

In a moment of complete decision, I pressed my lips together. I saw the buck blink, flick an ear, and drop his head in a way I could only call an acknowledgement. He turned and disappeared into the curtain of trees as the night fell on the clearing. I watched myself walking away, smiling.

Somewhere in the woods, along the bank of the creek, under the fall of pine needles and the creeping ivy and moss, lies the unattended grave of the man I could have been. And the bones are, only now, just beginning to turn white.

Clifton Joseph Lee *is a librarian, scholar, and poet from a small, rural town called Atkinson in North Carolina. In their free time they enjoy reading lots of sci-fi and fantasy, spending time with friends and family, and creating art of various mediums. This is his first published work. He is currently working on several fantasy and sci-fi projects, as well as a collection of poetry and prose centered around hope, nature, and their life. Of* Somewhere in The Woods *he writes, "I knew that I wanted to tell a story about the very human experience of not feeling like we fit neatly into the clearly defined rules that society and our peers set up for us, and that there was hope and joy in plenty on the other side of that rejection if we choose to be authentically ourselves."*

A Good Man is a Mother

Parker Durrance

Lines of cut grass stretched up and down across his lawn. "Ah damn… I can't even keep a straight line." He turned the mower and sought a new attempt once again. The heat of the day upset him more than his failure, but he didn't consider this. Especially, it being fall. Mowing the lawn required a kind of weather. It was that one get-away–from Joy and the kids–he could count on every week. If it was too hot or the mulching function abated, then the whole ritual lost its mirth.

Owen wiped the sweat off his forehead as he pushed the mower onto its last stretch. His hulking body swayed side to side with each step. Any passerby walking their dog might think to herself that he was the prototypical man. Well, American man. His five o'clock shadow had ticked off a few hours over the past forty-some years; his belt took a different route. And why shouldn't it? What's a Coors after a not-so-9-5? A few more notches on the leather were only proof of the man hard at work. At least, that's what he thought to himself. It's doubtful that our passerby would get this far in her analysis of the man. After all, he didn't hold your attention for long. He looked as he should.

Owen cut out the mower and pushed it into the garage. He reached to open the fridge and, as the light shone over the silver cans, he remembered they were going to his sister's. He closed it.

He walked inside to the sounds of his family. Joy was putting together the diaper bag for Jack, speaking to Elliot in the process. "I want you to know that it's okay. Being strong isn't about not feeling things. If you stuff it down, you end up weaker in the end." The nine year old stood there, sulking, eyes latched upon some torn out thread from the living room rug.

"Buddy, do you hear me?"

"Yeah… okay Mom."

Owen seemed to come in at the right time. "Y'alright bud?"

"Yeah it's fine." He avoided his father's gaze and turned to head upstairs.

"Well hey, listen, why don't you grab your mitt and we can throw around a bit at Aunt Christine's?" He had approached his son with a warm glance and a paw to the shoulder.

"Whaddya say?"

Elliot's face brightened a touch, "Oh yeah, that would be fun!" He ran up the stairs, barely avoiding a stumble as his socks slipped upon the slick, hardwood steps.

Owen turned back to Joy to ask about their conversation. Something at school again. The boy couldn't seem to hold his own with the others in his class. Owen had tried to toughen him up with a hard-line approach, but despite the boy's thin skin, Owen's rules and words ricocheted with tenacity. It was only in these moments–dejected, red-eyed moments–that the boy's sensitivity graduated to vengeance. Only, this vengeance singled out his father. Owen was puzzled by the irony, let alone his own failure. So he swallowed Joy's new-age soap opera with gritted teeth and a stomach in knots.

They pulled up to Christine's around six. Orange and red leaves were strewn across her driveway and lawn, making patchworks fit for a Mesoamerican shawl. Owen shut off the Ford and opened the door with a grunt. He lifted Jack from the car seat as Joy and Elliot leapt out on their own.

Christine's place was one of those small, mid-century homes nestled along the hills just outside the city proper. Each neighborhood had its own name, but they each converged in Owen's mind. Just "one of those places" where people of her ilk flocked. It was a kind of culture. Making meaning out of worn out, single-story homes. Everyone on her street sported a front porch with white columns of varying designs. Aged, but updated to post-modern appetites. Christine's had some wildflowers growing out front, with a vegetable garden sprawling over a good bit of the lawn. The warm, falling sun reflected off the trellis, bare as it was from vines. Her carrots and leafy greens seemed prime for their harvest.

Funny how time had remade the social landscape. At one point, these were homes for low-pay workers at the bottling factory. One could imagine the daily stressors: men returning home after their twelve-hour, oscillating between a quiet collapse on the couch and barking demands at their wives, children etching out a place beside their mothers in the kitchen, polluted run-off from the city diverted into the neighborhood, elders on their porches wafting cigarette smoke away and into the lungs of their grandchildren; only remnants of these existed as scars in the minds of descendants.

Christine was sitting on a porch swing as they pulled up, a blanket draped over her knees. She turned her head around as she heard her brother's truck eke up the driveway. Laying her novel and glass of wine down on a side-table, she leapt up to greet them.

She rested her arm gently on one of the columns as the Carey's ascended the porch, "Hey you guys! I hope you're hungry!"

"Always, always." Owen hobbled up the stairs and gave his sister a bear hug. She smiled warmly.

The screen door smashed against the wood boards and Joshua ran out with his new puppy. The cavalier leapt down the stairs and danced in circles, coaxing Elliot to play with him. His brown and white coat flashed like the Tasmanian devil in the grass, turning up pieces of finely cut blades in his wake. Meanwhile, Joshua rushed down the stairs, hollering to his cousin.

The boys were only a few months apart. Elliot was the quieter of the two, and though he hid his true feelings, he was often annoyed by his overzealous cousin. He let it slip once after a weekend in the Smokies. Christine had taken the boys up just before Jack was born to give Owen and Joy a much needed babymoon. Just walking in the door, Elliot seemed exhausted. So much so, that the prying was brief. Joy was a bit taken aback by the revelation.

"Okay, okay, hey, they just got here, we don't want the food to get cold."

Christine pulled back from her brother, rolling her eyes with an awkward smile. She grabbed Jack from his arms and welcomed Joy with as much of a hug as she could give. Jack buried his face against her chest.

The aroma of her classic spaghetti sauce had found its way to the foyer. It was the kind of smell that invited all who experienced it to come and see what a mother's labor had borne. Christine had always possessed random skills. Making homemade sauce was only one of her specialties. She had trained quite heavily in rock climbing, studied sewing under an indigenous Mayan family, and started a popular blog reviewing yearly album releases. She could do a little bit of everything; which in Owen's mind, meant a lot of nothing. She was the idealist, lost in the clouds of incessant need—for what, he couldn't quite place.

For a time, he thought it was finding a man for herself. Christine was a serial monogamist through school. Every time Owen would come home from Auburn, he'd have to do the song and dance all over again. Always some famished-looking, pale-faced boy, who for all his politeness and eyes for Christine, could never make a lasting impression on her brother. Always Owen asking questions and pretending to listen. Always a new boy, each time.

It wasn't too different in college either, except her taste had graduated to varying degrees of the avant garde. The one she had for the longest was a theatre major attempting a production of *Crime and Punishment* reimagined for 90's suburbia. Owen couldn't get past the boy's obvious need to make something *original*; when he actually saw it performed, he made no attempt to understand it.

So when Christine brought Andy to thanksgiving one year, it shattered his understanding. Andy was a financier: as polite as any other guy, but marked by a confidence that made you question if you really mattered to him. He hailed from the Midwest. Played division-one ball at Akron, busied himself with fishing trips on the Upper Peninsula, and never missed harvest season. He didn't care that he was prototypical: he was content to live in normalcy.

Christine seemed engrossed in him, but the dysfunction was as glaring as the engagement was short. She must've stayed at Owen and Joy's a half-dozen times in their first year of marriage. Usually for a weekend; always complaining about his emotional distance and his work hours. Owen tried to remind her that Andy was just trying to provide; "maybe he doesn't have the energy at the end of a long day to talk through his feelings?" Of course, by their one-year anniversary, Christine was pregnant. A baby boy. They seemed to come together in the journey of parenthood even as their emotional separation grew.

That's what made his sudden death so uniquely tragic. Not just leaving a kid behind. Not just leaving behind a spouse. But leaving behind a thin marriage. How was Christine to mourn? Theirs was a marriage too broken to be remembered for its joy and he was too "normal" a man to be forgotten with gratitude. She displaced her true feelings in the care of their son. Joshua shared Andy's eyes, and the more he smiled the more she remembered the good. Still, there is no smiling without remembrance of pain.

The cancer took Andy quickly. He was a bit older, but no forty-one year old expects a two-year diagnosis. As his body remembered more and more the earth from which it came, he tried to get his affairs in order. He made sure that Christine would be okay without him. Regardless of their strife, he did *know* her. He understood that she would never make enough on her own—because she would always be her own. After he passed, Christine had enough to move to a good school district and work a job she enjoyed with little thought of its minor salary. For the past few years, she had taught English at a school in Midtown.

Christine had time on her hands; time to reflect and be what she wanted without the socio-economic struggles that, generations before, men and women had experienced in her place. Her interests swarmed about their home; its walls and tabletops carrying signs of her habitual exploration.

As the Carey's entered the home, Owen noticed a new figure perched on the side table nestled against the stairs. A tribal man—made of iron—stood guard over her Book of Common Prayer. It lay open on the table, displaying the Psalter. Owen had gone to his sister's small, Episcopal church once a few years back for a midnight, Christmas Eve service. It had taken Christine awhile to convince him—accustomed as he was to evangelical spaces—but he eventually gave in. That night, the priest was adorned in full vestments. The liturgy hummed about the semi-circular room as the congregants responded to the priest's rituals. Needless to say, Owen politely declined any future invitations from his sister. Even years later, he talked about the experience as if he was still recovering from a noxious dose of *liberal* theology and ancient custom.

Opposite from the stairs, picture frames dazzled the Carey's with their reflections—as they always did. Guatemala, Thailand, Maine, Croatia; you name it, Christine had been there. There was one picture of her, Andy, and Joshua, watching fireworks from a dock on the Fourth. It centered the others on the wall.

The dinner was as good as ever. If there was one thing Owen could appreciate about his sister, it was that she knew how to make you feel welcome—the warmth and fullness in his gut included in that feeling.

Owen returned with his second plate into the dining room. Joshua was giggling as only a small boy could. He leaned his head back as he laughed, bearing his missing teeth. Owen smiled at his nephew—he looked like a vampire with that set.

Christine released her smile and took a sip from her glass.

"Mmm, Elliot! Your mom told me you've been enjoying orchestra! What is it you play again?"

"Oh, I… play violin." The boy sat up taller in his chair.

"Ah, you know that's what I used to play! That's not an easy one to learn. I remember just how much extra time I had to spend with my conductor to get certain sections down. Do you feel like you've had trouble getting used to it?"

"It was kind of hard at first but Mr. Sanchez helped me a lot."

"He's been *great* for him," Joy emphasized.

"He's so cool," Elliot continued, "he's played in famous places before! And, he'll play with us sometimes too, but he plays cello. Yesterday, he was playing with us and Daniel was on the viola, and

Mr. Sanchez grabbed another one and totally owned him. He can play, like, almost anything probably."

Christine could always get a little more out of him than his parents. They understood each other. Maybe because she was the cool aunt, maybe because they shared a disposition. She was soft, too. Not that his Mom wasn't–Joy had a voice that could soothe any catastrophizing of the mind, and a touch that made you forget. No, for the boy and his aunt, it was more passive. Their hearts were like fields of cotton balls. Any offense sunk like a stone, burying its weight until it was hidden. But the offense was there; it altered the composition of the heart. Past hurts gathered among the southern thread. If you pressed too hard, you might find a greater defense than you expected.

"He's been doing so good," Owen joined in, "you should see the way he swings… I swear I could never hit it like that, no matter how hard I trained…. I've talked with one of my buddies about getting him into a local gym in the off-season. With just a little guidance," he glanced proudly at Elliot, "he could step out in front of the other kids."

"Well, he's got his concert series in the fall though, so it might be hard to find the time." The bite in Joy's tone registered to Christine a history of similar exchanges. She continued, "he's so much like you Christine, he's into about eighty different things, you –"

Joshua interrupted, mouth half-full of mashed potatoes. "Oh, Elliot, we should throw the ball outside after dinner. Jake got me a new glove!"

"Yeah we should… right Dad?"

Owen sat back thumbing the side of a Michelob with pride.

"Definitely."

"So, you like Jake a lot Joshua?" Joy leaned forward to look at the boy, "he seems like he's really nice."

"I know, I can't believe y'all still haven't met him yet," Christine interjected. "He was going to come tonight but he had to pick up someone else's shift."

"Yeah he's so cool, he took me to a motocross race and we were right at the front. It was so loud and you just heard the 'Vroooooooom!' every time they passed by. He said he'll teach me how to ride one soon. He has one, and he used to race, he told me."

"Wow, well that's just great, I'm glad you have fun with him." Joy looked over at Christine as they shared some unspoken words together.

Owen curtailed the conversation with the hard press of his bottle against the table.

"Alright, well boys, why don't we toss that ball around?" He slid back his chair. "Joshua, go get your mitt, we'll meet ya outside."

Joshua leapt up and bound into the living room; the cavalier followed him. Joy unbuckled Jack from the high chair as the rest began to clear the table. Joshua's excitement made itself known across the house: drawers opening and closing, self-mutterings on the verge of frustration, and that final "yes!" after a treasure unfurled. His excitement lifted well above the clanging of metal on porcelain. Owen took the plates into the kitchen to wash them off. As he started working on them, Joy came up behind him.

In a hushed tone, she said, "Hey, why don't I watch the boys outside? You and Christine can spend some time together." She could see his eyes starting to roll. "It's been a while, you know, I just think it would be good for you two." She touched his arm, and his defenses seized.

Joshua fled into the kitchen laughing, the cavalier nipping at his heels. Owen turned to see him huffing. Elliot had his mitt in his hand, just looking out the window.

Owen turned back to Joy, "Alright, sure… hey boys, you two play together. I'll maybe join you in a little bit, okay?"

Joshua frowned,"Oh, okay. C'mon Elliot, we can practice hitting!" They bolted outside.

"Okay, but wait till I'm out there you two!" Joy wiped her hand with a dish towel and followed after them.

Christine joined Owen in the kitchen with the placemats. She slid them into the bottom section of the pantry and called to her brother from below, "What say you Boog?"

"Ha! Now, it's been awhile since I heard that," Owen reached up to his right and opened up a cupboard. He turned and grabbed two cocktail glasses. A highball for himself, and a Margarita for her. "It's probably been awhile since you had a *proper* drink, too." He turned and held them up like trophies, grinning.

She rose up to meet him with suspicion, "Okay but none of your whiskey-shit. In fact, there's a bottle of Buffalo in there you can take home with you. It'll get better use out of you!"

Owen squeezed a fresh lime into her glass to finish off her drink. Luckily, she had Cointreau; proper ingredients indeed. He handed it to his sister across the countertop while he started fixing up his Old Fashioned, careful to not be too liberal with the bitters.

"Ladies first," she said with a smirk; she took a sip with raised eyebrows. "Well, well, you weren't lying, Boog."

"Yeah, yeah, so tell me about this Jake of yours. I keep hearing his name but I feel like I know nothing about him. Where did y'all meet again? The roastery?"

"Ha, that's a good one. No, to be honest," she straightened her posture in the barchair and leaned against the counter, "I started bartending at Juniper's on the weekends every now and then back in April; I met him on shift one night. He asked for an Old Fashioned with Cognac, so–"

"So, you had to ask him for his name didn't you?"

"Of course! I mean, who orders that?

"Anyways, we get to talking, you know, and before I know it, I've got these, like, two has-been debutantes yelling at me about martinis. They were all dolled up, with some unwitting guys–trying to navigate a midlife crisis, probably. So, I tend to them, but I'm just checking over my shoulder, praying he's still there."

She imitated her presence in the scene like an overzealous side-character in a high school play.

"Sure enough, after I serve them and their dates, he's waiting. Just looking around, thumbing his glass and content as can be. I don't know… something just drew me to him; a confidence in who he was or a kind of presence. Either way, we just kept talking and, I don't know Owen, he's *different*. It's only been confirmed the more I've been with him."

Owen stirred his mix with a tired look. Christine didn't notice; she kept staring at her drink in thought, just spinning the glass in a circle to create a whirlpool. After a moment, she glanced up at her brother and explained herself.

"He reminds me of Andy, you know, at least a little bit. He's sure of himself. He's headstrong. But he's also tender. It's not like a hard-exterior thing; he's sure of his own tenderness, and he won't let anyone take it from him. It's what makes him so good with Joshua."

"Hmm." Owen sipped his drink. The burn wrapped around his throat with just the right intensity. "Well, it seems like Joshua's doing okay."

"Oh, he's got the usual stuff–actually, his grades have gotten better, but he's still struggling socially. Jake just responds so well to him, he–"

The sliding door opened and Joy peeked her head in.

"Hey, Christine, I'm sorry to bother you, but I might need you out here. Joshua's shutting down."

She bowed her head down and sighed faintly. She pushed off against the counter and joined her sister-in-law.

Owen pressed against the counter and took another sip of his drink. He walked into the living room and wandered around. It had been awhile since he had really spent time at Christine's–hence his wife's pressure upon him to make something of it. He had found himself over by a tall glass table that sat behind the couch before asking himself why he was exploring a room he had been in a hundred times. He picked up a collection of poems by Walt Whitman. It was well-used; coffee stains and marks feigned a sepia blur before his eyes. He put it back down on the counter.

Peering over the room like a hunter speculating over familiar land, he turned around to see a painting that he didn't recognize. It hung at eye-level, and was just big enough to command one's attention. The hunter was caught; an animal with hybrid colors, too striking to bear down upon, had stepped out from the growth before him–what was his role again? At this moment, it was to bear witness. To see behind the bright, abstract scene before him.

An odd shape, formed by quick strokes and splotches, took up the bulk of the frame. It was symmetrical; two small, round splotches on each side of an inverted, oblong triangular structure. A darker shade formed its center, while the tone bled lighter toward its edges, matching the color of the round shapes. While there was an obvious structure to the painting, its key strokes obfuscated the meaning.

It was for the viewer to draw their own conclusions. That being the case, Owen was certain that the painting was *meant* to hurl you into an ancient wonder; and so it did. He was right there with Peter and the Beloved, racing toward Christ's tomb. Only in this depiction, the two approached from opposite sides. These human blurs, almost circular in their kneeling, reached for their savior with long, emaciated limbs. The tomb itself lurched upwards from the earth; the stone was out of sight. Light rushed out from the darkness within, tracing itself along the subdued red of the earthen tomb; a decision in color that he didn't quite understand. The light was almost the color of the canvas. Was it unfinished? Was this a work of his sister's? Had the artist purposefully left the background the same as the light? As if to say, "this light makes all things as light."

The sliding door screeched open and shut as Christine came back into the house. Owen turned, half-embarrassed toward his sister.

"I'm gonna go ahead and apologize now.." She stuck her hands on her hips and sighed, "Elliot may've seen a different side of me." For all her attempts to differentiate herself, Owen's southern drawl had found its way into her statement.

"Oh, I doubt it, you never give the boy too much of a branding."

"You'd be surprised… especially recently. I don't know, I feel like I'm just losing more and more of my patience as I age."

"Ain't that the truth…"

"Entranced by feminine icons are we now?" She gestured toward the painting.

"Huh? The heck are you talking about?" Owen turned back towards the wall and winced.

Christine laughed and glided into the kitchen to grab her drink. "Oh never mind, c'mon let's sit. I just got these chairs. Facebook marketplace, can you believe it?"

When she returned to the kitchen, Owen had already plopped himself down in one of them. They were a deep, green Chenille. He spun around to face her with a grin on his face.

"I swear, you will never *not* be a child," she smiled and sat down in her own chair, "and I mean that as a compliment."

"Yeah, yeah, so what was that all about?"

"Well, I guess I first need to apologize for Joshua… as I was saying, he's still struggling socially. He's so sensitive and everything he perceives as an insult just piles up in him until it explodes. Anyway, I guess they were trying to see who could ground a ball better out there, and Elliot caught all of 'em but Joshua didn't," she waved her hands back and forth with exhaustion, as if she was weighing the validity of the outburst. "So, he started crying and shouting about how Elliot wasn't as good as him, and I guess as soon as Joy tried to calm him down, he just shut everyone out and went and sat under the blossom.

"Of course, I didn't make anything better by going out there. He's still sitting there now… I don't know Owen, I just struggle to get through to him. Ever since he started having these outbursts, the only way I could think to approach it was to be stern, and —"

"That's the only way you can do it… you gotta give firm boundaries, that way they can grow into them."

"Well, I'm not sure it's working."

"Do you take anything away from him? Maybe you just gotta be a little more harsh with—"

"It isn't that though, I can take any toy or game, or whatever, it just doesn't help him control his emotions in the moment. You know I've always been hesitant, but I've thought recently about getting him on medicine for his ADHD. He just has zero impulse control. Everything is an offense, and every offense is worthy of a response to him."

"Well, I don't think that's the answer… all that's gonna do is hook him—and talk about problems—he'll be stuck in the hands of Big Pharma for the rest of his life."

"I know, I know, 'medicine is evil, doctors are fake'. I just don't know what else to do."

"Yeah it ain't easy… how does Jake deal with him?"

"You know…" she smiled, "it's amazing. I couldn't ask for him to be better with him. By looking at him, you'd think Jake would be some lazy bum. You know, he's got his motorcycles, he's on and off with his band; he's this adventurous, bold guy. That's probably why Joshua likes him so much. He takes him on rides, to all these events, helps him complete levels on his Playstation… that's why Joshua listens to him. Jake's been able to get on his level, and he's just more willing to hear him."

"So… he's soft?" Owen chuckled.

Christine tilted her head with a mix of disappointment and expectation as she glared at her brother, "No, he's courageous…. Like I said, he's not afraid to be tender. Regardless, Joshua listens to him. There's no static when it comes from Jake. It's like they're tuned to the same station and I can't even find the damn knob!

"Honestly, as hard as it's been with Joshua lately, seeing Jake with him… it has me thinking about the future for the first time in a while." She downed a decent bit of her margarita and drifted off a little.

Owen gave it a second. "I'm not tryna be offensive Christine, but… you sure this is the kind of guy you wanna build a future around? I know I haven't met him and, sure, he could be alright, but it sounds like he needs to grow up a little. Now, I know you don't want to think in these terms but, he's gotta be able to pull his weight. Provide a little. As good as he may be with Joshua, at the end of the day, the boy needs a father figure, not a friend."

"Owen, he's —"

"No I know, I know, but I just want you to hear me. It's 'cause I care about you. I could be entirely wrong, but I'd rather be wrong than be a weak brother. It's my place, whether you like it or not. I'll always see myself as a protector."

"Owen, you seem to think that Jake being on Joshua's level means he can't be a good father. Besides, I think we have different visions in our heads about what it means for him to father Joshua. Joshua needs someone who asks him questions—not just me, but a man. A man to ask him how he's feeling. To help him work through his emotions and questions.. He needs someone to help him figure out and follow his passions. He needs someone who will drop everything just to be with him."

"Kinda sounds like you want Gee Gee, not as much a father," Owen retorted.

"That's my point. Think of how much time she spent with us—that's what he needs. Look, he may not fit your definition of what the average 'man' should be, but he doesn't have to. I feel like he will be the kind of father figure that Joshua needs. As good as Andy was, Joshua always needed more than he could give him. It's almost like sometimes—"

"Christine—"

"He was burdened by him," her voice raised over his with a hint of unsurrendered pain. "As good as he was, he wasn't always *there*. I don't know..."

She paused, clearly questioning her own words, "At the end of the day, I see in Jake an empathy and a longing to nurture others. In a sense, yes, this is 'soft.' Soft in that he..." She struggled to find the words, "doesn't have this protective shell. It takes strength to be that defenseless."

Owen sipped his Old Fashioned slowly. He couldn't get past her use of "nurturing." Burying itself in his consciousness, he feared it might get stuck there; like some cobwebs you know have been out of place too long but you keep forgetting to clean. In this fear, he tried hard to turn her words around on her. To help her see how misguided her logic was.

"So you're saying a good man is like a mother?"

Christine smiled with a hint of expectation.

"Well, if *Christ* is our measure, then yes." She calmly settled back into her chair, taking a long sip from her glass.

A kind of fire burned behind his forehead. All manner of dust had been scorched. Christianity was the *one* topic that they struggled to side-step with humorous jabs. While Christine had abandoned the faith of their childhood in high school, Owen had carried the flame in earnest. She would eventually come back, but to a perspective Owen labeled too "free" to be considered orthodox.

"C'mon now Christine, are you about to tell me God's a woman or something? I mean, where does it end with you?"

"Well… it ends with Christ going through 'labor pains' for us, I'd imagine. Even more, didn't he see himself as a mother hen?"

"Ah, that's just a metaphor." He waved her away.

Christine took a slow sip of her margarita and placed it gently on the glass table beside her. She held a quizzical look at her brother for a little longer than he appreciated. He began to stir in his seat.

"Look, let's leave the whole question about Jake aside for a moment, and why don't I just get right down to the point and ask you. Why does the mere thought of God being identified with a woman make your skin crawl? Why does it make you protest?"

Owen was taken aback by the forcefulness of the question. He sunk back a little into the couch before leaning forward and straightening his back.

"I know what you're trying to do Christine. Gosh, you haven't changed a bit since we were kids." He said this with a smile before regaining a serious disposition. "You're trying to say how I'm really just against women or something of that order. But that's not gonna happen. You know me. You know how much I give to Joy and the kids. You know just how much time and effort I put into making sure they got nothin' to worry about. And if I remember correctly, didn't I house you during graduate school while you were getting your English degree? That's what a real man does. He lays his life on the line, especially for his wife and kids. If that's not Christ-like, then I don't —"

"Owen, you're avoiding the question…"

He sighed and sank back into the couch. He placed his leg over his thigh, as men do.

"You know why Christine. It's got nothing to do with gender. It's got everything to do with being true to Scripture. All throughout, from beginning to end, it refers to God as a He. There's no getting around it. Now, that might offend you, but that's just what it says. All I'm trying to do is be faithful to it. This is the problem with today. The whole culture, and especially the universities, are trying to adjust what it means for something to be true. Nowadays, the truth is whatever you want it to be; but I hold to an older standard. The truth is the truth. It doesn't change with the times. That's how it is with Scripture. It's the Word of God, and the word of God don't change. So if the Word of God refers to God as a Father, then I'm gonna go with that."

"I'm not disputing anything about the Bible, Owen. We both already know that we have different approaches to the text. What I'm trying to say is, even from your perspective, you've missed the full picture the Word is trying to paint for us. Christ identifies with the reality of women. He reveals his resurrected body to *women* first. Mary was the first one to go around proclaiming the resurrection. Don't you know that she was deemed the 'apostle to the apostles' by the early church? Then if we turn to Christ's word, it gets even more interesting. Not only does he compare himself to a mother hen, but he also compares his suffering to a woman's labor. What higher comparison can you have?

"After all, I think at the end of the day, there's still a difference between Jesus, our mother hen, and what you're describing about being a man. The mother hen gathers her brood out of no regard for herself. How is it that every time a man announces his care for women, it always ends with him on a pedestal?"

Owen rolled his eyes to the side before taking on an annoyed look. "Well you've been avoiding my question too, Christine. I've been asking you. Are you saying God is a woman, or not?"

"I'm saying that if Christ is who we should follow, then 'being a man' is a lot more like being a woman."

Annoyed, Owen tilted his head with a scowl, but before he could think of some snarky response, Joy opened the sliding glass door. "Hey Owen, Jack's starting to get fussy. I think we better head on home. I'm sorry we gotta cut our time short... I hope you two had a moment to catch up." She frowned, warmly at Christine.

"Oh, it's no problem," she glanced over at her brother, "I'm just glad y'all could make it at all. It's been too long, for sure."

"I'll be right in; I'm gonna round 'em up back here."

Owen glanced back at his sister as Joy slid the door shut.

"Owen," Christine sighed, "You don't have to relish my theology but... trust me when it comes to Jake, okay? Just meet him–I know y'all will get along." She drained her margarita and stood up from her chair. Owen joined her.

"Alright, alright, you know I will. I just care about you is all... that's why I'm making such a big fuss. I wanna see you and Joshua taken care of."

"I know, I know," she gave him a big hug. "Maybe just be open to the fact," she said as she pulled away, "that you might not have it all figured out. Or at the very least, there may be a way of seeing things that is just as valid as the way you see them."

He nodded to her and put a hand on her back to usher her before him. They went outside to help Joy.

Between Jack's crying, the boys tracking mud into the house, and Joy apologizing for not being more diligent, goodbyes were curt. The drive across town wasn't too bad, given that traffic had died down. Jack had already fallen asleep. Elliot was working through some game on his tablet. The sky bore streaks of pink and red, obfuscating the barrenness of the overpass.

Joy turned to Owen. "So, how was it getting to be with your sister? You finally convince her to share a whiskey with you?"

"That'll be the day… It was good, it was good. You know her, she's always gotta be different. Always… taking some wild thought and making it seem wise or something. I don't know, I guess she's always gonna be like that.

"But yeah, we talked about her new guy and everything –"
"Jake, right?"
"Yeah that's right."
"So he seems like a good guy?"
"Yeah I guess. She sure likes him… I don't know, I'm not sure he's the kinda guy she needs at this stage in her life. All adventurous and scattered. You know Andy, he was…. different than most guys she's into. He brought some stability to her life. She could still be, ya know, her, but he balanced her out a bit. He was good for Joshua too. Seems like without Andy around, she's having trouble disciplining him."

"Well, he's definitely a handful… but I'm sure she's doing her best."

They pulled into the driveway. Owen admired his work from earlier as he hopped out of the car; like any man would a tarpon or a twelve-point, hanging on his wall. Joy took care of Jack and the family started off for the garage. Owen walked slowly behind them, lingering in that feeling of admiration. He was grateful, and partly for his hard work. The house, the kids, his marriage—what else could a man need? What else could a man work for?

As Joy opened up the garage door and they flooded inside, Owen paused in one last glance to admire the sky above. It was as if God himself was smiling down on him. "A man after God's own heart." There were times he had doubted this, but a good tree only bears good fruit. Contemplating this, he got lost in the streaks of red and pink, like the final screen behind the final scroll, tearing away the old with the new. It was beautiful and ravishing. "Birth pangs;" for some reason, this line overcame him. He thought of Elliot's birth. A cold, January night, freezing his ass off grabbing a spare blanket from the car. Why have the parking garage connected through a breezeway? Damning the poor design and planning, he walked the long hallway to their delivery room, and from about halfway down, he could hear Joy's screams. Of course it had started while he was away. The nurse had said that it could happen this quick. Panting, he hurled the door open and froze. Seeing his wife with gritted teeth, and the blood… the blood had rendered him thoughtless. A nurse grabbed him by the arm and took him to Joy's side. He spoke and knew not what he said. He held her hand and knew not what it achieved. A kind of powerlessness, foreign to his experience, seized his heart; even more when he watched behind glass as the doctor performed the cesarean. Where would he be, if something went amiss? How could he carry on alone? Who would he be, without her and the boy to love? Of every moment he could recall, there was none more terrifying; all the more for how it was burdened by hope.

Owen came to himself and the sky had shifted. Clouds had converged on the intensity of the colors, making curious shapes. Like a child experimenting with playdough. They had come together in part to form a scene. It usually came pretty quickly to him, but he struggled to name it. An elephant and its ears? No; the oblong center cloud bearing itself vertically upon the sky was only thinly connected to the two round clouds on either side of it. He took a second, but then it dawned on him and he laughed to himself, "it looks like one of those textbook pictures of the female reproductive system." He chuckled to himself, shaking his head and turning to the garage, but something prompted him to return his gaze. A deeper red streak formed the womb, with thin white streaks of cloud connecting the ovaries to it. It felt important, somehow. Like the scene reminded him of something. Puzzled, he felt like he could narrow it down, but just then Joy called from the house, "Owen, you coming inside? I could use some help with Jack…"

He shouted back to her, "Yeah, sorry I was caught up in something, I'll be right in."

Before heading in he glanced once more at the sky, but it had shifted again already. The scene had abated. He shrugged it off and tended to his duty.

Parker Durrance *is a high school history teacher from Atlanta, Georgia. In his free time, he enjoys studying theology, singing Bob Dylan songs to his one-year-old, and finding the perfect* I Think You Should Leave *quote for every social interaction.* A Good Man is a Mother *is his first published work. He writes poorly structured poetry over at his Substack, (@parkerdurrance), and is currently working on his first novel, tentatively titled* Where Shall I Flee? *Of* A Good Man is a Mother, *he writes, "I wrote this story to evaluate how Christian theology and masculinity influence one another."*

Beginner's Luck

Peyton Popp

My stepfather's big jar of pennies lived up on the shelf in his dining room. The coins may have been shiny once, but now they were so old they were a dull brown, almost black. The jar was brought down from the shelf one Friday night a month, and the Taylors would play Texas Hold 'em. Whoever won got the bottle of bourbon in the middle of the table. Clint, my stepfather, hosted every weekend, but Cotton, the oldest, always took home the bottle. He would hold it by the neck and crack his crooked cowboy smile. He was the only real card player among them.

Cotton loved the game for what it was and grew quieter and quieter as the game swelled; Clint tended to grow louder and louder. I got the sense that the youngest brother, Clark, was just there because he couldn't stand to be left out. He never allowed himself to be late to a party.

A few years after Dad's death, Mom and I moved down to Frankfort, and we quickly began to join the party. I would sit at the end of the table, next to Mom, and watch them all play hand after hand. There was something I liked about it. When Mom won a hand, which wasn't very often, a dimple appeared on the right side of her mouth.

I was never allowed to play; Clint said children shouldn't gamble. But one weekend when I was twelve, Cotton and Wilma were running late. We sat at our usual places, and the adults tried to talk around the two empty chairs.

"I wonder where they could be," Clint said. He was a big man with a face that always seemed flushed, and his voice boomed throughout his house.

We'd moved into his house not long before this, after Mom married him. I left all my boxes in the room that was supposed to be mine and sat at my spot at the poker table. I got up on a chair to reach the shelf, hoisted the jar up onto the table, took a deck of cards, and pretended to play a game of Hold 'em by myself. I tried to bridge. I tried and tried, and at some point, Clint lumbered up behind me. When he tried to talk to me, I jumped.

"Woah there, Jon. Didn't mean to startle you." Clint's forehead was shiny with sweat, but he still had his big, goofy smile on his face.

He started gathering up my pennies and putting them back in his jar.

"I was just playing with them."

"I know, I know. It's okay," he said as softly as he could manage. "You're just not old enough."

"Fine."

Mom stood in the doorway with a glass of water. I was going to complain to her that I should be allowed to pretend to be old enough, but she spoke first. "Listen to Clint, Jon."

She put her hand on Clint's shoulder, her new wedding ring a line of thin silver on her finger.

I said, "Okay."

The cards still wouldn't cooperate.

A chair groaned under Clint's weight. He hid the deck in his huge hands and tried to show me an easier way to shuffle. "This is how I learned," he said.

He spliced the deck and put the two halves together at one corner, letting them flip down slowly, and he shoved the halves back together. I looked at Mom.

"I know how to shuffle," I told Clint. "I want to be able to bridge as well as Cotton."

He looked at Mom.

"Say," he said, "we're almost done getting y'all's stuff inside. Why don't we take a break and have a catch? Huh? Whadda ya say?" He was out the door.

When his big smiling face returned, he had two large leather pancakes in one hand and was wiggling a baseball with the other. Red cheeks and beads of sweat framed his eyes. I tried to go back to practicing, but he plopped a glove down in front of me.

"C'mon, champ."

"I'd rather play cards."

He sought support again from Mom, who shrugged.

"It'll do us good to get some air," he said. "Some fresh air."

I looked at the jar of pennies on the shelf. "I don't want to."

My cards buzzed as I tried to bridge again.

"Oh, c'mon—"

Mom put her hand on his damp back.

"Okay, okay. I can play cards. You like Go Fish?"

"Not really." The cards made a stupid teepee as they crashed into each other, again.

Mom tried to whisper, "It's okay, Clint. Let him get used to the place."

As they started to leave, Mom rubbed the necklace she'd worn for longer than I could remember.

Cotton was long and lean, like my father, and quiet, like his father, who I never met but everyone always talked about admiringly. Cotton worked for the state but worked weekends on a tobacco farm, leaving him hard and tan. His empty chair kept staring at us.

"Maybe they had to stop for gas."

"Yeah," Clark's wife, Marie, said. "I'm sure that's it."

Her smile was soft, like Mom's, but she had deep red lipstick on her front tooth. "So, Jon, how's school going?"

Mom and I had lived in Kentucky for almost three years, but I still longed for the anonymity of Chicago. I felt naked under the eyes of the entire town.

"It's going well," I said.

Mom smiled half-heartedly. "Well," she said, "does anyone want a drink?"

"Y'know," Clark said, "I could go for a beer if you can spare one."

She started to rise from her seat, but Clint motioned at her and heaved himself up from his chair. "No, Jackie," he said, "let me get it. I'll do it." He flashed a cheesy smile at her and turned to Marie. "So, two beers. Do you want one, Marie? Something else? Okay, three beers. What about you?" Back to Mom. "A beer?" He winked.

"Oh, Clint," Mom said sweetly. "No, baby, you know that." She laughed.

This drew a look from Marie.

"Just checking," Clint said.

He headed for the door, lurching like a boat in a storm. He attempted a stuttering dance as he went under the doorway into the kitchen. Mom giggled, but I wasn't amused. Clark removed his hat, leaning back in his chair and tossing it onto the back of Cotton's chair. He lived over in Lexington and worked at a bank. He insisted on driving a Ford Bronco he couldn't afford and wearing snake-skin cowboy boots, his flat brimmed hat no cowboy would ever wear, and to top off his ensemble, patterned golf shirts tucked in around his basketball belly. We could hear Clint rummaging around in the kitchen like a bear scavenging for snacks to go with his beer.

The phone rang, and Clint's aggressive chuckle broke through the doorway.

"Y'all reckon that's them?" Clark asked.

"Hopefully," Mom answered.

Marie added, "I'm ready to get this show on the road."

"Bet when they got gas," Clark said, "Cot had to finish his precious cigarette. Bet he took his sweet time."

Marie laughed a little.

"There he is!" Mom grinned as Clint returned, arms full of drinks and bags of chips.

He started distributing the snacks. "There we go. Junior, I thought you and your mom might want some Cokes." He slid me a Tab and Mom a Sprite.

His laugh stole the air from the room. "He hates when I call 'em that," Clint explained to Marie. "Call any Coke a Coke 'cept a Coke. In the big city, they call 'em pops."

Marie nodded.

"Any-*who*," Clint popped a finger against the table. "Wilma called. Claims their battery died. They're getting on their way, but we're good to start without."

"Ah geez," Clark said.

"I think they had to scrounge around looking under couch cushions for their share," Clint said. He tapped the red wax seal on the top of the bottle. "You know he'd be the first to call somebody out for not checking on their battery."

Clint and Clark bent their voices into a joint imitation of Cotton. Clark had to lower his voice, and Clint would contort his cannonball voice into a grotesque attempt at Cotton's tree-sap baritone. Together, the brothers sounded like two TVs turned to the same channel, just slightly out of sync: "Didn't Red teach us to check our damned batteries so we wouldn't get into messes like these?"

They cracked up. Clint funneled a handful of chips into his mouth and clapped his hands together to get the greasy crumbs off.

He draped his arm over the back of Mom's chair. She and Marie both laughed too, but I didn't think it was so funny.

Once Clint and Clark got over themselves, Clint started to deal the cards. I helped Clark count out the pennies and distribute them to everyone but me. Once everyone had cards and pennies, Clint dug around in his pocket and plopped a dime down in front of Mom and a quarter down in front of Marie.

The first couple hands were dull. Nobody bluffed, and both hands, Mom folded as early as she could. I sipped on my Tab. Surprisingly, Clint won both hands with ease. The next hand, Clark's nose got itchy, and he bluffed to try to win a hand for once. Clint's goofy smile widened as he raked in his third helping of dull copper.

Mom sipped her Sprite and smiled at me. "Wanna help me play for a bit?" She looked around the table. "Anybody mind if I play with some extra help?"

She looked at Clint, who hesitated. His eyes flashed briefly to Cotton's chair, but he shrugged.

"Welcome to the big boy table," he said finally, smiling as though he'd never stopped.

Mom dealt the cards, leaning a little over the table to make sure everyone's cards lay neatly on top of each other. I peeked at our cards. They were terrible. Mom tossed in the first round of coins without looking, but when she did look, she pursed her lips. The flop gave us a pair, so I was able to keep her from folding.

"Play it cool," I whispered.

She cupped her hand around my ear. "Should we bet big?"

I rolled my eyes. Everyone was playing timid, and a single pair didn't mean we should go making any statements like betting more than anticipated. If we bet too much, even Clark would get suspicious. I wanted to last long enough to still be playing when Cotton arrived.

"No," I told her. "Just the minimum."

I tried to keep my face as calm as I could, neutral like hard limestone. Mom sat back in her chair and rested her hand on Clint's shoulder. Clark bet the minimum, but Marie and Clint both folded. The river gave us a second pair, and I tried to play it zen.

"Minimum again," I whispered.

She put two pennies in the middle. Clark put four. We had him. I had to reach a little to call with two more pennies. We showed our cards, and Mom beamed as she helped me rake in our winnings.

Clark took a swig of his drink. "Mr. O'Hara came to play!"

"Mr. Taylor, actually," Clint said. "I adopted him when we got married."

He and mom grinned at each other.

"O'Hara is still fine with me," I said.

"How groovy," Clark said. "Another Mr. Taylor."

Clint tousled my hair. "Smart playing. Just . . . Just don't smirk like that when Cotton gets here."

"Oh, Clint," Marie smiled at me. "Let him enjoy himself. It's his first time."

"Okay, okay." He leaned back. "You're right."

Marie dealt, and Clint glanced at his cards.

Clark wiggled his can up in the air. "You mind if I have another?"

"'Course not," Clint said. "Help yourself."

He looked for a long time at the cards. Clark's boots clicked against the floor. Just as the fridge door opened, the doorbell rang.

"I bet that's them," Clint's voice echoed through the house.

Finally, I thought.

Marie started taking up the cards to deal Cotton and Wilma in. Clint flipped his cards to her — pocket aces. Clark burst through the door laughing at a joke he hadn't told yet. Behind him, Cotton held a beer. Over Cotton's shoulder, you could see the top of Wilma's hair.

"Look what the cat dragged in," Clark said.

Cotton's sleeves were rolled up, and he was popping the tab on his can. Wilma's stern face hovered next to him, her dark eyeliner making the blue in her eyes as blank as an empty winter sky. She quickly took her seat next to Cotton without removing her black leather jacket. She flashed a powdery smile, but one eye went kind of squinty, and she aimed her blank eyes at the table. Her arms were crossed as she told Marie that the delay was no big deal. Cotton sat down his beer and started gathering up all the pennies. Clark tried to ask about their car trouble.

Clint interrupted. "Woah, woah. Cot, what're you doing?"

Cotton kept gathering. "Just got here. The real game starts now."

"What?"

"I said I just got here. Didn't you miss my pretty face?"

Clint's jaw tightened and released. "Well," he said, "I was going to have everyone give up some of their pennies, but I guess we can start fresh."

Mom stroked his back. Cotton and Clark finished doling out coins, and Cotton had started shuffling by the time Clint finished tightening and relaxing his jaw. Cotton was the best shuffler I ever saw. He bridged perfectly every time, clapping the edge of the deck on the table after each shuffle, letting the cards flip neatly into two halves, bridging again, clapping again. He tossed the cards so they landed in neat little pairs in front of each player. He was all business.

"So, you get your car trouble sorted out?" Clark asked again.

"Huh?" Cotton took a drink of his beer then continued, "Oh, yeah. You could say that."

"Y'know, if you check the battery regularly—"

Cotton's laugh was hollow. "Oh, poor baby doesn't know the first thing to look for."

"Hm." Clark chewed on his cheek. "Clint ain't that big of a baby." He chuckled to himself a bit.

Cotton looked at him. He took the non-cowboy hat off the back of his chair and dropped it on his baby brother's head. He took another drink, crushed his now empty can in a neat line down the middle and leaned back to set its corpse on the counter behind him. He looked at his cards. The new hand went poorly for Mom and me. We clashed on when to fold and when to stay in. Every time I won and we stayed, nothing came to fruition. The second Mom convinced me to fold, the cards we needed turned up. Mom would scoff and whisper about her luck.

As expected, Cotton came in firing. Marie lost out quickly, and Wilma seemed strangely out of it. While Mom and I squeaked by, Clint began to fold more often than before. Clark played as randomly as he always did but managed to stay afloat. As we played, Cotton's cool, limestone gaze repeatedly focused on me. Not maliciously, just that I could tell he noticed me helping mom after the first couple hands. Maybe he was rooting for me not to suck.

Cotton stood and calmly walked toward the door to the kitchen.

"I'll have one, too," Clint said, "if you're getting —"

Cotton was already gone.

When he returned with two beers, which he sat in a pair right behind his wall of chips, Wilma looked at her meager stack of coins and made eye contact with Mom and Marie as though they could communicate telepathically. Mom smiled, and we played one of the fastest hands of Hold 'em I've ever seen. First thing, Wilma went all in, and Mom convinced me to fold. There was no bidding war. Clint and Clark both looked at Cotton from the corner of their eyes and folded after the turn. Cotton won the hand easily over Wilma's pocket twos. Wilma and Marie went off into the living room.

"Jon," Mom said. "How would you feel about playing the rest of the way without me?"

I shrugged, already plotting my comeback. She went off with Wilma and Marie to talk about whatever they always talked about.

Clark hoisted his can up over the middle of the table, "Boy's game!"

Cotton raised his eyebrows unimpressed.

Clint clinked his empty beer can against Clark's. He plopped back into his chair.

"Say," Cotton looked at me. "Y'ain't played bad yet. Let's see how it goes now that the training wheels are off."

"In a few years," Clark said, "I bet you'll be teaching a little brother or sister how to play."

He smirked at Clint, who flashed a warning eye.

"When they're both old enough, of course."

"I can't even have a little brother," I said. "My dad is dead."

Cotton, now with a glass of something dark and iceless, dealt the cards. Clark sunk back in his chair. Clint's mouth hung open, and he sat there blinking for a moment. Cotton's stone eyes reminded all of us we had a game to play. Clint closed his mouth. His eyes narrowed. By force of will, he won both of the following games. Cotton looked for a second like he wanted to spit, like he couldn't process what was happening. The expression dissolved back into cool cowboy limestone.

I folded the next hand to avoid his wrath. Clark stayed but had nothing. Clint's eyes shifted. He had yet to smile. Cotton's face was neutral, normal. He kept checking his cards. The three boys flipped their cards over. Cotton had two pair, but Clint had a flush. A muscle quivered in Cotton's jaw.

"You got something up your sleeve there, Clint?"

Clint's stomach shook with the weight of his forced laugh. "You accusing me of something, Charles?" He looked Cotton in the eye and straightened the cards on the table.

"No," Cotton said. "No, I guess not."

Clint made sure his pennies were properly stacked, and Cotton went for a refill.

Cotton took the next hand, and the game proceeded quickly from there. I focused on my plan. My first goal was to edge Clark out, which was easy because he probably never in his life let an itch go unscratched. Then I went for Clint because he would be easier to deal with than Cotton. No one played like Cotton, even with Clint in his newfound trance. But my stack was still measly, and I needed to be careful not to let my focus on Clint cost me my own chance.

I had something in my hand that I liked, and when the river added to it, I put in a bigger pile of pennies than usual. For a moment, all eyes were on me, and I could hear the women in the other room talking.

Marie's soft voice asked, "Is he always so quiet?"

Then, when she realized how quiet the little house was, she added an involuntary, "Oh."

And the truth is I had always been pretty quiet. It came in handy when Dad got really sick. He got so thin he was little more than a whisper of a man, and when I wasn't at school, Mom and I were at the hospital by his side. Sometimes, we'd go there instead of school. I would sit and listen to him and Mom talk. All Dad wanted to do was talk, and all I wanted to do was be there to try and memorize every word. And, of course, I don't remember much other than the goopy ghost of his soft voice.

Clint broke the silence with a laugh. "Woah now, Jon thinks he's got something!"

But Cotton was not afraid. His face twisted, just a little, and he raised me slightly.

Clint folded. "Y'all're too rich for my blood."

Cotton grunted and polished off the last of his latest drink.

The last card was the ace of spades. It took all my energy not to smirk at the royal flush I saw before me. I reminded myself to be Zen, like stone. Cotton bet big again, and I called. He quickly flipped over his other two aces: four of a kind. I flipped over my cards and started raking in pennies.

Cotton's eyes sizzled against his muted face. "Impossible."

"Read 'em and weep," I said, heat rising in my cheeks.

Clint shot me a nervous look. Clark's laugh stopped when he saw Cotton's face.

Cotton let out a hollow chuckle. "Good hand, kiddo. Good hand." His jaw danced.

He started shuffling, dealing. His eyes, aimed at the middle of the table, still seemed lost in disbelief. And despite Clint's worried glance at his brother, I wasn't deterred. If I had the cards and played smart, nothing could stop me. If I didn't have the cards, so what? But why would I ever not try to win? Cotton wouldn't do that, and neither would I.

On the next flop, two sixes and a king showed, which nicely complemented my pocket fours. Cotton put a stack of coins down, and Clint hung with us to see the turn, but then quickly folded. It was hard to get him to bet big. He looked at Cotton and chewed on a fingernail.

Cotton eyed my pile of pennies, looked again at his cards, and smirked. He put in just enough for me to go all in. Clint sighed. Clark all but gasped. I didn't hesitate. When Cotton finally flipped the river, another four smiled up at me. A full house. My risk had paid off.

All Cotton had were the sixes looking up at him and a second king from his hand. I started raking in coins again from the center of the big dining room table. I was giddy about having the most coins, and I was giddy to have survived Cotton's crazy bluff.

His jaw flinched again. He growled, "You're cheating."

I stopped mid-rake. "What?"

"You gotta be. You're cheating, you little weasel."

"No, I just won." I started pulling in coins again.

"Now, Cotton," Clint began.

"C'mon, you think he's gonna flip a royal flush and a full house back-to-back?"

I couldn't keep the smile off my face.

"I knew you were bluffing," I said to Cotton.

He didn't respond, only reiterated the odds. "It's bullshit's what it is," he said to Clint.

Cotton aimed his eyes back at me.

I froze. His eyes were burning; his stone face was melting into an animal's scowl.

"Okay, okay," Clark said. "Let's keep it civil here. What if, what if we just act like that last bet didn't happen? Cotton'll take back his big bet, and Jon'll take the rest of the pot. How's that? Fair?"

Clint shrugged and half-nodded. He moved onto another fingernail.

"No," I said. "Not fair. I won. I won the hand fair and square."

The last of the pennies made a satisfying noise as I pulled them across the table in groups. When I leaned over the table to reach the last group, the red of the top of the bourbon bottle poked me in the chest. There was a grunt, the sound of an animal. Before I realized Cotton had made the sound, he twisted back and swung with all he could muster. His hand must've been as big as my whole head, knocking me like a skipped stone over the edge of the table.

The glass slid with me along the wood until its red wax neck met the back of a chair and severed. As I fell to the floor, the brown bourbon blood glugged into the chair's seat and overflowed, trickling onto the floor beside me. The red wax bottle head rolled along the floor and settled near my face. At the clap of breaking glass, I popped up dizzily and fell backward, knocking my head against the hardwood floor.

My vision went blurry. Red, then black. I heard heavy footsteps and Clint's voice—booming like a cannon—striking against the red of Cotton's babbling. Mom was there. My head was in her lap, her voice a singsong of worry beneath the shouts of the two brothers above us.

They were apart and then rushed together. They wrestled. They rolled around on the floor and rose as tall as oaks. Clint had his arms around Cotton's neck, slammed his thick foot hastily down in front of his brother's, flinging Cotton over his body and onto the floor. Cotton's back flattened with a dull thud. Clint stood over Cotton's body, then stepped over it. As he approached me and Mom, his eyes were soft and goopy.

From behind, Cotton rushed at Clint. His angry jackal eyes hovered in the space over my stepdad's shoulder. He wrapped his arms around the trunk of Clint's throat and tugged. He pulled him back and choked him and tripped him down onto the floor, which echoed with the sound of my stepdad falling. Clint gasped for breath, and Cotton settled onto his chest and started punching, spewing and babbling all the while. Wilma was calling his name, and Mom's frail singsong shifts over to Clint now.

I rush forward, fumbling out of Mom's grip toward the brothers.

"Get off him! Get off him!" I shout, I don't know how loud.

I stumble, either shrieking or whimpering, "Clint, Clint, are you okay?"

It's Clark who catches me, sits me down in the bourbon-soaked chair, and goes to pull his brothers apart. His snake-skin boots saying *clack-clack-clack.* I stare into the broken shattered glass on the floor.

"You spineless fuck!" Clint's blood-gargled voice bellows.

Mom is holding him up, like she'd held me. Above his right eye is swollen. Below his left eye is busted open, a slit of red trickling down. His wide nose oozes red so dark it's black. He wipes his shirt sleeve across where the blood gushes, keeping it from his mouth. And even as he rages and his voice booms throughout our small house, gooey tears trickle from his soft paternal eyes and mix with the tracks of blood down his cheeks.

Peyton Popp *is a banker from Kentucky. In his free time, he enjoys playing cards with his wife and trying to teach his son baseball. Peyton's work has appeared in* Words & Sports Quarterly. *You can also sometimes find his ramblings on Substack (@theretype). Of* Beginner's Luck, *he writes, "I wanted to explore the way our perception affects who is a hero and who is a villain."*

Twins

Nate Hanrahan

I

"Take care of your mother for me." These were the last words spoken to Jane by her father before he left for the front. Not to the front straight away, but to a base in the South, then a port in Europe, then to the front. The days were the hardest to bear when he was not at the front, but was gone, training for war. Preparing for conflict in a state she had vacationed in the prior year with her family.

She watched oak leaves tumble over frozen asphalt. She walked a sidewalk-less street briskly, as if pursuing something, or fleeing someone hideous; an empty envelope addressed to her sister gripped in her ashy hand.

Being a twin is the mildest of curses. A sentence to reiterate answers to a droning line of inquiries from strangers and acquaintances: do twins run in your family? How can I tell the two of you apart? Do you have a twin language? The anodyne questioning batters one's belief in novel thoughts, or the existence of novel thinking. Everyone wonders the same way; makes the same droll conversation, fixates on the duplicative, mirror-like nature of the two women they see.

A small white truck passed Jane quickly enough to be perceived as traveling too fast.

Where the embellishment of twins' sameness was always banal, any attention paid to the difference between the sisters was cruel. Estimates of who was smarter and who was prettier and who was funny and who was in charge slipped out in jokes and remarks, seeming to praise one, but which only brought discomfort for both. "Our sameness or our difference is our value as twins" was the observation of Jane's days; very little premium was ever based on the individual, only the juxtaposition.

"What then was the value, the difference, between myself and Madeline," she thought, "that Dad would write her a goodbye but not me?" She dropped the envelope and it scampered hastily away with the leaves in the bitter wind, as though the letter itself knew it never belonged to her.

Jane's father, Madeline's father, the father of the twins, had died. The officer who knocked on their front door delivering news of his death did not tell them what had killed their father. He likely did not know, although he surely would have lied had he been asked. Most people probably ask, Jane would later think. Jane did not care so much if it was a bullet of the enemy, or of a friendly, a slip and fall leaving a trench, artillery, or shock. Knowing the method could not have been a duller knife than his not telling her goodbye when he sensed that he would meet his end.

"A good father loves his children equally and uniquely" was what he had said to them both, individually and in front of each other. The "uniquely" being stressed, providing the cover for any disparity in treatment, in gestures. Jane remembered thinking it was wise policy when she was young, and a pragmatic deflection as she aged. No one really loves everyone equally, not even the genetically identical. She revolved the phrase in her mind: "they must have a favorite and it must not be me." This phrase was a guard, allowing her to play as a dutiful runner up, bowing out of the competition in an effort to enjoy the game. The ruse of equanimity was enough, the great consideration provided to console, but not to accurately depict her status.

The officer delivered two letters. One for their mother; one for Madeline. No letter for Jane. No goodbye when one could have been sent. This stripped away any semblance of equanimity. Jane's mother assured her that her letter must be lost, that one was certainly written, en route, or lost on a battlefield, but nonetheless very real and swelling with meaning and sorrow and affection, like hers was. "Your father loves you. He was not cruel."

Jane once admired her father's strength in matters of fairness. His commitment to appearing to love her and her sister equally was a calmer, quite meaningful love in its own capacity. This fueled warmth in Jane, not pain. She believed this devotion, unstirred by passionate affection, was actually the stronger cord in their home.

A dog barked three times from behind the glaring window of a brick house that Jane passed by.

Her father's dutiful devotion was a staying comfort. All she required was his keeping up the demand made by modern decency to treat one's children equally. Until this last communication, he had upheld it. Whatever preference he maintained for Madeline must only have taken precedence in his final days. His obligation to equality caved in the face of death, fear crumpled him, made him forget the woman in his home whom he loved the least, she thought.

Jane considered a reversal of fates. Had it fallen to her lot to die in battle, what would she have said, and to whom would she have said it? She reflected that she would only have written to her father. Her sister and her mother already knew what she would say. To put it in writing would dampen its hue. It could only obscure, or understate, what they already saw so clearly: the love they all shared, which they spoke of often.

But she did not ever convey to her father that the way he said that he loved her always meant a great deal. He would often say "do you know why I love you? Because you're my daughters." This always reflected to Jane the foundation of her stability: he would love her and treat her as a daughter should be treated, simply because she was his.

II

Madeline was awake at two or three in the morning, propped upright in her hospital bed in a spacious corner room, two days after giving birth to her twins. A twin who gave birth to twins. Her husband was asleep on the couch by the window. Each of the babies was swaddled and catatonic in their respective clear plastic bassinets. As she watched them inhale and exhale, she thought that she now would begin to understand something more of twinhood. Throughout her 28 years, she understood it in an intimate way, the way a whale understands the ocean: from beneath, as a part of its undulations. But now she observed it as a sailor does: from above, rocking on a vessel that precariously surfs the waves.

There, on the wheeled bassinets, breathed her daughter and her son, and she wondered how the relations between twins alter when they are not the same sex. This disparity, she thought, caused the whole arrangement to be quite different from hers and Jane's. This boy and girl, in the same blanket, in the same hat, differentiated by nothing she could see, would not be mistaken for the same person for very long, and thus the differences between them would not be so sought out.

In the process of plumbing whether she harbored some preference for her daughter at this early hour, she wondered alike whether her husband would love their son more. Did he want someone to fashion into himself; to bond together over their similarity? She thought of her father, how he would look at herself and Jane warmly when they had done something strange and say "with daughters like these, what man needs sons?" I do think he meant that, she thought.

He never said anything to betray that he would trade either of them for a boy to call his own, but they never doubted that at some point he clearly would have wanted a son.

A clergyman had once mildly, maybe jokingly, accosted her father for Jane's being highly opinionated. He responded that "what is good in one sex cannot be bad in another." Her father later attributed the quote to one of the Roosevelts. Madeline remembered thinking that maybe being opinionated was not good in either sex.

Her father was defensive of their femininity's equality with masculinity. These defenses were often made on the heels of some action taken, or some word spoken, by Jane. When Jane behaved as others expected a young boy to behave, he asserted her right to do so. Madeline began to see now that her father viewed Jane somehow the way he would have viewed a son: needing more guidance, but less affection, giving him the space and the material to be his own man.

"This may be the separation between her and I as young girls," she thought: "my father treated me as if I were wise, elegant, witty, and sensitive. He treated Jane like he would have treated a good boy—hardworking, dogged, intelligent and brave." He said that what can be good in one sex can't be bad in the other, but he operated from a place of separate expectations for his daughter and his proto-son, Jane.

She worked chronologically through her life, observing her memories through this lens and seeing if the theory held up.

She ultimately saw him preparing for a great battle where he may die, and determining what last correspondence his children needed to hear. She saw him determining that his daughter Jane, she his only son, was strong and needed no consolation, or would be made weaker by receiving it. "But what son did not need consolation when his father was killed?" thought Madeline. He was not so dull as to miss this point, nor to neglect it.

The babies stirred, opening their mouths, but the sound did not emanate for a moment, and then simultaneous wailing filled the room, pleading for their mother's attention and her warmth. She did not know who to console first, this little boy or little girl. Her husband rose from the couch that was too small for his body. He handed her one of the babies and he held the other.

III

Two days after the assault which killed the twins' father, the enemy conducted a counter-offensive and assumed the trench that he had lived in for months. A sergeant inspected their new ground. In the corner of a room that was six feet wide, eight feet long, carved in the earth with walls and a roof reinforced with wooden beams, he found a damp letter:

My Dear Wife,

I wish I could receive your response in an instant. I hope your thoughts are revealed to me by writing to you. In two days, we're beginning a new assault and we are expecting quite heavy casualties in the first and second wave. I am part of the third wave and I don't think that I will be killed, but I thought writing these letters would help avoid the eventuality. I find that the bad things that befall me aren't the ones I ever fear or prepare for, so I am preparing for this one in hopes of escaping it.

I have been thinking of how I would tell you, Jane, Madeline, and my parents how I love them if I only had one more chance. What precisely would I cite as being the prime attachment that our loves are wrapped up in? I'll tell you about our love shortly, but your letter is the easiest to write and the hardest to bear. Easy because I know you share it so completely, hard because I can't imagine receiving such a letter from you and not feeling as though I had been sawn in half.

I need your help and your words. I need you to edit my letter to Jane. Jane's letter is elusive to me. My love for Madeline is a very sensible one. She's sharp and witty. She cares for animals and she makes jokes more clever than yours or mine. She's accomplished, and I have no doubt she will do such great things, but I will be certain to tell her that even if she never does anything worthwhile in her whole life again, I'd still be proud that she is mine. But Jane has something in her eye that only she and I share. I saw it when I picked her up when she was young and it has stayed there ever since. I don't know if she's aware of it. But she is the most like me on some elemental level. In Jane I see myself. I want to tell her this, but I cannot see how I could.

To tell her that with her I feel a kinship that I don't feel for anyone else could not help her grieve me better; it wouldn't help her love Madeline better, and if Madeline were to learn of it I know that could do nothing but hurt them both. But to send a letter and to explain my love without elaborating on that glimmer that I see in her feels as though I am hiding something: that my final communication was some sleight of hand to reveal the truth without saying it. She would not see what I wanted to say by this slight of hand, only that I was obscuring something, which again could do her no good.

The letter stopped there and had a curved line running diagonally through the page. The soldier did not understand English. He balled the paper and placed it in a wooden ammo crate along with other waste and worthless personal effects abandoned by the previous tenants and continued his inspection of the muddy room.

Nate Hanrahan *is an engineer and writer from South Carolina who loves his daughters equally. In his free time, he thinks about, designs, and builds chairs. His work has appeared in* Magazine Non Grata *and* The Hacker Quarterly. *He is currently working on a novel about 2nd Samuel and the 1968 Republican National Convention in Miami Beach. Of* Twins, *he writes, "I thought of this story while feeding my twin daughters at night in the hospital after their birth, mulling over a post-game press conference during which Deion Sanders claimed to power-rank his children every week."*

Sidewalks

Rasmus Rosenkrantz

Tag det roligt og pas godt på dig selv.

Those were the last words my father spoke to me. "Take it easy and take good care of yourself." All he ever wished for me was to walk on my own feet, to take small steps unattended. He wished for me to not cling to the sidewalks, where my feelings had always resided, but to slowly extend myself unto a larger world that he—or perhaps God, as he would say—had envisioned for me.

***

There's nothing quite like waking up to glance at the lakes of Copenhagen from behind my window's wooden casing. I prepared for the day in haste and stepped out into the streets where my neighbour Martin greeted me. He was accompanying his dog Lucky for a morning stroll. I was compelled to join them but had to get to work. I mounted my bike and started pedalling as I wished them a good day.

The sea wind blew through my hair. At the traffic light I looked for the withering leaves of autumn and found them swaying rhythmically. I arrived on time at the King's Square and entered my office. I was the first and only one who met at the office that day. Apparently I'm alone in not seeing the advantage of remote work. Maybe it's because I live so close by that I insist on going every morning, even if I know it to be likely that I shall contend with my own company. At home I'd always be distracted, so there wasn't much of a choice for me.

Working in the city centre is quite lovely. I can freely observe the square and even some of *Nyhavn* with its colourful houses, always attended by curious tourists: Swedes, Dutch, Germans, and Americans alike flood the tiny street with canned beers in hand, singing and dancing. I could only imagine what tunes they carried with them.

Oh, how wonderful it would be to join them, I'd sigh, daydreaming, being able to see them so vividly, yet separated by a glass pane. *Why did it have to be transparent?* Only giving me a glimmer of all this humanity yet none of the warmth. I pulled the curtains so I could get some work done. The city was too distracting.

After the first couple of reports and an uninspired internal meeting, my curiosity couldn't help it any longer. So I pulled away the curtains once more to embrace the distractions. While working I alternated my gaze between the two monitors, but my eyes always wound up wandering back to the streets. There I caught a glimpse of a little girl with a big ice cream covered with pink and blue crumble. Her mom was standing to the side, carrying a stack of napkins, in case she should spill on her dress with white orchids. In another life she could have been my daughter and in this life I wished to grab her hand and take her for a stroll. But her mom pulled her away, likely saying "it's time to go." The ice cream fell out of her hand and then both of them faded from my eyes, having gone down the alley next to the French Embassy.

Saddened by this tragic scene, not being able to buy the girl a new ice cream, I pulled the curtains a third time. Then I returned to my double-screen setup. *That's enough of the real world for today.*

* * *

It's not easy turning 40 and still be living alone. One could consider me wealthy, absolutely, but even money fails to make me happy. Instead it's my youth I remember as having the key to my long-lost happiness. Back in those days when I was an idealist and saw the world through a magnifying glass. Back when the sky was always blue, and from early evening to late night I would be in the company of friends painting dark clouds lighter shades of green. Back when it felt like life was blossoming.

I remember when it all changed. The dinner of my 30th birthday. Gathered with the family at the steakhouse down the road where we all used to live. The constant questions directed at me: are

you thinking about settling down?—have you met a girl at work yet?—
when will you start thinking about having children?

Now that I was turning 40–10 years passed and nothing
changed, I refused to commit the same mistake. Towards the end of
my workday I turned off my phone, but not before catching a
glimpse of a longer message from my mom: "Happy Birthday,
honey! Who are you passing the day with? Have you met someone?
How about that gi…" I deleted the message, determined not to be
disturbed for the remainder of the day.

Instead I made my way to a nearby pub: **Charlie Scotts**.

Inside pints of Guinness and sleazy but reliable company
awaited me. On Mondays, the jazz quartets played. This evening
was the same, only I became entranced by an intoxicating figure
doing an inspired but unconvincing Billie Holiday impression. She
stood on a small inclination above three other musicians. Her hair
was long and black with small flecks of brown scattered throughout;
when she wasn't singing, she let it slide down across her face forming
a mask. Occasionally she would spin 180 degrees, turning her back
to the audience. Her green dress was low-cut both front and back,
revealing generous cleavage and exposing her lower-back tattoo: a
black rose.

I suspected she was in her mid to late thirties, still singing in a
mid-tier jazz quartet in small pubs on Monday evenings. It certainly
seemed like she was accustomed to modest living, but judging from
her smile it seemed that she possessed a happiness similar to the one
I now considered estranged from me.

She announced the next number *I'll be seeing you* would be the
last, and I was determined to try and converse with her, once she
would be done.

By some divine coincidence I was in luck. After she uttered
those final words *'I'll be looking at the moon. But I'll be seeing you'*, rasping
into the microphone, she headed straight for the bar where I was
sitting.

"A Guinness, please," she asked.

"Make it two, and I will be paying." I followed.

"I can pay for myself."

"Sure, you can. But why should you?"

She sighed, looking towards the ceiling, like she really wasn't in the mood for this, but also had nothing better to do or perhaps she conversed with whatever figure she believed resided up there.

"Alright, I will grab a beer with you," she said. "What's your name?"

"Michael."

"Nice to meet you, Michael. I'm Simone." She stretched her hand. I shook it, looking deep into her brown eyes. She grinned ambiguously as she took the first sip.

"I enjoyed your performance."

"Oh, did you? You do look like a man of poor taste."

She was right; I have never had even the faintest comprehension of music or any sort of art for that matter.

"Today's my birthday, you know?"

"Really?"

"Yeah. I'm actually quite happy to say that you're the first person I've talked to today."

"How come?" she asked before emptying her glass.

"I just don't feel like turning 40 is something to celebrate."

"But why not? It's just a number. Didn't you celebrate your 39 other birthdays?"

"Yes, that's how I know I've had enough of them."

"Alright, fair enough," she said. "Next round is on me then, birthday boy!"

I smiled, surprised that being called that didn't bother me in the slightest: *Birthday Boy*.

"Two pilsners please," she said before turning towards me. "I've had enough Guinness. I always grab one to get going at the bar only to drink virtually anything else the rest of the evening. My mouth just starts to dry up if I have any more of them. Do you know what I mean?"

I nodded in agreement. "Cheers, Simone!"

"Cheers, Birthday boy!"

"Do you enjoy your work, Simone?"

"These concerts you mean?"

"Yes."

"Well, you could hardly call it work. More like a side hustle. But it's for fun, not like actual work. Instead, I work in a call center getting screamed at, and rightfully so, by angry people who don't enjoy me invading their daily lives, offering them market-leading discounts on tele-services. Now that's work!"

I laughed softly and said, "Aren't you too pretty to be working in a call center?" Immediately, I gushed at how much cornier it sounded, said out loud, than in my head.

"Aren't you a charming fellow, Mr. Casanova? 'Too pretty to work in a call center', what's that even supposed to mean?" There was a biting sarcasm in her voice, but as I hid my embarrassment behind the beer she added "But thank you anyways, Michael. I can tell you mean well."

She downed the beer and reached for her coat, hanging on the chair next to her. I grabbed her arm, pleading "Don't go, Simone, please!"

Her eyes were dismissive. She put on her coat. "It's been a pleasure, Michael."

"Please don't go, Simone. Walk with me, at least some way? Won't you keep me company just a little bit longer?"

"Alright…" she said and laid her right hand on my left shoulder. I tried to give her a kiss on the cheek, but she grabbed my face and kissed me on the mouth.

"Alright, Michael. Let's do this."

We stumbled out of the bar into the streets. Both of us walked unevenly. I heard Simone laughing, and looked up towards the sky—the clouds were green for the first time I could recall in 10 years.

The night sky bathed our drunken silhouettes in hypnotic spots cast by the moonlight. Simone walked unconcerned and began to dance, performing alluring pirouettes, swaying through the park's yellow leaves, like she was acting in a movie from the 60s.

"Let's sit by this bench," she said.

"Fine," I responded. "But it's a whole lot more luxurious back at my place."

"Five minutes, Michael!"

I sat down. She kissed my neck while pointing towards the duck pond. "I went skinny-dipping in that pond, when I graduated," she laughed, letting go of my neck. "What's the craziest thing you've ever done, Michael?"

I came to a halt, sighing, "I have no idea."

"No, Michael! I don't believe you. Tell me."

"I don't think I've ever done anything wild or crazy in my life."

"Fine." She spat towards the ground. "If you don't want to tell me, then let's just get going to your place."

"Okay," I muttered, saddened by not having any worthwhile stories to tell this beautiful woman on the night I turned 40.

Simone spoke for the rest of the 10-minute stroll to my house. I limited myself to humming in agreement and nodding my head. Truthfully, it was nice to just be listening for a while, even if the only reason was that I had nothing to say myself.

We arrived at my house next to the lakes. Simone marveled as I turned the key. "You sure are lucky to be living in a place like this."

I shook my head. "Lucky?" I think she must have interpreted this as me being cocky, but that couldn't have been further from what I intended.

We entered. She found her way to the sofa and started undress-ing.

"Do you know, when was the last time I had sex, Michael?" she asked.

It was a question that didn't interest me. In fact I would have preferred not to know. I mostly found her appealing because she was a mystery, and because she seemed innocent and dirty to me at the same time. She had a vulgar figure, almost pornographic, with shambolic ink-drawings up and down both her sleeves. But her face was so pretty; her gaze had a despairing quality to it, like the little girl who lost her ice cream that morning—big brown eyes searching for something out of sight, out of mind, something inconceivably distant.

"A year?" I asked, playing along with her game.

"Oh almost, Michael," she said, smiling. "The answer is two years."

"Me too." I answered. She then embraced me.

It was not true, but I've never been the type to tell the truth on a one-night stand. Talk is quite superfluous in the heat of the night, for passion speaks in a foreign tongue, and what the mind tries to hide, the body reveals as it expresses itself loudly and violently. It's in the night, between the sheets, when the two souls momentarily become transparent, that hearts communicate telepathically without a message, without a purpose. It's in the night that time stands still and one gets lost in the arms of the other, having stripped down the soul to guiltless nakedness. It's in the night when sweat blocks your eyes, and your airways clog in the ecstasy of the moment that it's no longer necessary to breathe or think or even be. It's in the night and only in the night that humans are free!

I heard Simone moaning from pleasure, but I didn't feel much of anything. I kept thrusting. I could have gone on endlessly, though I was numb in my left leg. My shoulders sank deeper into the cushions. I merged with Simone's shapes and felt how they were much more pleasant than mine. Some of her warmth transferred to me as she kissed me on my right cheek. "Keep going, Michael."

I did as she said, kissing her passionately and continuously until our intercourse reached a prolonged conclusion. She then cuddled up in my arms and said *goodnight* in my dreams.

There was silence in the apartment and a reluctance floating in the air. But I did appreciate not waking up alone, and Simone's figure complemented the striped pattern of my bed-sheets perfectly. The day was young and my head was dizzy. I could no longer sleep.

In the kitchen our gazes met like two ghosts shaking hands into empty air.

"Coffee?" I asked. She lit up a bit and nodded her head. "How do you drink it?"

"Black and strong, no sugar, no milk, and no cream."

I prepared her order and brought it to the coffee table where she was sitting.

"I really enjoyed last night," I said.

"Don't, Michael. No small talk, please."

She took a sip of the coffee and smiled for the first time since last evening.

"Good?" I asked.

She nodded and got up from the couch, reaching for my singular bookshelf.

"*Enten-Eller?*" she asked.

"Yeah, that's the only book I own."

"Why?"

"I don't know…"

She started reciting from a random page: "For greatness is neither this nor that; but to be oneself, and this any man can muster, when he desires it."

"Nice quote," I said. "Your reading is lovely."

"Are you yourself, Michael?" she asked while putting the book back into its solitary place on the shelf.

"Yes, I would say so, or at least I think so, probably."

"Alright, Michael. I have got to get going."

I rushed for a napkin and a pencil before stumbling into her at the entrance.

"Please give me your number, Simone. Will you?" I asked, holding the napkin to her face, "I need someone now more than ever, and I think I want you more than I want anyone else."

She grabbed the pen and napkin and wrote the numbers down in silence.

"Here," she said and handed me back the napkin. "Thanks for now, Michael."

"I'll be seeing you," I said almost as a half-question, as the door slammed. I then heard her fading steps from the staircase. Once they disappeared completely, I ran to the window trying to look for her, and there she was: her small figure walking down the streets, slowly being reduced to an insignificant dot that only vaguely reminded me of the woman I had held in my arms through the night. And then the dot disappeared, leaving only the memory, and the scent of her that was still lingering in my apartment.

134

* * *

Duty was calling once again, and the struggles of everyday life stared straight into my tired face. Despite my hangover, my heart feeling ever so slightly stirred by last night's happenings, I insisted on going to the office rather than working from home. Before grabbing my bike, I sat for a short while on a bench by the lake and drew a sketch of Simone; something that would remind my eyes of the face that absorbed my mind.

It was a windy morning and yellow leaves blew around me. The water in the lake created small waves. This agitated the swans and ducklings, making them bash their wings, creating tremendous noise. Finally, one last orange autumn leaf fell into my notebook and onto my drawing of Simone. *Alright, that's enough. I've got to get going.*

I kept my drawing in the inner pocket of my jacket as I cycled to work. It was a terrible drawing, even for a sketch, bearing no resemblance to Simone or really anything at all. My imagination would compensate for the lack of decipherable subject that had come from my pencil strokes.

At the office I arrived once more to sit alone. Tuesday still wasn't a day that people liked going to the office.

I started my daily routine, attempting to finish my work as quickly as possible. I kept the curtains open, daydreaming of going down to the square and joining all the people. The whole time I kept the napkin with Simone's number in my hand, nervously pondering *Should I call her already?* and ultimately answering *No*. It was too soon.

By two o'clock I had finished my most pressing tasks. I stood from my seat and stared out into the grey afternoon. It was cold and windy; soon it would rain. Still, the streets were bursting with life. The same tourists from yesterday sat by the port drinking beer, cheering like they would always do. A kindergarten class gathered around the boats for a trip around the canals. Next to the French Embassy I once more saw a young girl crossing the street with an ice cream. It couldn't possibly be the same girl as yesterday, but her presence reminded me that life moves in patterns, and though people find themselves crossing the same streets, I suspected that they were happier than I, who remained locked in place.

I shut off my computer two hours early without alerting my boss or anyone else. Then I stepped out into the streets.

As I leapt across the sidewalks, I thought back on my father's words and the steps I had always refused to take. I stared back at the sidewalk in front of my office, and saw how small its inclination was, much like the step Simone took onto her imaginary stage. There she could ascend, physically only a couple of centimeters, but travel miles in her head to a universal place; there people would meet her and see her for what she was: something beautiful. Something transcendent.

I thought of the journeys I could have followed, and which journeys may still be in front of me. Now, as I finally walked the streets I had marveled at for days, I counted every single step. I wondered if my life had begun anew. Each step felt as the first I ever took.

Rasmus Rosenkrantz *is a writer from Denmark. He writes the Substack 'Arthouse Poetry' (@rasmusrosenkrantz). Of his writing, he shares, "I draw from multicultural influences in an effort to connect the longing of dreams with the grit of reality and to find peace with intensely felt experiences. In Side-walks, a man imagines with fear that his life will not be fully lived. He decides to revolt in order to redeem himself and give adventure a second chance."*

Flight of the Rain Machines

L. Christopher

For Gimlet. One last mile.

When you wake up to handwriting, you are waking up to William Blake and all of his castles. It was on this half-assed principle alone that I found myself 105 miles from home in the center of Eastern Long Island, in damn near a typhoon, perched upon a motorcycle nearly ten years my senior. There were six dollars of quarters stacked haphazardly inside the zippered leather sleeves of my borrowed biker jacket. The coins were waiting to be exchanged for nearly 100 miles of gasoline tax and bridge tolls to pay for safe passage back into the Garden State.

Some things were worth fighting for, even in that day and age—a hair after the millennium turned. And I had not a snowball's chance in hell, and knew this, but did it anyway. Some might say that's the sort of thing that fools are made of. They'd be right, of course. Others might point out that it was thinking like this that kept the concept of being principled alive in the first place, and I'd hasten to agree with that one, too. But if the truth of the matter was ever to be boiled down into five words, I guess I would have to say that I never had a choice. Believe what you want. I am free.

My name is Jacob Rader, and this is a recording.

***

It seems sometimes I am forever penning a note against the flat of my hand.

Writ upon a gasoline receipt the texture of onionskin, just outside a window of a cozy ranch house with cherry stain and a lawn that is healthier than the President's. In contrast, the dark skies overhead are falling in behind me, back the way I have come. If this were a war, this would be a front dictated by barometer. Eastern Long Island; The Shortest Peninsula, they called it once.

The rain dissolved the translucent slick paper like spun sugar candy; the ink ran around the webbing of my fingers at a frolic, staining my hands, making them slippery, making them come alive in the fuchsia wash; slapping and virile as river dancing without shoes along the Mississippi. Because when you wake up to penmanship, the last few crusts of sleep still twisting on your eyelashes, you are all the things that ever were, are, or could ever be. It is a telephone ringing into the infinite, waiting to be picked up and the voices inside the cradle handset to be released. You are your dreams and your dreams are still there, nearly visceral, streaming, caught in your hair, your cheek. Spiraling off and up from the headboard of your bed to the ceiling and back again. It is the best time to be making decisions. It is the best time, Miranda told me, to be alive.

I had awoken early in my second-floor Northern New Jersey tenement apartment to a sense of panic so serious that it was damned near paralyzing in its urgency. The one with the hallway that always smelled of refuse and just-spent shell casings and freebase. All of my hard currency was round and heavy, jingling in my shirtfront like a well-dressed monkey's carillon turning over. It was a week until my job tossing luggage for Newark International Airport would come through with paper again, my check, the kind of paper only banks could read. There was gas in the peanut tank of the Davey from the sound as I slapped it and the motor caught—

this time. Twenty-three miles later I would take the Holland Tunnel hard, spurring the tachometer into the red with a cinch of my wrist, *come on come on come on, you lazy bitch*, and the HD, she begs me to stop, rods pulling themselves to their limits like a dental assembly, playing a backbeat cacophony on a gasoline organ, hydrocarbons from a thousand becalmed automobiles that I shot past effortlessly as I balance the double-yellow line, visor up now, gearbox gnashing, licking the hydrocarbons from my lips, bellowing out of the half-mile pipe that led me out from under the water.

Her metal spine a fist in my ass, my ass in her dropped saddle, oil pan weeping softly to the city blacktop a foot below. The motor wound down and I dropped the clutch, knowing if I caught a false neutral in the heavy-traffic-oil-soaked Holland Tunnel they would be scraping me off the walls with a putty knife. I imagined electrons spinning off it like curlicues. My Harley-Davidson wasn't going to blow tonight, not yet. I camber into the left lane following the reflective green signs bordered in yellow, heading for MANHATTAN, ignoring BROOKLYN to the right, as everyone but Hasidic Jews and poor Black families had done since time immemorial. Alex Cox's seminal Sid & Nancy shot through my mind, the dealer at the Chelsea Hotel who came back with nothing after all day through the five boroughs: *I even been to BROOKLYN,* he said, acidly. **Hate* that fuckin' town.* I slap my visor up to free my sightline and rocket through the off-ramp, nearly getting clipped by two bright yellow taxicabs dueling over a transexual fare and stamped the forward control shifter with my left Satan-Resistant John Fluevog Michael, two-toned, jet black with blood red vamps riding up the instep and tongue. *I was dressed in the height of fashion...* and my mind was off again. Focus. The engine was running hot tonight. I could feel it boiling underneath me. Couldn't get pinned down in traffic. Any rider worth their salt knows that the silver fins of the air-cooled 1200cc

Sportster only truly cooled the engine while the bike remained in motion. *An object in motion will stay in motion. An object at rest will remain at rest.* I split the lane and shot down West Broadway, looking desperately for my exit. I only had enough fuel to do this once.

The city night was charged with anticipation and possibility. A night in Lower Manhattan at a time when the Towers still stood, beer ran from my chin in amber rivers, the smell of cannabis entrenched me at every apartment door I called upon, a meal—a feast to end all others—Japanese food prepared at a Chinese restaurant, dancing, making fun of the tourists, the squares, a fistfight, police, waking up alone and feeling for my keys, my teeth, where am I, where are You? Then the procrastination leaves me. It's gone, the delirium, the need to purge the task at hand away, the chance to pussy out. It had been a downpour since the bridge that dumped me onto the Northern State from Manhattan Island. I allowed the thought that this flight of spontaneity might have been a very bad idea to surface for the first time. And by then of course it was much too late.

I tapped my knuckles against her windowsill. A beat, and then a striped tiger cat leapt to the sill. I had rescued him from the urban townhouse attic apartment we shared off of Remsen Avenue and Tabernacle Way. *We live upon the crux of a platform of sacrifices*, Mira said, once. The tub filled the entire tenement bathroom. When there was shooting I would make her go and lie inside of it, take out my pistol, and wait. For 540 dollars a month, we could afford it, and that was all that mattered. *Poverty knows no color*, my father had said once. I thought: I wouldn't go saying that around this side of town. *Are we poor?*, I asked him once, five years old. *We will have enough*, he said, but his eyes were flinty and unsure, and it scared me, seeing my male model for God flinch like that, and so I never asked him anything else again. It was the first and last time we ever spoke about money, either directly or indirectly. We named the tiger-cat Wyndham Earle, after Special Agent Dale Cooper's hornfit nemesis, because In A Town Like Twin Peaks No One Is Safe, and we both felt that way every day of our lives until we found one another.

Wyndham meows at the skin-saturated figure and rubs himself against the glass, giving me a dubious look—*And just where the fuck have *you* been, Dad?!*—before settling into a tasteful designer armchair tailored in plush mauve fabric. He dragged a live bird three times his size into our top-floor apartment the third night he was home, and Mira just gave me a look from under the electric blanket: *Go get your cat, Jacob Rader.* It was a killdeer with a wingspan so large I couldn't understand how our new pet direct from the Serengeti pulled it through the safety bars locking the window closed. I freed the bird and got a *what the fuck, man* look from the cat.

The day was off to a flying start, and my memory reel trailed out of the projector, and I was standing outside again against a gray pastel smear of weather circling the earth. It was so enormous in its totality that it cast a reflection into the cat's wide green eyes. The smell of ozone carried across the flat one-point-four acres of property, and the rain machines have just began to close down when she arrives.

Miranda Ubiquitous pulls up into her driveway in a late-model luxury Mitsubishi, a great black Japanese beetle of a car. It was on its last legs when her father had handed it down to her two years before, which meant that it was certainly down to its last rites now. The exhaust system sounded like a vacuum cleaner being channeled through a cheese grater that was then recorded at low speed and played back through a vuvuzela. The valves were tapping maniacally, and when she killed the engine it reminds me of ironclad pipe organ, stuffed with blankets, all keys flattened simultaneously. I step back and away from the house, my two-toned Fluevogs slipping on the wet stone ballast and landscaping chaff surrounding her home, dumping me ass over teakettle onto the carefully sculpted front lawn. Fantastic. I right myself, brushing rainwater from my leather sleeves. The clouds had shifted into a cocked cirrus fist but had not yet left the sky. They continued to walk the invisible line between gas and liquid forms, for now. It was not quite noon.

Mira gives me the look she has been giving me my whole adult life. *Of course you're here*, it says. She has some parcels from the grocery store and hands me the bigger brown paper bag that weighs a little less than a tuba, an antelope, or the caboose coupled to the ass of a locomotive.

"Would you like some tea?" she asks in her way, and her voice, all Jewish affluence and New York Suburb and Twining's Earl Grey, hooks its thumbs into my forebrain. They are the first words she has spoken to me in five months and in-between the seas. The Mitsubishi's engine, now still, begins ticking over, punctuating the again-silence with an unseen second hand, making me feel like I have just entered the bonus round on some asinine television game show. She is dressed simply in blue jeans and an ancient designer button down shirt with a collar large enough to form its own gravity—probably her father's by the size and scope. A short violet scarf is tucked into her back pocket.

"Tea would be nice," I say, circling behind to follow her in.

She leads me through the garage into the house, the electronic garage door rattling up on unseen tracks before returning to the ground behind us. Past the Honda snowblower, the riding lawn mower, her mother's off-the-lot Nissan flagship. I could start a landscape company with the equipment here. All of it dusty, the gummed warning labels still brightly affixed. Tools this clean did not shine of maintenance, they spoke of disuse. They could be promoting a livelihood. Providing for a family. Disemboweling a politician. I used to smoke cigarettes here when the weather was cold and the snowstorms flew up the coast to throw themselves against her development like a tsunami. The coil of the antique space heater would glow red and push the bluish exhaust from my lungs up into the air on rising heat currents. I have not been smoking lately, not tobacco, but would be willing to fall blissfully into remission the moment opportunity presented itself. I weigh the chances of her mother having since installed a cigarette machine into her childhood bedroom in my absence at slim to none. I don't bother asking if she's got a spare pack lying about the place. Mira only smoked when she was upset. She never got upset anymore.

Her bedroom has not changed. That was the first thing. I wonder what other catharsis had transpired; if she had taken her car to get the oil changed at least once in the last half-year, what new books populated her closet shelves, if she still favored unders with strings that hooked themselves into orbit around the pale swells of her hips, if he had paid for them with money he had earned from his night job throwing baggage at Newark International Airport. I look over as she looks away off the turn of his head as if on an oiled swivel. *Ballet*, he thinks. *A pedestrian ballet.* Two emotional prizefighters that secretly respect each other, even after the name-calling and event propaganda has been billed on every wall in town. Catcalling from the rafter seats after every ticket is sold. Every man in the house looking for openings, from the crude matchstick bleachers, praying the other doesn't shit their gamble down first. I skin a stick of gum from the paper and break it in half, swallowing my share and offering her the rest. She takes it and thanks me with her eyes. My stomach was terrible, on the verge of boiling over, my bowels cinched more tightly shut than a park fence after dusk. Silence. This wasn't productive at all. There was no sense of forward motion in empty moments like these.

"Give me your shirt," she says, and I peel mine off, somewhat embarrassed of the weight I've gained in her absence, thankful that it is largely muscle. She smiles when she sees the nicotine patch plastered to my skin just above the bicep. "I knew something was up," she says, laughing softly, and the tension decreases just a little bit more, although there is still no sense of fear in her voice, just kind customer service so far, just la-di-dah and I could be anyone. She could be a laundress working at the cleaners in the bowels of town, somewhere. Miranda leaves to get the tea, singing to herself as she goes. I lug my motorcycle jacket down the hall to the mudroom without being asked, the zippers dancing at the end of the sleeves as I go, like marionettes. Her voice carries, like always, a midshipman's boom. A train conductor screaming *All Aboard* for *New York, Philadelphia, and All Points West.* It is a song I have never heard before, and I lean into the strains of her voice, trying to hold onto the words, knowing I will have forgotten them by the time she returns. I walk back down the hall the way I have come, passing her parents' bedroom, Mira's bathroom, her father's financial studio still settling from his years on Wall Street in Ivan Boesky and Michael Milken's day.

We sweep through the house as if we are guided by wire. It is a pith of analogy. Always precise movements, all motion like hospital corners, as swift and precise as baccarat—exacting, like surgery. We are old card-players. Our faces reveal nothing. *If we were older than this, we would know better,* I thought. The excavation of the Kitchen Ubiquitous has been complete and total—the cats seem afraid to stay in it for very long, perhaps fearing that they might be the next subtraction to the decimated Formica landscape. The coffeepot has plaster dust scouring its opal surface. Her mother can be heard in the sitting room, talking on the telephone. She skirts the periphery but says nothing. I wonder how much her mother knows. Of the other men she had taken from the surrounding honky-tonks. A lover in Italy, others. How he had shoved her to the ground in frustration upon finding out the truth when she wouldn't give up the local boy's name. Her normally-omnipotent mother seems aware of the tension, but does not seem upset that he has come: leather jacket, wild hair, lips that had pulled too many toxins inside between the last year's perennial nascent and this one. Should be no contest, there. Just a goy. Not to worry, never to marry. Always a bridesmaid, never a bride. No worries and no fear, love. Shhh.

I open my eyes and I am in Mira's bedroom again. My picture is gone from the bureau, although I still carry one of you in my billfold. Her bedspread is almost-white, the color of cream with a single drop of vanilla spreading through it, like melanin. This is where they sleep now, her boy and her. Where they sleep, where they dream, where they love. Where for all of their adult acts, they consummate the silliest, most animal one. Her parents never held concerns over things like these, where my own father—if I had been born female and our roles had been reversed, would have led me to the curb by the ear, probably pinned to the end of a shotgun barrel. I am perspiring slightly. I can hear the dryer being switched on in the far room, the room with the gas furnace the size of a shopping cart—yet somehow powerful enough to heat the two-bedroom ranch house comfortably even during the most terrible winters, the winters with no Christmas tree, just eight candles, a match, and five paragraphs in Hebrew I could not understand.

This development was the Levittown of the hoi polloi; Strathmore, what once was considered the middle-class. I look up then, out of my reverie. She is there, watching me, two cups of amber steaming in her hands. The smell of bergamot washes over me. I take one.

"Thank you," I tell her.

"Hush," she says, and I hush. She takes my arm then. She takes my arm and pulls me through the house and out into the backyard, through the rock garden, towards the swimming pool. Her touch travels up my arm, like current. She hasn't asked me why yet. She hasn't asked me why because she doesn't have to. Mira was the one who pulled the trigger.

We sit on the diving board; her in-ground pool has since been filled halfway in with topsoil and chipped cement leavings, a parachute's worth of blue plastic tarpaulin, scrap. All it would need is some cattails and perhaps some pheasants and they could have registered their own swamp. We hadn't gotten around to untethering it from its concrete moorings. The trees keep them company, whispering secrets as the wind picks up. We cannot see the house from here.

"Your pool is gone," I say, stupidly, to break the silence. Mira looks at me like I have suddenly become marginally retarded. *No fucking shit, mister.*

"The lining went rotten. My father didn't see a reason to have the contractors replace it." Mira was a magnificent swimmer. She trained butterflies through the water.

She held my heart in a paper bag four stories above the street at all times. And she would not be coming back here.

"Want to go swimming?" I ask, looking down at the oversized mud puddle beneath us. Like a giant had taken a bite out of the earth and then decided it had gone rotten and spit it back. I cannot swim, not for my life. I couldn't paddle a dog with a Louisville Slugger in one hand and a fistful of filet mignon in the other. She knows this and swats me playfully, her fingers lingering long enough for me to raise my eyebrows slightly. Her arms hug her knees to the hand-made sweater she hides her body behind, Angora, red and white, two-thirds American.

"Shut up, you. Drink your tea while it's still warm."

"Yes'm," I say, as dusk begins to really dig its heels in.

We do not speak again, not really. I want this moment to go on forever, but it can't. At one point I think to myself: *The last time we were naked with each other, we were wearing masks.* He looks across the blue Lucite of the diving board, her beautiful white knees pushing through holes in the denim, the smell of chlorine so thick it was nearly maddening, a contact high of the atmosphere. Mira was blushing, looking at his hands. The grease under his fingernails from the cycle. The ink-stains from his failed note three hours ago.

"It turns me on," she said, once.

"What, that I'm dirty?" I laughed back. Putting my tools away, our second apartment together.

"No, that you can't get it out. It's permanence. I'm a girl. I like permanent things."

Back in the desert of the real, the rain begins to pick up again, matting the curls of her dark hair, her Jew-fro, her Jesus-wave. Four years ago she had shaved it to the scalp. Ozone fills the air. We take off our shoes and dangle our feet into that ruined hole like lunatic fishermen. We stay until the tea is gone.

Inside the evening grows warmer and we retire to the bedroom after refilling our cups. Mine has plaster floating in it, clotting the surface skim like an artery. I drink it anyway. Mira notices this and takes it away from me, frowning at the stupidity that comes with being born male, asking me how I take my coffee now. I say *it doesn't matter*, and that is the truth—and also the right answer to a woman's question, which is convenient. She returns while the coffee is brewing and shakes a chessboard out onto her yellow coverlet and begins to arrange the pieces. After a few minutes have gone by I get up to retrieve it, setting aside a mug for her mother, who has retired to the dining room and is working on outlining a sewing pattern in blue chalk. It looks like an envelope of a person, all fabric, no skin or soul.

"Are you hungry?" she asks, not looking up.

"No, Mrs. Ubiquitous."

"How is she? She doesn't tell me anything."

"Lovely."

"You think it's lovely that she doesn't talk to her mother?"

"No ma'am." Jesus. H. Christ.

"You boys. Doesn't anyone own a telephone anymore?" Boys. There are sharp snapping sounds coming from my sides. I look down and my knuckles are cracking reflexively.

"Um."

"Mow the grass," she says, without looking up from her pins and stitches. I reflexively check my watch. 9:13pm. Long since dark out.

"Right," I say, and head for the door.

It takes me about forty minutes and he keeps looking at the night sky, come on rain, you bastard, rain. I need one night to fix things and rain will do that. I can sleep on the couch. I'll sleep in the compost heap, I'll sleep in the fucking hole in the earth outside like an Iranian refugee, and make mudpies til sunup, but help me out here. Just this once. I am not old enough to believe in a God so I suppose my pleas go out to Order, but it doesn't happen. The sweet smell of a lawn with a fresh haircut surrounds me. I feel a crash against my back and Mira is there and shouts, "Go boy! Get us down to Mardi Gras!" and I take out one of her next-door neighbor's prize shrubs swerving to avoid the Ubiquitous's mailbox and go through their gravel driveway instead. It sounds like a demilitarized zone with a Honda emblem and a fire-engine red paint job shooting past the designer homes, the carefully manicured lawn, sparking off the curbsides like a fusillade. I finally lift the lawnmower blade up, throwing levers, pulling switches. Her hands clutching at my back, her bare knees, the way her skirt rides up and how she shuffles her behind to get it back to a PG rating unconsciously in that way that girls do. Lights coming on up and down the boulevard street. We're in a movie, I think. Still forming new memories. I let out a whoop from somewhere I've forgotten and she laughs and squeezes me tighter as we take a left onto Wich-ita Street, passing my sleeping motorcycle, long cooled. I don't want to ride it home across the Holland Tunnel with a crick in my neck from the helmet's heavy anchor and both shoulders screaming for rest. I want to go back inside and marry her and never come out. They could soap up the lawn tractor with the Just Mar-ried intaglio and honeymoon in the ruined in-ground swamp of the backyard—the burial ground of fourteen-hundred swimming lessons and her tenure in the family nest. Make a fort out of blankets and telecommute from home via her dialup connection. Her laughter, the vibrato of the engine, the thrumming of my heart. The sky doesn't change. It will not call the rain to wash away, make new.

When I come inside she has already changed again into a pair of blue men's pajamas—she never could wear anything for more than twenty minutes at a time. No bra or unders either, by the look of things. Christ all Friday.

"Can I clean up?" I lift my hands, palms out. They are nearly black. There is grass in my hair and an oily scrap of cloth I used to wipe the mower down with afterwards.

"No," she says, drawing a record from its sleeve. "We've no time, come here."

Duke Ellington's *Money Jungle* begins spooling out of the hi-fi as we set up our chessmen for a most localized race war. Her new boy, Michelob, has taught her how to play, and she is good—almost beating me the first game; me forfeiting the second by turning my king face down to kiss the checkered game board in the universal sign of self-defeat. She chides me about this, shoving playfully. A faux-argument ensues, light pushing. Soon there are smiles and then we are rolling over the board and around the bed, tickling, each knowing the other's weaknesses, each both knowing that we must do it with care, that we must not upset apple-carts stacked by others in absentia. The room is electric in the palpable static of our shared, since-discarded sexuality; the tensive charge in the air we begin to give off is almost maddening, animal. *Animale. Adorare.* Pheromones go everywhere like invisible confetti.

And regardless of what ground has been made up tonight, I know that ultimately I cannot stay, that an invisible line of demarcation has been rough sketched—perhaps has been drawn months ago, ages, years before we met, before we were born. I know that it is useless to talk of such things as oil slicks, and the dry rot that is eating up my tires like cancer; the leaking seals on the raked Frisco fork I had put in myself with no help from anybody, a thousand individual variables that could twist and spill him out onto the pitted, seemingly-always-under-construction asphalt. Of fatigue and the myriad dangers of the New York roads at night, as seen from behind a pair of chrome baby ape-hanger handlebars. I could tell her that *Organ Donors* were what they called motorcyclists, in the backs of the Emergency Room smoking areas and Police Stations of this world of ours. All of the things I had been deliberately ignorant of on the ride over, the hundreds of minutes before the hours passed on and I knew that I would have to leave, one hundred and seven miles in, at the very Eastern edge of these States United.

Our feet are touching and Wyndham, the cat, is sleeping contentedly between them. It feels as warm as when I looked through the converse side of the windowpane a light year ago, watching me

spinning outside her reach, a pericynthion of a lovesick boy on a
two-wheeled horror machine.

"Do you love him?" I ask her, because it seems right to.

"We're getting married," she says, simply, and everything stops.
Shifts over four inches to the left and comes apart like a jigsaw puz-
zle flushed down a toilet.

"Yes," I say.

She looks at him with eyes like fine violence, so deadly in their
compassion, so female in their desire and ability to strike without
physical violence or threat of arms.

"Yes," I say again, my mind cycling, frantic, oddly at peace.

"You're giving me tiny heart attacks," Mira says. She slides
over and puts her head down on my chest. "Your heart is beating
so fast," she whispers, and I can hear the tears welling up fast in the
back of her throat. They have not reached her eyes yet.

Oh babe, I think, drawing her close. *Oh babe, you have no idea.*

I stiffen helplessly against her and she pushes back, hard. There
is a near-pregnant pause and I know I am supposed to take her.
Make that indecision mean something. Make her mine again. I
know this and I know that she would give in, open herself to me. I
know that she would even come back. But I cannot. It is not my play
to make, and there are no Umpires for games like these. We stare at
each other for twenty minutes entire. We are both weeping in silence, holding each other's hands, beaten.

She takes my now-empty mug and goes to fetch my clothes,
knocking two knights and a queen from the bed to the floor. I peel
off the sweatshirt with the logo of a University I shall never qualify
to attend emblazoned across the front and fold it neatly, then begin
to make the bed tightly–her one lapse in an otherwise perfect domestic routine bordering on obsessive compulsive disorder, to sort
the fancy lacquered chessboard for the next time she plays. I seat

the pieces carefully in their bed of green felt. I know that I will never see them again.

In the laundry corner, next to a boiler so impossibly small that it looks like it could fit in the trunk of her car, we are folding clothes. My dry clothes smell like the past apartment we shared together, like spring—like being born, I imagine. They look weary—a ward of the state encapsulated in cloth in the basket alongside hers, which are bright, thick fabrics that are not missing threads or buttons. I don't like it; wish I had others. I feel the light that first sparked the idea to visit this afternoon begin to fade, like a hallucinogenic tonic leaving my system after the peak has come. My chest thickening as she walks me to my motorcycle, all black and chrome and dangerboy. All of the things I secretly love to be known for and yet wish that there were stereotypes for the person that I really am. The same way she hates the fact that these things attract her to me, when all she really wanted was to be old shoes together with some rich kid with floppy hair and a bourgeoisie record collection. My hair falls in my eyes as I pull the helmet on over my face and I am reminded how she used to cut my hair with paper scissors in a time when we called each other by names we would never use in public, not then, not ever. Her mother's laughter carries across the lawn, holding the day inside of it. It has teeth and is more raucous than cheerful; like I am the clown, the *payaso*, instead of the other way around.

"Is this yours?" Miranda asks me astride the Davey with the 3% rake in the front fork, and she means *Do I Own It, Is It Paid For* and I say yes, and she tells me that it is very pretty. She doesn't ask me if I made it myself because she knows I have made everything that is important to me in this life. First out of necessity and then for the love of the game. She doesn't bother to remind me that I owe her money, and I am glad for that if nothing else. I do not know if she is scared for me, worried that I might splatter my head all over the pavement like Mark Farina or Fast Bobby Dylan. Her hair is dark and shining and shot through with drizzle and dew. We hold each other as the streetlights turn themselves on and there is something there, underneath, swimming in the emotional ether. Something like an amalgam of feeling and regret. There is an instant where I feel she is going to climb on the back with me and sail down the dark-slicked straits of Interstate 495, the L.I.E. Ironical, that. Her eyes are wandering and her mother's hand trembles. Tears are invisibly mixing themselves into the rain. Neither one of us will move.

"Go inside before you catch your death."

"Let it come."

"*Now*, Miranda-Boleyn." And I am uncertain that she'll listen to me, but something in my voice has returned, some power I once had, and she submits.

Then she is gone.

***

I cannot go as fast as I like, the roads are still slick, but the smell of the manicured lawns and fresh sea salt air fills my synapses to brimming where loss was just beginning to take hold a moment before. The trip alone gives me purpose, but the goal is no longer highlighted in amber at the end of my directions, and it is harder this time. I could own a house like one of these in ten or twenty years, but the motor powering me now would be long gone before that. Having sweat my last dream out upon the machine shop floor where I repaired the electric suitcase cars the baggage handlers drove out on the tarmac to the planes at what I used to call The Airplane Station. When I was lucky. Where I was allowed to work alone, and smoke my cigarettes–they always grounded me, stupid fucking things. And think of her, of course. Wondering which sky she was in tonight, where I was going, where I had been. Thinking of penmanship by morning-side, of moon rabbits and Peter Pan. Of waking up to a living dream.

The last time she wrote me, I awoke aside a red owl mask in a Doctor's house that neither of us owned in East Setauket, on the Long Island Sound. Playing house as a rhumba was tossed off from the television. They were Mr. and Mrs. Jacob Davenport, Em Period Dee Period. It was the morning I awoke to William Blake and all of his castles. The ashtray had been cleaned and a single pristine cigarette left in one of the slots cut in the green glass to cradle it. A book of matches from Tara's Pub in nearby Port Jefferson. There was a cup of coffee that had not quite ceased to steam pinning a cream-colored college-ruled page to the teakwood. ***Don't Think Of It As The End***, it said simply, outside the orbit of the ring stained through the page. Beneath her careful script was an early-edition Blake she had culled from the library for which she worked, the call signs stamped into its paper flesh. PR4142.S74.1924. DISCARDED. A castle had been drawn across the cover in a practiced hand.

But people grow up. Sometimes they do. Sometimes dreamers wake up. I open the visor even as the LIE approaches fast on my right and feel the tears get blown back behind my ears before they have a chance to draw wavy lines against my pale face, to swan dive to their little liquid deaths. I open the throttle as wide as it can go. I lean.

I think it will begin raining again and I am not wrong—the sky opens up about eight miles in even as the castles of the north disappear behind my chopped fender skirts. I am happy for the opportunity. With motorcycles, weather is something that can always be defeated. Cageless, without a roof to constrict you, you can always track the distance you make as you plot your course to overcome the eye of the storm and allow you out the other side.

There are analogies in nights like these and he doesn't mind the solitude. In the sky, dozens of miles above them, the rain machines are starting up again, a low growl, the rift that holds distance between two points open even as the warm and cold fronts hammer themselves apart. It is feeling on layaway, of waiting rooms, of hourglasses upturned and then turned again. It is both baptismal and funereal. It is the knowledge that some doors never close.

FIN, lchristopher. Sunday, October 26, 12:34AM, Fort George, Manhattan Island, NYC.

About Flight of the Rain Machines *, L. Christopher writes: "I'm kind of from the old school. When you courted a woman, you threw stones at her window after working all night and she would come down all wrapped up in a white sheet so crisp and clean you knew you couldn't afford to sleep in her bed. And she would smile and unlock the door and let you in and you would make the coffee and fill the water pitcher while she went off to bathe. You'd go to class and work and she'd go to class and work and at the end of the day you would pet the cats you shared and think about the future. You would talk about what you wanted from life. You had all the time in the world." Find more of his work, including poetry and short stories, on his Substack (@lchristopher).*

Any Reasonable Person

Daniela Clemens

The world outside One Horse Bar is cased in layers of frozen rain and the storm is far from spent. Branches in nearby trees grow heavier. Occasionally, one cracks off and lands on the frozen earth in a blast of frosty shrapnel. Electricity in town is tenuous and anyone who drives to the old watering hole outside of town is taunting fate, but Father Bartholomew Claghorn can't just sit at home.

When he enters One Horse, a neon glow is pooling on varnished tables and coyote skulls are mounted on the wall across from the counter. Father Bart asks for a beer and takes a seat on the first of seven stools, furthest from the register. An aging cashmere scarf girds his neck and his nose is still burning from the wind. While he waits he cleans his spectacles.

Father Bart has never been to One Horse before but it's the only spot open in the storm. One Horse is never closed. It's *that* bar—the sticky, hard-up, bottom-rung, three-finger bar for truckers and divorcees and anyone whose second job is whiskey.

He's relieved to find only five quiet strangers inside because tonight he doesn't want to chat. He doesn't want to be a priest. He wants to not be home.

When his beer arrives, he only sips at it, without hurry. Temperance in all things.

Father Bart was called to Natagwa twelve years ago, when a stroke snatched his predecessor mid-dream. The freshly-collared clergyman arrived with a trunk of books, an east coast education, and a desire to serve. Now, the dwindling parish he inherited—and the promiscuous tabby that came with it—are both on their last legs.

Father Bart's glass dips to three-quarters, the half mark, the quarter mark, and then the front door of One Horse swings wide, letting in a wet lash of wind. A twenty-something girl stomps in, whipping a knit cap from her pink hair and unzipping a quilted black coat in a single motion before the door even settles back into its frame. She hangs her coat on top of another coat on the rack in the entrance, and blows a long breath as she scouts the room.

Father Bart sees her.

She sees him.

He turns away. The girl shows up at Murphy's sometimes, his usual spot on 5th and Jericho. She's a heat-seeking sort, a bar-hopper who leaves on a different arm every night. Father Bart wears his collar at Murphy's so she might place him, too.

"Sarge." The girl greets the ex-marine owner behind the bar, climbing the stool next to Father Bart. The priest glances at her for just a second. Her lids are black and her t-shirt is too small. Any reasonable person would be wearing a sweater in this weather.

She catches his glance and fixes on him with a twist to her mouth, like finding a priest in One Horse is a punchline. "You're here, too," she says.

Without a word, Sarge pops the cap from a green bottle and drops it on a coaster in front of her.

"Father Bart, right?"

He nods without looking. He could move to a different stool but it's not going to help. The other five patrons are too old or too drunk so she's going to stick to him until something better shows up.

"Bart's an old man's name," she observes, wrapping her fingers around the bottle, nails as pink as her hair.

Father Bart takes a deep breath and his shoulders ride the exhale. The girl pivots her body toward him, anchored by an elbow on the bar. "But you aren't old though."

He sips his beer and stares ahead. A mottled reflection returns his stare from the mirrored backbar. She's going to wear him down one way or another. He needs a smoke.

"Must be a family name," she guesses. "Bart. Bartholomew."

"It was my father's name."

"Father Bartholomew's father was Bartholomew," she says. "It's a tongue twister."

Father Bart truly needs a smoke. He draws an antique silver holder from his pocket and folds it open on one thigh. When he tucks a cigarette in the corner of his mouth, Sarge scowls. "Sorry, Father. No can do."

"C'mon, Sarge," the girl intercedes, leaning her breasts on the bar, eyes shaded by heavy eyelashes. "All the wires are broken and trees are falling. We're all gonna die on the drive home. Let him smoke."

Sarge snaps a towel from its post under the bar and walks away.

Father Bart offers her a smoke and she accepts. He strikes a match, protects the flame, and touches it to her cigarette before his own.

At the far end of the counter, one of the old men squints at the lawbreakers, and fishes a foil pack from his flannel shirt. Then the old man by the door takes a pack from his own vest. Tobacco clouds begin to fill the room and blur the neon signs.

"I'm Bridgette." The girl passes her cigarette to her left hand and offers the other. "Bridge."

"Nice to meet you, Bridge."

"You're a priest," she says.

"That I am."

"How about," she proposes, "since it's the end of the world, I'll be *your* priest tonight. You can confess your sins and I'll forgive them."

He still avoids eye contact, to prevent any misunderstanding, and studies the foamy peninsula in a sea of brown beer. "That's a good offer," he says.

"C'mon," Bridge coaxes, "confess somethin."

Sarge slides an ashtray down the bar.

If it wasn't for her, Father Bart wouldn't be holding a cigarette. He plays along. "Forgive me, Bridge, for I have sinned. This is my second pack today."

"I don't actually know what a priest does next."

"Tells you what your penance is," Father Bart says.

She squints. "I, Father Bridgette, sentence you to three beers and two whiskeys. Drink, and be forgiven." She tips her bottle skyward and swallows until it's empty.

Father Bart smiles. He finishes the last of his own beer. "One time, I quit for four days." He motions with the cigarette. "Then after two hours on the phone with my insurance company who wouldn't pay for a dent in my car, I saw old butts in a dustbin. They were covered in vacuum dirt." He grimaces. "I smoked them anyway."

"That's desperate." Bridge motions Sarge for another round.

"Want to know the lesson there?"

"Take out the trash more often?"

"No," he crushes the dying cigarette. "When you walk away from something, don't keep any trace of it."

"You oughta use that in a sermon."

"Yeah," he says, "and I'd lose the seven people who still come to mass."

They drink for a while without speaking. Father Bart notices Sarge watching them with his Semper Fidelis arm bent on the counter. Bridge signals for another refill.

"How'd you end up here?" Bridge asks.

"In Natagwa?"

"At One Horse. I've never seen you in here."

"It's the only place open."

They spend the second beer of Father Bart's penance on black ice stories and the worst of Colorado winters and the likelihood that they'll have to sleep on the floor of One Horse.

"Gross," Bridge says, looking like she just tasted the floor. "So, what happened today?"

"Nothing happened."

"Somethin did. This place is too fuckin low rent for you. You're the kind a guy that stays home in a storm, with his little scarf all tied up." She shakes her head. "Somethin bad happened today."

Father Bart simply drinks.

"Tell me," she presses. "Tell Father Bridgette."

Two beers down. Wind pushes at the door, trying to get in.

"I talked to my mom today," he says. "My parents live in Rhode Island. They've been married forty-three years."

"And they're gettin divorced," she guesses.

"They're getting divorced," he repeats. "Forty-three years. They're the kind of couple everyone puts in the forever category."

"Kids always put their parents in that category."

"Yeah."

"Well," Bridge offers, "I had cramps, so my day was worse."

Father Bart chokes on his beer. He pinches off his spectacles and considers the challenge. "I also burnt my eggs. I had to go hungry all day."

"My horse broke his leg and I had to shoot him."

"I was abducted by the FBI."

"I was actually abducted by aliens."

"Well, at least you weren't alone."

Three beers down. A slide guitar mourns in the speakers overhead. Father Bart calls, "Sarge, can we get a couple of whiskeys?"

Just as the barman grips a red-label bottle by its neck, One Horse's front door slams open. A big brown man wrestles through the frame in his dripping parka. Bridge twists on her stool to see the newcomer.

"Y'all hiding from the storm?" asks the man.

One of the old-timers looks up from his door-side post. "You hiding from your wife?"

The man laughs. "Hey, Abe," he says.

"Juan."

Bridge turns back toward Father Bart. "You believe in angels? Or demons?"

"Of a sort."

"That's vague," she twists her whiskey with two fingers. "You pastors just love holdin back."

"Technically I'm not a pastor."

"You're a fuckin bouncer is what you are." She focuses on her shot glass, weaving slightly like she just left a merry-go-round. "You guys are in charge of a door that people wanna go through. The more people think you know secret shit, the more powerful you are. And the crazy thing is, is people *want* you to know secret shit." Bridge leans toward him. "Because if you know the answers, that means there *are* answers."

One whiskey down. Father Bart looks up and notices Sarge eyeing them again—no, her. He's eyeing Bridge. "So you have a history with the church," he says.

"You could say that. I grew up in the big one."

"Grace Tabernacle?"

"When I was in high school, the elders cast demons outta me. Rebellion and Independence. Also Lasciviousness. You know what that is?"

"I'm a priest."

Chatter disappears as the neon signs falter. All nine souls in One Horse wait to see if the electricity will hold and it does. As drinking resumes, Sarge opens a cabinet. "Bout to get romantic in here," he warns, stacking tealights on the counter. "Anyone got a light?"

"You ever done an exorcism?" Bridge asks.

"I've yet to meet someone possessed." Father Bart uncoils his scarf and lays it across his lap.

"Oh, this place is crawlin with possessed. Accordin to my church elders, this town is a spiritual battleground."

Father Bart frowns, "Your church says that?"

"It's what all the churches say."

"Why are they possessed?" He offers her another smoke.

Bridge tucks a white cylinder into her mouth and leans into the flame Father Bart is offering. An orange reflection flickers in her pupils. "Because of the Lumines and the demonic activity they left behind."

"I thought Lumines were like off-brand freemasons."

"They were. And also thugs, and kind of like warlocks. Churches ran 'em out of town but apparently the demons stayed behind."

"What makes your church think that?"

"Haunted trees," she inhales. "And an old woman who lives in the ground and comes out at night. People acting nuts." She exhales.

"A woman who lives in the ground?"

"There's always been a weird hole in the middle of Seller's Field. When we were kids, we used to throw trash in it. Lumines said the Auspex lived down there. She'd come out at night and sit on a flat rock by the woods."

Father Bart smiles like he knows how that particular magic trick is done. "What does the Auspex want?"

"She marks people," Bridge replies. "Story goes, you wake up with your hair cut off and sprinkled in a circle around the bed."

"And then what?"

"Don't know," Bridge confesses. "I don't think it's happened in a long time." She draws a finger along the rim of her empty shot glass. "But my ass hasn't seen a pew in forever, so who knows."

Suddenly, One Horse's door bursts open and wind howls in, flinging bitter drops on the linoleum. A patron who already has a fist through a coat sleeve heads into the storm. Two others are right behind. The door swings closed and the six remaining souls get back to it.

"Final round," Sarge pours a jet of red whiskey in each of their tumblers. "On the house." He drops a glass between them with a bill curled inside and aims a hard stare at Bridge. "Since when are you two friends?" He tucks the bottle under one arm and gathers empties.

There is some history between them that Father Bart can only guess at. "In a town this size, people don't have to meet each other to know each other," he says. "Especially if they're both a little different."

"It ain't gonna end well," Sarge declares. Then he turns to clean and close the place.

Bridge squares herself to Father Bart. "What do you mean 'different'? It ain't like you're Chinese. Or gay."

"You don't have any idea what I am."

"I have some idea."

"I'm the only Catholic priest in a Protestant town, Bridge. I don't get a lot of invitations to dinner."

"Tragic," says Bridge. "Fine. How am *I* different?"

"You're in a bar in the middle of a storm while everyone else is sleeping."

"I thought maybe you meant because I'm a slut." Bridge tilts the shot glass to her bottom lip and swallows the last liquid offering of the night.

"No one deserves that label," is what Father Bart would normally say, but tonight he doesn't. "Why do you take people home?" He knocks his own shot back.

A long moment passes. "I don't know." She stares at the warped mirror. "Every night, I'm standin on a bridge and I never know if I'm gonna get down or jump off." Her forehead wrinkles. "In the mornin I couldn't tell you why I was fuckin on it in the first place."

As if to make the point, she jumps off her chair. "I gotta visit the ladies'." In that same instant, the neon signs blink off and black night floods the bar.

"Here we go," announces Sarge.

In the obscurity, Bridge's fingers find Father Bart's arm, "Come home with me," she whispers. "It doesn't have to be…it can be…whatever." In the background, a match head hisses to life. Sarge begins to light candles along the bar.

Father Bart is drunk. He can't remember the last time he had a conversation as a man instead of a collar. His answer is to tie his scarf, rise, and lay his hand on the small of Bridge's back.

Sarge comes to inspect the twenties that Father Bart and Bridge left on the counter. He shoves Father Bart's bill away and plucks Bridge's twenty, stuffing it into the bill glass. "Don't do it, priest," he warns. "A priest with the clap won't stay secret for long. You can say *adios* to your seven Catholics after that."

Bridge salutes the bartender with a middle finger.

Sarge salutes back. "Drive safe."

Bart is zipping a toddler's raincoat. He's pinching the serpentine head of a jumper cable because Bridge left the headlights on. He's reading ghost stories to grade schoolers. He's topping the Christmas tree with middle schoolers. He's burning eggs for his wife in their empty nest. Another life passes in less than an hour in the middle of a freezing rain storm, with Bridge's left arm hugging his waist. It's what could be. Father Bart is relieved that he's the front spoon. He doesn't want his erection to ruin the unexpected harbor of a shared blanket. He didn't ask and she didn't try. Rain ticks against the bedroom window, building fresh layers of grey ice. Wind rattles the glass. The muddled forms of dark branches weave into and out of view. Shadows sweep over their feet. Father Bart thinks about how many men have laid on Bridge's sheets and about the cigarette burns in his own and about what can be washed from a sheet and what can't. First stones and all that.

Daniela Clemens *is a graphic designer based in Bologna, Italy. One of her stories was published by* Indignor Playhouse *and others have been longlisted for short fiction competitions. She's currently working on a short story collection set in the fictional town of Natagwa, Colorado, as well as a fantasy noir novel about class warfare. Of* Any Reasonable Person, *she writes, "Most of my stories are about marginalized characters who are either fighting power or finding each other, I love unexpected connections." Other Natagwa stories can be found on her Substack (@dmclemens).*

And the Thunder Rolls

J. T. Morel

Bedtime always took longer than it should have. I never thought that was a bad thing.

My wife walked around our living room, picking up dinosaurs and dolls. Riley and Ripley groaned as she approached them.

"Please, can we stay up?" Riley asked.

"No, not tonight. Your dad and I have plans." My wife looked at me and gave a small wink. It was the first time I had heard excitement in her voice in weeks.

I didn't say anything. Just felt the pressure of the promise I made fall over me.

The twins argued and bargained but their mom quickly put a stop to it. She flashed me another grin, then shuffled the pair upstairs.

I turned the TV on and started flipping through the channels. A weather alert flashed, and the camera cut to our local station. I heard the chime of my phone and picked it up, ignoring the warning.

After some time, my wife's silhouette appeared at the landing next to the stairs. She let her robe fall to the floor and wore nothing but lace and a desperate expression.

"Honey, come to bed." Her voice was soft and tinged with hope.

I barely glanced up at her, refusing to leave the conversation on the small screen in front of me.

"Claire, I better catch the weather. It might get bad tonight." The words were distant and carried on a half-truth. The weatherman on the TV was flanked by a radar that showed a nasty thunderstorm was headed our way.

"Okay," she said as she picked up the robe and wiped at her eyes. The quiver in her voice carried a finality to it. "Well, the twins are in bed, and your lunch for tomorrow is in the fridge."

"Uh-huh," I said.

"I love you, Bo. Come to bed soon."

"Yeah, I will. Just need to watch this storm." I felt guilt tug at me, but I'd gotten real good at ignoring it. I typed up a reply, then directed my attention to the TV.

"Folks, if you're in the Oklahoma City metro area, you've got about thirty minutes before this storm is on top of you. Radar indications show that it is weakening, but as this front pushes on through, anything can happen. Stay with News 9. We'll keep you advised." The weatherman was replaced by a couple of helicopters flying in over a mountain range, and the haunting M*A*S*H theme poured out of the TV speakers. I stood up and grabbed my cigarettes.

A return to regularly scheduled programming was the universal all-clear in Oklahoma during severe weather. I figured I might as well get a smoke in before the rain got here.

The thick air greeted me as soon as I stepped outside. I watched as lightning danced across the sky and began to count.

"…Six Mississippi, seven Mississippi." A rolling clap of thunder interrupted my counting. "Oh yeah, it's not too far off now." I put a cigarette to my mouth and lit it. My own face stared back at me from our large glass windows; its features bathed in a fleeting orange glow. I turned away. The eyes of that reflection seemed hollow and unfamiliar. The man I saw in my reflection was a stranger. I didn't like him or the things he did.

I moved toward the towering oak tree that stood as a sentinel in our yard. Thunder continued to roll in the distance. I felt like a ghost moving through a graveyard of memories. My hand found the heart etched into the trunk of the tree.

"Claire and Bo forever." I traced the lines I had carved so many years ago. "I sure fucked that up."

The cigarette was almost done, and a familiar hankering for whiskey was sneaking up on me. I was about to make a run for my liquor cabinet when my phone rang.

"Hello?" I spoke.

"Hey, Mr. Duncan, I just wanted to call and confirm the meeting with Phoenix Oil and Gas in the morning."

The voice of my mistress was an unattended bottle at an AA meeting. I was an addict, and I needed a fix.

"Cut the act, Justine. Claire's already in bed."

"Did you get the pictures?" I thumbed through my recent messages and felt all the blood and decision-making ability in my body race below my waist.

"Oh shit. Yeah, I did."

"Well? You never answered me earlier. Are we going to meet up or not?" My eyes lingered on the lingerie that I had bought for Justine just last week.

"Yeah. Can you make it to the guest house in twenty minutes?"

"I'm already on my way, Mr. Duncan. You think a little ol' storm would slow me down? Bring the red wine I like."

"Justine, I told you last time we only have three bottles left." I made the mistake once of telling her they were Claire's favorite. My wife had picked them out while we were in Italy some years ago. I spent a small fortune to bring the ten vintage bottles home. Once

Justine found out they were Claire's, she made it her mission to squeeze every last one out of me. The harlot wasn't content with taking a husband; she wanted everything from my wife.

"Pleeeeease," she pouted. "I got the nail polish on you like."

"Okay. I'll bring it. Don't forget to—"

"I know, I know. Turn my headlights off before I get to the gate."

"I'll see you soon, then."

"Love you, Mr. Duncan."

"Don't say that, I told you not–" Justine hung up before I could finish.

I threw the cigarette butt down and let my head fall to my hands. The rain began to fall along with another clap of thunder. The tears in my eyes stung.

I couldn't help but be jealous of the great oak tree beside me. The tree was grounded with strong roots that held to its foundation. The oak knew who it was, and it refused to waver. Wind, rain, fire, or snow—the tree took it all in stride.

Me? I was frail. Just a sapling bending under the weight of my own desires. I tried to be unwavering in the commitment to my marriage. I was strong for a while. Justine was fresh out of college and had taken a job at the energy company I inherited from my father. The advances started slowly: a low-cut blouse here and a lingering touch there. She tested the waters to see how I would respond.

I was strong in that I didn't reciprocate but weak for not putting a stop to it. Time passed as it always does, and I thought I had put the matter to rest. Justine became less forward, and the monotony of the day-to-day took hold until one moment last spring.

Justine wore sandals that day, and I couldn't help but stare when she kicked them off and slid into her seat. I was on the phone with a client, stuttering through a drilling report while she playfully tapped her feet under her desk. I think she heard the tremble in my voice and spun around to catch me staring. I turned away, but not before I saw the smirk spread across her face.

The next morning, I walked into my office to find her sitting in my chair with her bare feet perched on top of my desk. The rest is history.

Heartbreak grabbed at my chest as the rain picked up.

I jogged back toward the house, dodging the puddles forming in the yard. The wind strengthened as I reached our garage door. I turned the handle and stepped into safety.

The garage was quiet as I moved through the vehicles in search of the light switch. After I flipped it on, I went to the large vault door that served as our panic room and safe and typed a code into the keypad. My efforts were met with three shrill beeps and a flash of red light.

"What the hell?" I said out loud. I put the code in again. "Seven, seven, two, zero, one, five." The beeps were louder this time, and the light flashed twice.

"The twins were born on July 7th, 2015. That's the code." I struck the cold vault door with my fist. Justine wanted the wine, and if she didn't get what she wanted, then neither did I.

I located the service number on the side of the vault and punched it into my phone. The line rang twice before a man answered.

"Good evening, Safe and Sound Home Security. This is Mark speaking. How may I assist you?"

"I'm locked out of my vault. I think the storm's messing with it. Can you unlock it from there?"

"I understand your frustration, sir. For security reasons, we don't have remote access. I see here there were two failed attempts to unlock it. Let's try resetting your code. Can I verify your identity first?" I rolled my eyes as he spoke.

"Sure, just hurry it up."

"Thank you for your patience. I'm sending a code to your phone now."

"976-234," I read off the code as soon as it arrived.

"Thank you so much. Now I need you to open the Safe and Sound app. Can you verify the security questions there, please?" I sighed and leaned against the hood of my truck as I typed out the answers—mother's maiden name and all that.

"All right, done."

"Awesome. Now you should see a digital pad on your app. Go ahead and type the new code in there."

I hit the 9 key repeatedly until the code was confirmed.

"Okay, you should be set, Mr. Duncan," Mark told me. "Please don't forget to inform everyone in the household who might need access that the code has been updated."

"Don't need your advice, buddy, but thanks." I hung up the phone and went back to the vault.

With the updated code, I was able to pull the heavy door open. A set of concrete steps and stale air were waiting for me on the other side. I began my descent with Justine on my mind.

I walked past the shelves lined with canned goods and water and went straight to the wine rack. I blew the dust off the label and looked at it under the buzzing fluorescent lights. The Italian translated to 'Light of the Vine Estate'. It was a red wine from the Montalcino Reserve, bottled in 1931 on the banks of the Arno River in Tuscany. At least that's what the old man told Claire and me when he sold it to us.

"Light of the Vine for the light of my life," I told Claire when we packed the bottles into her suitcase. "There is nothing I wouldn't do for you."

My stomach turned as the memory came back to me. I hated myself for the way in which I had betrayed her. I gripped the neck of the bottle as if it were my own and headed back up the stairs, shutting the vault door behind me. The locks clicked with a loud, haunting echo.

The wind grew louder outside. I slid into the driver's seat of my truck, and the cold leather sent a shiver up my spine. My fingers blindly groped the dark recesses of the glove box. I shuffled through forgotten receipts and old mail until the rubber grip of my revolver met my hands. I kept the gun back there, but it wasn't what I was looking for.

I sighed and pulled my hand out. The dimly lit cabin didn't offer many hints, and I could feel my frustration mounting. I looked up to the heavens as if an answer would fall to Earth, and to my surprise, it did. There, clipped securely to my visor above my head, was the garage door opener. A sticky note from Claire clung to it. "I know things are rough, but we'll make it through this. I love you, Bo."

I hit the button on the remote, and the garage door groaned to life. I crumpled the note and tossed it as I put the truck in reverse and backed out.

The guest house was only a half mile from our main home on a small gravel road, but between the wind and the rain, it took me some time to make the trip. When I pulled up to the drive, Justine's car was already there.

I stepped out into the storm, dodging hail as it started to fall. The wind and rain carried me to the porch where Justine was waiting on me.

"It's kinda funny, ain't it?" she asked.

"What's funny?"

"Men." She adjusted her hair while looking at her reflection in a window. "You're just so easy sometimes."

"What exactly are you getting at?" The hail beat at the metal roof of the porch with heavy thuds.

"Look at you, Mr. Duncan. It's in the middle of a storm. You drug yourself out here away from your family and brought me that bottle of wine. And for what?" I fumbled with the keys at the door.

"Don't start with me."

"You did it all for this little body of mine. We both know it." Justine smiled and twirled her finger around her hair. "But me—I do it for the control. I've only ever wanted what other people have. Always been that way."

"I'm sure that's why your sister loves you so much," I told her as we went into the house. She took the bottle from me and fell onto the couch laughing.

"If her fiancé cheated with me, he woulda cheated with any-one." Justine popped the cork and took a big drink of narcissism. "I saved her the trouble."

"You know, the less you talk, the better." I laid down on the couch next to my addiction and slid into the familiar embrace of ecstasy and regret.

The rain battered the windows, its fury mirroring the tempes-tuous turmoil I felt inside my soul. Justine's hand began to caress mine. I leaned in to kiss her when a flash of lightning struck. For a brief moment, Claire's face was in front of me, washed in a fear I had never seen before. I pulled away, then a terrible noise rang out from my phone. I picked it up and read the words every Oklahoman fears: Tornado Warning. Take cover now.

I jumped up from the couch, causing Justine to tumble down to the floor.

"What the fuck?" she said as she stood up.

"I have to go. Get in the cellar right now."

"It'll be fine. It's probably not even by us."

"Justine, I'm not arguing with you," I said as I pulled my boots on. "Get your sorry ass in that cellar if you want to stay breathing."

"Don't talk to me like that." She followed me out to the porch. "Where are you going?"

"Where in the fuck do you think I'm going?" I jumped into my truck and pointed to the cellar just beside the house. The wind shook the trees around us, and baseball-size hail pelted the ground. "In there. Now."

I didn't wait for any more arguments as I threw the truck into gear and sped toward my home. I hit the power button on the radio, and my heart pounded in my chest.

"The National Weather Service in Norman has issued a tornado warning for Oklahoma County, Cleveland County, and Lincoln County until 12:45 a.m." I gripped the steering wheel with white knuckles as the electronic voice went on. "At 12:00 a.m., National Weather Service Doppler radar indicated a severe thunderstorm capable of producing a tornado two miles north of Nichols Hills."

My wipers worked with a Herculean effort to keep the rain off my windshield until a piece of hail crashed into the window. The windshield shattered, and I was left flying blind against the rain. "Doppler radar showed this tornado moving northeast at sixty-five miles per hour."

I slammed my fist against the roof of my truck.

"Locations in the warning include Chisholm Creek, Edmond, Guthrie, and the John Kilpatrick Turnpike."

"Fuck!" I screamed. "It's right on us!"

In that moment, I saw the towering behemoth illuminated from the back by power flashes and lightning strikes. The power of nature incarnate was a deep purple and moved slow across the land, destroying everything in its path. I felt my truck begin to rattle and shake as it was pushed around by the storm.

Sirens began to sound all around me—the final warning for all the sitting ducks caught in the path, just like me. I bore down on the accelerator, praying to a God I had ignored for most of my adult life.

"Damn it! This can't be happening," I said between sobs. "Lord, I know I'm a shit father and worse husband, but let them be okay. Please. Send me to hell where I belong, but don't take them."

Another power flash sprang up just outside my window, and dirt and debris shot into the cab of the truck. All the windows exploded, unable to bear the immense pressure of the tornado. I ducked, but shards of glass and wood pierced my skin like a thousand burning knives.

The truck spun out of control, and I felt myself tumbling end over end. I tried to make sense of the world as I spun through the air. The truck came to a stop with a crash, and I found myself hanging upside down, looking at my home through busted headlights.

"Claire! I'm here!" I called out as I struggled to free myself from the seat. I was only about two hundred yards from the house. "Just hold on! Dad's here."

I kicked the windshield out and scrambled to my feet. With blood and twigs covering me, I began a frenzied sprint toward my family. Every step was painful, every breath heavy with desperation. I felt like I was running through a battlefield, with hail raining down like cannon fire from the heavens. The wind bit at me from all directions, cutting me with the shrapnel of everyday life.

I was bloodied and beaten, but every step brought me just a bit closer to home. A power flash lit up the world, and the scene before me knocked me to my knees.

The tornado was at my doorstep, wrestling with the giant oak tree that stood in our yard. The sentinel fought back against the wind with its thick branches. The oak stood firm, refusing to let the storm move another inch closer, and the two seemed to be deadlocked.

I felt a cold breeze drift across my cheek and head straight for the pair. The cool air surged the tornado forward, and it folded the oak in half with the creaks and moans of a dying man. The branches of the tree snapped and splintered as the oak struck the house. An explosion of glass and wood filled the halls as if they were carried forward on the waters of a great flood.

The wind howled louder than it had all night. The storm celebrated its victory and continued to march forward, pulling the roof off my home.

"No!" I ran toward the massacre. "Please, God, no!"

The muddied ground slowed my footsteps as I raced to find the answer to a question no man should ever have to ask. The sirens continued in the distance, and the wind pushed back hard against me. It seemed to scream with laughter ahead of me, where I could hear the tornado tearing into more homes.

I saw a shadow looming in my periphery that seemed to get bigger. I turned to see what it was and heard a fleshy crunch as the branch hit me in the face. Pain erupted from the point of impact, and my vision blurred. I could hear a woman screaming as I hit the ground just outside the house.

"Riley! Ripley!" I reached toward the door hanging from its hinges, and then everything went black.

I woke up in a pool of blood coated along the edges with mud. I couldn't see out of my left eye and went to rub it. My hand touched what felt like a ruptured grape hanging on the end of a bloody vine. I shuddered and tried to stand. The world around me was eerily quiet. Far off in the distance, I could make out what looked like the lights of emergency vehicles.

I groaned in pain and forced my body to get up off the ground.

"Is anyone there?" I called out as I fell into the rubble that was once my home. I moved to the garage where the safe house was, doing my best to avoid arcing electrical lines and glass. "Are y'all okay? Please answer me, babies."

I ran into a large nail sticking out of a wall and whimpered as the metal tore deep into my flesh. Half of the garage had fallen in, and I could see the sky plainly above me. I reached the vault and began to dig into the pile of wet sheetrock and scattered lumber that was stacked against the door. The debris cut my bare hands, but it did not slow me down.

I uncovered the keypad and felt bile rise in my throat. I turned away from the door, and a soup of shame and remorse left my body through my mouth. Bloody fingerprints covered the number pad, but the nine had no indication that it had ever been touched. Did I really just lose my family over a bottle of wine and an office whore? I fell to the ground and screamed, cursing the God I prayed to just minutes earlier.

I lay there for a while, wallowing in self-hatred, tears, and vomit. I stopped and stood up when I thought of the advice the weather-man would dish out as a last resort: If you can't get to a shelter, then go to the centermost part of your home on the lowest level. We had a bathroom just down the hall that fit the description. I allowed a small sliver of hope to fill my chest.

The memories of the life I built with Claire and my kids were scattered all over the house. Our wedding pictures lay strewn about the wet floor, covered in insulation. I tripped over my children's toys and longed for the day when they would be able to play with them again. Warm tears fell down my face as I was confronted with the reality of my affair. I was the one that treated all of this stuff like garbage. The storm was a mirror that I couldn't look away from.

The remains of the oak stood between me and my goal. The heart I carved into the tree so many years ago was now judging me in the aftermath of disaster.

"I get it! I fucked up!" I lashed out at my broken promise. "Claire, can you hear me? Riley? Ripley?"

I wound my way through the branches, doing my best to ignore the gentle thuds of what remained of my eye as it bounced across my cheek. The limbs were a maze, and the tough bark left deep scratches all over my skin.

I reached the bathroom and did my best to see inside with the occasional flicker from a sparking power line.

"Kids? Claire? Are you there?" I stepped farther inside, ducking underneath the branches.

Sparks fell like a gentle rain over the mattress that covered Claire's body. She hung halfway out of the bathtub, where she and the twins had tried to take cover. The tree had fallen directly on top of them, and the weight of the wooden lances left them skewered from every direction. I couldn't see both of my children, but I knew they were there under the foam and springs.

"No! No! No!" I collapsed under the guilt of what I had done. "I'm sorry. I'm so sorry." I reached up and yanked the gelatinous mess that was my eye and severed the optic nerve. The pain coursed through my body and burned with a white-hot intensity, but all I felt was relief.

I screamed, and I wept.

"I can't do this. I can't." I stood up with a resolute confidence I hadn't seen in myself in years. "I won't do this."

I began the crawl back to my truck, doing my best to keep the images of what I had just seen at bay. I made no attempt to avoid injury as I stumbled out of the house. I stepped on a nail and welcomed the searing iron as it pierced my foot.

"You're almost there," I said through gritted teeth. "Come on, Bo!"

I limped away from the rubble toward my overturned truck. I beat on the bumper until my fists were bloody.

"Stupid piece of shit! You're nothing but a stupid piece of shit." I fought with the jammed handle and twisted metal of the door until it swung open. My focus shifted to the glove box, where my ticket out of this nightmare lay. I reached inside and hit the release. A .357 revolver fell inside the cab, carried on a waterfall of meaningless paper. I fished it out of the broken glass and stood up.

I could hear footsteps running toward me from behind. That bitch, Justine.

"I want you to know this is all your fault. Don't you ever forget that." I placed the barrel firm against my head.

I turned to face the skank. Let her reap what she sowed. In the small moment between the flash and my life ending, I realized no hell was punishment enough for what I had done.

It wasn't Justine running toward me but my little girl, Riley—cut up and bruised, carried by the wind to God knows where, she was racing toward the safety of her father.

"Daddy, no!" The cries of my daughter were the last thing I ever heard.

J. T. Morel *is a homesteader and tribal citizen from the Seminole Nation reservation in Oklahoma. In his free time, he works to preserve the traditions of the Seminole people and hunts and fishes wherever he can. His work has ap-peared on the* NoSleep Podcast. *Currently he writes his horror musings on Substack (@hogbellyhorror). Of* And the Thunder Rolls, *he says, "This story came to me when I was deciding what kind of husband and father I wanted to be."*

Ruminate, Inc.

A. A. Kostas

The Steering Committee is like the bridge of a ship, that's what Godfrey always says. But this ship has a rat sitting with us in the bridge. And I know who they are, and Godfrey doesn't know that I know.

Godfrey knows there's a rat because he planned to fire Martha before she took maternity leave. But Martha published the plan on her LinkedIn before the Steering Committee could implement it; she had documents proving the whole thing. The plan was for her to be caught accessing Godfrey's own personnel file, specifically his financial records, which would be accidentally-on-purpose linked in an email. Right about now she should have been packing up her desk and handing back her laptop, crying and holding her pregnant belly, but instead she's on podcasts quoting Godfrey's exact words from the last Steering Committee meeting.

G: She won't be able to resist the temptation to see all my bits and pieces.

Gross. I winced when he said that, then recorded it in the meeting minutes.

Back to rats and ships. Some traditions describe Noah's ark as perfectly round, a giant coracle holding life afloat during the floods. I imagine the ark as a panopticon, dark and musty, the animals under constant observation. Old man Noah sitting in the centre, flitting his eye over all the beasts. A few shards of light knifing the gloom. Who sees more than the man at the centre of the panopticon? Only the spider. Throwing up webs in the upper corners, manifold eyes peering through the dark. Silver threads catching whatever delicate light can be found. To be a spider, then, is the only way to survive a company like Ruminate. To spin our delicate lines toward those who would help us, then to scuttle and hide and watch. To pray that our threads will hold onto what little light remains.

Ruminate sells digital surveillance products, but the company is also the sandbox for each new feature. We're test dummies for whatever fresh humiliation Godfrey conjures. There's no hiding from the darkness of his gaze: every tap and click, every hovering cursor, every message, every draft. Our laptops have eyeball tracking software. And every data point is fed into Ruminate's fully integrated artificial intelligence entity. Which Godfrey, of course, named G0DFR3Y.

The personnel file Martha was supposed to access was false, created by Kay, and I was tasked with dropping it into my email chain with Martha.

G: You'll be laying out the honey pot to attract the ants.

But Godfrey's not talking about honey anymore. He wants rat poison for whoever leaked the plan.

***

On the Steering Committee we're all chiefs of something, a confederacy of tribes. Tabitha is Chief Operations Officer, solving the daily issues; Jerome is CFO, an accountant with a fancy title; Kay is Chief Technology Officer and Chief Information Officer, I'm not sure what the difference is; Lorna is Chief People Officer, she was the Chief Diversity Officer until Godfrey made her delete our DEI policies; and I'm Chief of Legal. Between us we cover all aspects of the business. What, then, is Godfrey's function? To make us miserable would be a fair answer. He's achieved that KPI every single quarter.

But here's the more interesting question: why does he want to fire Martha? It's not about her pregnancy, though we have fired women for that before. There was a rumour from HR that Martha was preparing a sexual harassment complaint against Godfrey, but nobody internal could investigate due to a conflict of interest; Godfrey is technically everyone's boss and, more importantly, everyone is friends with Martha. Possessing the face of a Renaissance angel, tranquil and wide, and bringing doughnuts to work every few weeks, pronouncing them 'doo-nots' in her Polish accent. She's impossible not to love. Godfrey got wind of the incoming complaint and called an emergency Steering Committee session and began planning his honey pot operation. He was ebullient, diabolically gleeful.

But now he's seething, sweat beading the dimples on his misshapen forehead. I keep waiting for him to throw the stapler that sits on his desk, adding another dent to the walls of the windowless room he works from. Once, the stapler grazed Lorna's arm on its trajectory toward the back wall. She didn't flinch. It had become commonplace.

I'm the obvious culprit for the document leak to Martha, I sent the bait email. Except that in her LinkedIn post she named me as Godfrey's most loyal manservant. And the forensics team is unable to prove I've done anything aside from send the email then go home for the weekend. My laptop stayed locked and my phone was only used for mindless scrolling and playing online chess with my cousin.

So Godfrey turns on the other four: Tabitha, Jerome, Kay, and Lorna. If I'm innocent of leaking the plan and have no motive for doing so, who's to blame? On Godfrey's orders, I write letters of suspension for the rest of the Steering Committee and hire an external investigator, who produces nothing after three days except an extortionate bill which Godfrey refuses to pay so they commence debt recovery proceedings against us which takes up most of my time. Somebody in the committee is the rat, but for the first time in the history of Ruminate, Godfrey himself is in the dark. Martha's story is gaining momentum online and now there's talk of a lawsuit, even a class action. Godfrey is dithering, raging.

Back to panopticons and spiders. Is it strange to identify with arachnids in a company built on a tangle of webs? Is it Stockholm syndrome? We should be pumas, jungle cats, tearing through the cords of falsehood. But each of us on the Steering Committee grows more spidery the longer we work for Godfrey. Cautiously feeling our way through the darkness of constant surveillance. We gather information, we weave our webs, we wait.

At least once a week, Kay and I meet up after work, usually at a hotel bar or somewhere else parenthetically scandalous. Godfrey knows, of course–he tracks our phones' locations. But he thinks we're hiding an affair, which comforts him. We're non-threatening in our vices. This is the nature of men like Godfrey; they cannot imagine acting for any reason but self-gratification.

Kay and I aren't sleeping together, and our spouses know we're meeting. It's useful to have an established time and place to pass information in a way that doesn't alert Godfrey's suspicions. We've become good friends, comrades in arms. Aside from work we discuss dogs, kids, apartments, plans for the future.

Me: What would you do if you weren't at Ruminate? Another tech company?

K: Something more important, I hope.

Me: Like?

K: I'd open a little restaurant in the suburbs. I'd cook all my mother's best recipes—bibimbap, seolleongtang, japchae, tteokbokki. Only have a few tables. Serve them soju and beer. Send them home happy.

Me: There's not much greater work than that. That's the job of a lifetime.

To avoid unnecessary suspicion, Kay is the only member of the Steering Committee I meet with outside of work. Aside from me, she has fortnightly coffee meetings with Jerome, ostensibly to discuss budgets and forecasting, which allows him to pass any information he hears from Lorna who separately meets with Tabitha. A chain-link communication.

Me: Did Godfrey do it? Harass Martha?
K: What do you think? Who's more likely to be lying?
Me: True.
K: Regardless, he's planning false entrapment to stop her from making the complaint. That's illegal, right?
Me: If you can prove it.
K: Jerome thinks this is the one.

I've always thought Jerome was a creepy little cockroach, an accountant acquiescent to Godfrey's whims. Especially compared to Lorna who barely veils her contempt in half the Steering Committee meetings and Tabitha who maintains a steely tranquillity. But Kay says Jerome is the most level-headed and useful of the three. He understands that a campaign of subterfuge requires patience. Biding your time until providence reveals a chink in the armour.

***

My son is four months old. Not yet crawling or rolling, but old enough to turn his huge head and laugh when I enter the room. When I get home, I take him off the nanny and bring him out to the balcony so he can watch the cars on the griddled streets. My son's bulbous head reminds me of Godfrey's own skull, and I think of the five years I've spent doing his bidding, pushed and prodded beyond every ethical limit I thought I possessed. My red lines nothing more than gossamer threads, swiped away by Godfrey's fat fingers. How can I explain that? My son swivels his head to look at me and drool on my shoulder, and then he looks past me, to the cobwebs in the upper corner of the balcony next to the sliding glass. No matter how often we clean them away, new webs appear. Their creator is undeterred, spinning another web despite the destruction.

***

At our next regular liaison, Kay tells me about Tabitha's flower shop. How it could be used to provide Martha the necessary documents.

> *K: Godfrey doesn't know about it. It doesn't exist.*
> *Me: Meaning?*
> *K: It's not a business, not a registered organisation. It's a room on a street with flowers.*
> *Me: There'll be some trace, some paper trail.*
> *K: Nope. No staff, no rent, no ownership, no shipments. Just a place where she leaves plants and people buy them.*
> *Me: The money then. That can always be traced.*
> *K: There's a box where people leave cash.*
> *Me: That's not secure enough.*
> *K: It's secure. This place is a neighbourhood institution. She's been paid for every plant.*
> *Me: How? The honour system?*
> *K: Why not? You extend trust to people, they respond better than you expect.*

I visit the flower shop the next day, leaving my phone at home as a precaution, spending most of my time at a café across the street as a further precaution. It's barely a store; a stall enclosed in glass and filled with plants and flowers. A greenhouse in a trash-strewn alleyway. I observe it for less than an hour and five people come through. A ficus, two Zanzibar gems, a rubber plant, a peace lily, and a bonsai all leave. Every person reacts the same way when they see the cash box and read the sign. A recoil, a darting look around for a CCTV camera, a hesitation, then an unfolding of a crumpled bill, fishing for a coin. They are, for a moment, beyond the panopticon. Free to act like people.

What difference does the plant shop make? It's the vector between the spiders of the Steering Committee and Martha, an untraceable method of communication. Godfrey has broken the law and an innocent victim is finally willing to take action. Between us we have all the incriminating information, but need someone to use it for the right reasons. And the leak can't be traceable to any of us. Godfrey won't just fire us, he'll use Ruminate to destroy our lives. We'll never work for another company, we'll never get another credit card or bank loan, Kay will never set up her neighbourhood restaurant. G0DFR3Y's tendrils are everywhere, involved in everything.

I give Kay the go ahead. We'll get the documents out of Ruminate and into Tabitha's shop for Martha to collect.

***

So this is what it comes down to; a bizarre leap of faith. A disposable camera containing photos of computer screens, a handwritten note with an address and a date and a time, a hope for mutual understanding, a hope that communication from silence will say everything that needs to be said. Hope that a good person will recognise that spiders need the help of the innocent, even if it's too late to save themselves.

Friday afternoon. I wait in my office, deathly still, until the lights automatically turn off. With delicacy I reach into my bag and wind the plastic dial on the camera and take a photo of my glowing laptop screen, and then another, and another. The room remains dark, the CCTV cameras see nothing. Later that day I make the drop, the disposable camera ends up in the tupperware Jerome has left in the fridge with a sharpied note, 'do not eat'. Then, if all goes to plan, it will pass through the rest of the Steering Committee, each photographing their documents, to end up in the cash box at Tabitha's shop. And over the weekend Martha will visit and retrieve it, get the film developed, talk to her lawyers.

What is this, that we're doing? A meagre thing, a wish or a prayer. Small inching movements, as prey make when they're trapped by a predator. Actions so faint as to be nearly meaningless. Yet my heart races as I hold the camera in my hand, imagining its journey from my fingers to Martha's.

∗∗∗

Months later, Martha's lawsuit against Godfrey and Ruminate is coming to trial. I'm out in the park walking my dog when I run into Tabitha and Lorna. I've never seen them here before. Tabitha's grey bob wavers around her face as we make eye contact, Lorna raises her pencilled eyebrows. They're both walking dogs, which start sniffing my dog and we are dragged together. We begin chatting lightly, our breaths steaming in the cold air, saying nothing of substance. Cold War commissars feeling around for wire taps. Finally, the conversation turns to Martha's case.

> *T: We did the right thing. We got her what she needed.*
> *L: Of course. But will it be enough?*
> *Me: I've seen the depositions, the evidence. I don't think she can lose.*
> *T: So we did the right thing.*
> *L: Godfrey's finally getting what he deserves.*

What is this? Patting ourselves on the back? We haven't acted nobly. I think of the apartments we all live in, located in one of the most expensive postcodes on the planet. The holiday homes, the investment portfolios, the private schools, the premium pet food. We have demonstrated only the merest courage. Does that become something significant when it's multiplied by five?

I try to say goodbye and move on, but our dog leashes have become entangled. It takes far too long to unknot and disengage from each other. Uncomfortable silence as we work with numb fingers; our threads so closely joined. As I walk home I try to capture some of that certainty that Tabitha and Lorna expressed. But I don't feel it. I can't escape the thought that we will never be anything more than spiders, weaving our webs in our shadowy domains.

A. A. Kostas *is a lawyer at a tech company based in Singapore. In his free time, he shoots film and spins vinyl records. His work has appeared in* Inkwell *and* Republic of Letters, *among others. Currently, he publishes poetry, essays, and fiction on his Substack publication* Waymarkers *(@aakostas). Of* Ruminate, Inc., *he says, "This is a story of whether a few very ordinary people can do anything against the soulless evil of our artificial and technocratic era."*

The Line

Brock Eldon

I

Outside the kitchen window February pressed its face to the glass and breathed. Wind shook the maple like a wet dog, snowbanks hunched against the curb, salt dust shining under the streetlamp. The furnace coughed, caught, kept the house at nineteen Celsius if the doors stayed shut. Two pairs of boots stood by the mat, white-crusted, laces like wire. The street outside was half-plowed, a steady whine of tires from Queen Street, the CN Tower a dull ghost in the fog.

Jason sat at the table in a hoodie and sweats, shoulders up around his ears, phone tilted low so the glow wouldn't splash the room. The betting app looked clean, medical—blue lines, tidy fonts, odds that slipped when you blinked. He kept seeing the number he'd tried to stop seeing: minus ten thousand and change. After the Eastern Conference Finals, he'd sworn Tatum wouldn't torch the Raptors again. He'd told Sarah it was "small stuff," a flyer, fifty bucks to keep it interesting. Then the Raps stalled, and his stomach slid through the floor. Half went to the card. Half to a guy in Scarborough whose texts came late and friendly and ended in a smile that felt like a knife.

He chewed the inside of his cheek until the taste went copper. The Raptors were on a heater now. There was a way out—there was always a way out if you could see the seam. He'd been seeing seams since his MBA, since lecture halls on commerce where his peers—named after law firms—lost rent money to his good patience. He was good. He was still good. Just one clean hit and the air would return to the house.

"Jason?"

He locked the screen too late. The sound of his name had weight. Sarah stood in the doorway, robe tied over her T-shirt, hair roped back, slipper heels gone grey from salt. The overhead light was too bright, made both of them look tired.

"What's that?" she said.

"Scores." He tried to smile and found he couldn't get his face to do it. "Just checking scores."

"Give me the phone."

"Come on."

"Give me the fucking phone."

He slid it over the table; better to surrender than make it a scene. She didn't sit. She scrolled, thumb quick, mouth flattening as the numbers stacked. Futures, overs, a same-game parlay dressed up as a hedge. She breathed in through her nose, slow, bracing for a hit.

"You're betting again."

"It's not—" He pushed his chair back; the legs shrieked on the tile. "It's not what you think. Fifty bucks, just to—"

"Fifty," she said, and laughed once, ugly. "You said 'fifty' when you dropped ten grand on the Celtics."

"It wasn't like that."

"How was it, then?" She put the phone down like it was warm from someone else's hand. "Explain it to me again. The math, the edge, the little speech you give yourself when you're about to light our money on fire."

He rubbed his eyes with his knuckles. The furnace clanked, the fridge hummed, a pipe somewhere ticked in the wall like a metro-nome losing time. "It was a freak game," he said. "Tatum went off—

look, it doesn't matter. I can fix this. The Raptors play the Sixers tomorrow; there's a number the books haven't moved on yet. This is what I'm good at, Sarah. It's how we keep the lights on. The house, the car, the trip to—"

"Don't." She lifted a hand, palm out. "Don't fucking say 'the house' to me like it's proof you're a man. Everything in this kitchen is balanced on your bullshit."

He looked at the boots by the door. He'd bought those, too. He tried to speak calmly, the way his father spoke when a waiter made a mistake and the table had to be educated. "I know what I'm doing."

"You knew what you were doing when you were with those other women. Twice I caught you." Her voice went quiet, like it didn't want to be heard. "You knew what you were doing when you lied about the card. When you asked me to 'trust you,' all the while pocketing the cash too."

The word *twice* hung in the room like steam that wouldn't clear. He rubbed his thumb along a swollen seam in the table where the laminate was lifting, as if he could press it flat.

From down the hall came the little cough their son did in his sleep. The sound brushed the room like a hand through water. Sarah's eyes flicked toward the hallway; Jason felt his chest tighten.

"Don't talk like that," he said. "Don't say—don't start with divorce."

"I'm not starting," she said. "I'm finishing. I'm done, Jason."

He stood, then sat, couldn't find where his body was supposed to be. "A custody battle—fuck, Sarah, do you get what that does to me?"

She blinked. "To you?" Her laugh was small and cold. "To *you*. He's six. He shouldn't have to learn what a creditor is. He shouldn't see his dad twitch when his phone buzzes. He shouldn't think a man is just somebody who wins until he loses and lies about the losing."

"It's not like that," he said, and heard himself. "I can win it back."

"You always can," she said. "Until you can't."

The phone buzzed on the counter. The preview lit up the screen—someone from a group chat:

Lock of the night. Free money.

The words crawled across the glass and fell off the edge.

He wanted to say this wasn't degenerate luck, it was language. He wanted to remind her of the other winters, the ones with hotels and spur-of-the-moment flights, the way she'd laughed with her head thrown back when a last-second three made a stupid Tuesday feel like New Year's. He wanted to say *I'm still that guy.* But winter pressed against the glass, and the boots were white with salt, and there was a man in Scarborough who texted smiley faces with his due dates. The story didn't sound how it used to.

She picked up the phone again, thumbed to the banking app, turned the screen so he could see. "How long were you going to wait to tell me?"

"I was gonna fix it," he said. "I wasn't going to dump—fuckin' panic—on you."

"I live panic," she said. "I fall asleep with it in my mouth."

He reached for her wrist and she stepped back like the floor had moved. He let his hand fall. "Sarah, I'm asking you—just—don't blow us up tonight, please."

"You already did."

They stood there with the heat running and not quite reaching them, with the hums and ticks of things that only sounded loud when you were quiet. Snow pebbled the window. Somewhere a plow groaned and scraped.

"What do you want me to say?" he said. "Tell me and I'll say it."

"I want you to stop," she said. "I want you to stop and mean it. I want you to understand that you don't get to be the hero of this story just because you're good at math on a screen."

He nodded like he'd heard a thing he could agree to, like a meeting had wrapped with action items. "Okay."

"You don't mean it," she said. "You mean win it back first, then stop."

He opened his mouth. Closed it. The phone buzzed again. He flipped it face-down with his fingertips the way you put a lid on something that smells.

From the hall: the padded thud of small feet, a door hinge complaining. Their son's voice, sleepy and thin. "Mom?"

Sarah set the phone on the counter and wiped at her cheek with the heel of her hand like she could smooth her face back into what a mother's face is supposed to be. "Go back to bed, sweetie," she called, warm, steady, the voice she knew how to make.

Jason swallowed and found nothing there. He wanted to say *I'm here, we're okay, I've got this.* He wanted to be the kind of man who didn't need to say it for it to be true.

The feet retreated. The house listened.

Sarah's eyes looked newer when she turned back to him, as if something had been scraped down to clean wood. "Tomorrow," she said. "We talk to someone. Not you. Not your buddies. A lawyer. And you call someone who isn't a bookie and say 'I have a problem.'"

He nodded again. "Okay."

"Don't lie to me while you're nodding."

"I'm not."

"You are."

He put his hands flat on the table like a man about to pray, or push, or lift. The laminate gave a little under his palms. He felt very young and very old and completely himself.

The phone didn't buzz. The furnace settled. The wind found a new seam in the window and whistled there, thin, like a kettle you weren't sure you'd left on.

II

The radiator screamed like it was dying. One long hiss, then a metallic pop, then silence before the next round. The whole apartment pulsed with it—heat trapped in pipes, the air too thick to breathe. Outside, the garbage truck growled down the block, the metal chewing up the ice. Jason paced the length of the kitchen with his phone in hand, sweat prickling under his hoodie despite the cold that leaked through the window seams.

The Knicks were in Philly tonight. The line had moved again: -3.5, down to -2—it meant the other bettors were heavy on the Sixers. He'd fade it. He always faded the public. That was the rule. He could see the comeback already: one good night, a run of threes, a score that reset the universe.

He could still fix it. He had to believe that.

Sarah's voice came from behind him, small but sharp. "You're doing it again."

He turned. She was standing in her robe, coffee mug in hand, hair pulled into a rough knot. Her face looked pale in the light. She glanced at the phone, then at him. "You told me you stopped."

"It's just scores."

"Don't. Don't lie right in my face!"

He slid the phone into his pocket. He'd been guilted to it. "It's fifty bucks. Jesus, Sarah. You make it sound like—"

"Fifty?" She set the mug down, too hard; coffee splashed over her hand. "You said fifty the last time. Then you lost ten grand on the fucking Celtics. Ten grand, Jason. Our savings. Our rent. You think I don't know?"

He flinched. "That was different. It was a freak game."

"It's always a freak game." She laughed without humor, the sound brittle. "The Celtics, the Warriors, the fucking Raptors. Every one's the same. You think you're smarter than math."

He rubbed the back of his neck. "I *am* math."

"You're a gambler. And an *addict*."

He took a step closer. "Everything we've got—this place, the car—that's me. I've been carrying us. You think your paycheck covers this rent? Come on."

"Don't you dare." She pointed at him, eyes wet but fierce. "Don't you dare make this about how much money I make. You're lucky I have a job at all, or we'd be out on the sidewalk freezing our asses off."

Jason lowered his voice, tried to make it sound reasonable. "You know I can win it back. One hit, Sarah. One clean night. You've seen me do it before."

"I've seen you win," she said, "and I've seen what comes next. You can't stop. You don't want to. You just want to chase the feeling of not being scared."

He opened his mouth, closed it again.

Her phone buzzed on the counter. She wiped her hand, checked it, ignored the message. Then she said, quieter now, "You think I don't see what this is? You're not betting to make money. You're betting to not feel like a loser."

The words hit harder than any of the shouting.

"Don't call me that."

"You called yourself that first."

He turned away, leaned on the counter. The hum of the fridge filled the space between them.

She looked at his back and said, "Oh, and I called the bank today. We're three months behind on the card. If you think you can fix that with a fucking point spread, you're even stupider than I thought."

He turned. "Don't call me stupid."

"Then stop acting like it."

He laughed once, a sharp bark. "You think you're better than me? You think clocking in at that hospital makes you the hero?"

"I think at least I don't gamble the rent away to prove I'm still a man."

The kid's door creaked. Jason froze. Sarah closed her eyes.

"Mom?"

She straightened, called up the stairs with practiced calm. "Go back to bed, sweetheart. Mommy's fine."

Jason waited until the door closed again, then said quietly, "Don't say that. Don't say you're fine when you're not."

She stared at him. "You don't get to tell me what I am anymore."

He stepped forward, voice low and trembling. "Sarah, listen. You can't talk about divorce. Not in front of him. Not at all. I can't—"

"What?" she said. "You can't survive it? You're gonna give me that again? It'll kill you faster than cancer? The thought of custody papers makes you sick? What about *me*, Jason? You think I haven't been sick for years watching you do this shit?"

He pressed his palms flat to the counter, leaning hard. "You don't get it. A custody battle—that'll kill me. I'm dead serious: *I'll kill myself.*" She winced to hear him say it; Jason did not blink. "You don't know what I'll do."

She laughed then, short and sharp. "You'll spin any story to make sure *you're* the victim. You're thirty-one, Jason. Grow the fuck up."

He felt something hot rising in him, the kind of anger that came when he couldn't find words fast enough. "You don't know what it's like, Sarah. To have everything resting on you. To wake up every morning knowing the whole fucking world wants to see you lose."

"No one cares enough to want that," she said.

He slammed the counter with his palm. "Don't!"

"You know what I want?" she said. "I want my son to fall asleep without hearing us rip each other apart."

He looked at her, chest heaving. "Don't do this."

"I'm calling a lawyer tomorrow."

Jason pressed his hands to his face. "Please."

"I'm not asking anymore."

The fridge clicked off. The silence that followed was so thick it felt like gravity.

His phone buzzed in his pocket. Once. Twice. Three times. He didn't look, but Sarah did. Her eyes flicked toward his jeans, the faint glow against the fabric.

She said, almost softly, "There it is again."

He reached for it; she grabbed his wrist. "Don't."

He froze, and they just sat like that, breathing each other's air, the radiator whining, snow spitting against the window.

She let go first.

"Tomorrow," she said, voice gone flat again. "You tell your boss you're taking time off. You call someone—Gamblers Anonymous, therapy, whatever. You get your fucking shit together."

He didn't answer.

She turned toward the hallway, shoulders slumping. "And if you don't, you're gone. I'll kick you out. That's it."

He watched her walk away, robe brushing her calves, the light catching the edge of her hair.

The kitchen went still. The radiator hissed, then clicked off, leaving a quiet that felt more final than any door slam.

He took the phone out of his pocket, thumb hovering over the app, over the lines, over the blinking odds. He pressed the power button instead, blacking the screen, the reflection of his face disappearing with it.

Snow rattled against the glass. A plow groaned somewhere down the block. The sound came and went, like breath.

He stared at the dark screen until it became just another mirror.

III

Morning came in flat, the kind of light that didn't brighten anything so much as show all the dust. It seeped through the blinds and smeared itself across the fridge, the counter, the dinged-up cabinets the landlord swore he'd replace last year. Outside, the sidewalk was a slow churn of gray slush and cigarette butts, snowbanks sawed into by tires, the curb cut into a gutter of brown ice. Somewhere a bus hissed at the stop and then moaned away. The radiator did its routine—hiss, bang, silence, a breath held too long—before starting again.

The radiator joined in—hiss, bang, pause, start again.

Jason filled the kettle, poured last night's coffee. It tasted like coins. His tongue felt thick, eyes grainy. He'd slept in the chair again, neck bent wrong. He didn't look at his phone. He just set his hand over it like it might bolt.

The boy padded in, dinosaur pajamas, socks unmatched. "Morning, Dad."

"Hey, bud." The smile broke halfway.

Sarah came in behind him—scrubs, parka, eyes hollowed out by another night shift. Two bowls, Cheerios, milk. Motion without sound.

"I can do it," Jason said.

"It's fine."

He stood there too long, then retreated. Set the milk near her hand like a truce offering. The gesture stung.

The boy talked about gym class—Matteo, cartwheels, recess. Milk slopped across the table. Sarah caught it with a napkin, efficient. Jason watched her hands, remembered when that steadiness used to calm him.

The kettle whined. He shut it off. The silence it left was loud.

"I'll take him to school," he said.

"We're fine," she said.

"I'm off till noon."

"You're off till you call someone. Your sponsor. That's what you're doing."

He nodded, too fast. The sound clicked in his neck. "Right."

"Who you calling?" she asked, calm as a nurse.

"GA. My sponsor. Happy?"

"Write down the time."

He did. *GA, 10 a.m.* on the back of a five-dollar bill. The pencil tore the paper.

The boy looked up, milk on his chin. "Park after school?"

Jason's heart jumped. "Yeah, bud. We'll shoot."

Sarah's mouth tightened. "We'll see."

He nodded. She looked at him a second too long, then turned.

They stepped off the curb together. Their boots made the same sound in the slush—a rhythm he couldn't follow anymore.

She looked at him one extra beat, and he tried to hold her gaze without asking for anything in it. Then she turned with the boy and stepped off the curb into the crosswalk, their boots making the same sound in the slush, a mother-and-son rhythm you couldn't fake.

Jason watched until they were swallowed by other bodies, other coats, a city's worth of errands. He stood there a stupid amount of time, hands buried, breath fogging, as if the cold could cauterize something. A car splashed his shins; he didn't move. When he finally turned back toward the building, the wind took his breath in one clean piece.

Upstairs, the apartment had cooled, the radiator in its quiet between fits. He closed the door soft, as if he could keep the silence intact that way. He picked up the five-dollar bill with GA, 10 a.m. on it and propped it against the saltshaker like a sign you'd put in a shop window: OPEN / PLEASE COME IN. He stared at the digits on the clock—9:27—watched them change to 9:28, each minute loud.

He poured another coffee he didn't want and didn't drink, just held. He looked at his phone and didn't touch it. He thought about the corner, about the smallness of it, about how a life could be measured in blocks. He thought about being a boy and the first time his father had let go of his handlebars and how he'd pedaled two wobbly strokes before tipping over. He thought about the kid at the crosswalk repeating *eyes up* like a spell. He thought about the words he'd have to say at ten—*Hi, my name is Jason, I have a problem*—and how saying them didn't fix anything, but not saying them made it worse.

At 9:31 his phone vibrated, face-down, a small insect hum against the fake wood. He didn't flip it. He put his palm on it until the vibration stopped and the quiet returned, big and impossible, the size of a city. He took his hand away and left a print in the thin film of dust. He looked at the print like it might be proof of having been here at all. Then he wiped it away with his sleeve and stood there, listening to the radiator breathe like a thing you couldn't save and couldn't live without.

The apartment still smelled like her perfume, faint and chemical under the burnt-coffee stink. Jason hadn't turned on the light. The gray outside was enough. The radiator hissed like it was whispering at him to move, but he didn't. He sat in the chair he'd slept in, thumb tracing the dent in the fake wood table.

He opened the phone once, scrolled the numbers like rosary beads, closed it again. His reflection ghosted back at him in the screen: thirty-one, hollow eyes, hair sticking out in back. He almost didn't recognize the guy who used to walk into bars with his shirt pressed and his confidence loud enough to fill the room.

***

He'd come to Toronto for that version of himself. He'd arrived at twenty with a finance degree and a chip on his shoulder the size of Bay Street. His friends were all analysts in glass towers, working eighteen-hour days. He'd told himself he was smarter, freer. He didn't need a desk when he could read the market like weather.

Back then he'd sit in dive bars on Ossington Avenue, laptop open, betting NBA totals while the Knicks blew another lead on the TV above the bar. He'd quote stats like scripture. "Randall can't hit the corner three under pressure," he'd say to the bartender, who nodded like that meant something. He made five hundred bucks one night and tipped a hundred just to see the bartender's eyes widen. That's what being a man was: knowing the numbers, walking out ahead of the next fuckhead.

He remembered the first real win: a four-leg parlay that paid six grand. He'd taken Sarah to a steakhouse in the Harbour area and told her it was a bonus from consulting work. She wore a green dress that made every other face in the restaurant look like bad lighting.

He'd felt untouchable. He ordered the names of wine he could not pronounce, tipped double, watched her smile at him like he was building something solid instead of just rolling dice that hadn't come up snake-eyes yet.

He still saw her hand across the table, her nails short from hospital work, her palm open on the linen. *You're lucky,* she'd said, and he'd grinned and said, *It's not luck. It's just data.*

That line had worked then. Everything worked then.

***

The radiator clanged, dragging him back to the kitchen. The phone buzzed once, a quiet vibration against the table. He didn't look at it. He pictured Sarah at work, her hands gloved, hair tied back, the same precision she used here now used on strangers' bodies. He imagined her telling some nurse she was fine, voice steady.

He stood and crossed to the window. The snow outside had turned to sleet. A kid in a red parka was kicking ice chunks off the curb. Jason's reflection floated over the glass, ghost on ghost.

He thought about the woman from the gym—the second one, the one who'd laughed at his Knicks hat and said he looked "like trouble." He thought about how easy it had been to slip. How easy it had been to justify. How being wanted had felt like proof that he still mattered.

He remembered the night Sarah found the messages. Her silence had been worse than any shouting. The quiet after—the months of pretending, rebuilding—had felt like standing on a frozen lake listening for cracks.

He pressed his forehead to the cold window. The sleet tapped against the glass in quick, nervous beats.

He saw himself again in the old world, sitting in a dorm room stacked with beer cans, cards splayed across the carpet. The guys chanting his name after a big hand. The taste of cheap whiskey, the rush in his chest. He'd loved the moment just before the win—the suspended breath, the maybe. That was the part he couldn't quit.

He turned from the window, grabbed the phone. The screen blinked alive: *Knicks–Sixers, line moves to -2.5.* Beneath it, a message from Mike: *Bounce-back night. Trust me.*

He could hear Mike's voice in his head: *Man up, don't be scared of a little risk.*

He thumbed the message open, stared at it until the words blurred.

He imagined Sarah saying the opposite: *You're not brave, Jason. You're just scared of being ordinary.*

He put the phone down. Picked it up. Set it down again.

His chest hurt. He couldn't tell if it was hunger or panic. He hadn't eaten since yesterday, just coffee and adrenaline.

He opened the fridge, stared at the half carton of milk, the jar of pickles, the leftover lo mein in a takeout box. He took a forkful cold, chewed, swallowed, and hated himself for the small relief it gave him.

He wiped his hands on his hoodie and went back to the table. The phone buzzed again, louder this time, rattling against the wood.

He whispered, "There's no such thing as easy money." The words felt foreign in his mouth.

Another buzz. Another.

He picked it up, turned it over in his palm. The numbers on the screen looked clean, mathematical, safe. He knew if he looked long enough, they'd start to mean something, start to whisper the same old lie: one more shot.

He closed his eyes and saw Sarah again in the green dress, smiling at him across that restaurant table. He heard her voice, soft, before it hardened into the one she used now. *You're lucky.*

He almost smiled. Then the memory broke.

He slid the phone away, stood up, and pressed his palms flat to the counter until the laminate gave under his weight. He stayed that way for a long time, listening to the radiator breathe, the city shifting under the window, his pulse keeping time with both.

He heard the key in the lock and for a second his chest went thin, like the air had been pulled out of the room. The sound always did that—made the apartment feel smaller, as if the walls leaned in to listen. He'd been pacing for hours. The Lakers were down, the Raptors were down; he rubbed his palms together, slow, like trying to start a fire or something. He told himself he was done, he'd say the words at ten, he'd call GA . . . He told himself a lot of things.

The door opened and Sarah stepped in, coat zipped to her chin, cheeks red from the cold.

She stood in the hallway for a beat, took off her gloves, and looked at him. There was snow in the crook of her sleeve. Her eyes were hard and rimmed with tiredness. "We need to talk," she said.

"Where is he?" Jason said.

"Mina's," she said. "I dropped him after my shift. I needed ten minutes where he didn't hear us."

"So we're…?"

"We're going to talk. Not in that kitchen."

He wanted to say the radio said Knicks were -2 tonight, that the line was moving in his favor, that he'd already put it on. He wanted to say he'd pay it back, he'd double down, he'd—whatever. Instead he followed her down the block. The air outside bit the inside of his nose; it made his eyes water. The city smelled like hot pretzels and wet dog and exhaust. People hurried past in puffs of steam, hoods up, earbuds blocking the world. He pulled his collar up and matched her steps.

They walked without saying much, a nervous silence that was a telescope of thin sound: the scrape of footprints, the distant wail of a siren, a neighbor slamming a car door. The sidewalks were glossy with slush. Every few steps she checked her phone and then put it away like she was trying to ignore a ringing. He kept thinking of the line moving, of a number that could make their whole world tilt back. He kept thinking of the word *divorce* like a cold stone in his throat.

She led him toward the bus stop at the corner, the one with the warped plastic bench and the flyer for a missing cat stapled to the shelter's metal frame. No one was there—bone-empty, no one waiting for a late bus. The streetlights orange-bloomed in the puddles. It felt intentionally dead, like the city had given them a private room.

She stopped and turned on him in a way that startled him. Her face was wet with cold, her nose pink. "Why did you lie to me?" she asked.

"What lie?" His voice was too small; he tried to make it steady.

"The whole thing." She spat the words. "The house, the trips, the last-minute Jays pit tickets. You make everything look like this movie, and I believed it. I believed you. And it was all paper. It's all paper and IOUs, Jason."

He breathed in hard, the air burning his lungs. "I—come on. You know what I can do. You know I'm good at this."

"You're good at convincing people you're good at this," she said. Her voice snapped like a wire. "You're good at convincing *your-self.*"

He stepped toward her. "Do you understand? I lost ten grand because a game went sideways. The Celtics . . . shit happens. But I can take this back. I can fix it."

"You can fix it?" She looked at him like someone looking at a stranger who'd wandered into their life and started rearranging the furniture. "You call that fixing? You put a ten-thousand-dollar hole in our life and call it a rough spell. We have bills."

"You make it sound so simple. It's not about being reckless. It's about having a system. I've done this—"

"Stop saying the word 'system' like it's a shield," she said. "There is no system here. There are only consequences you don't want to face."

He felt the anger rise like heat. "Don't talk to me like I'm a child."

"You *are* childish," she snapped. "You run to numbers the way other people run to bottles. You throw away what we have so you can feel big for an hour. You're terrified of ordinary." Her breath clouded. "You're terrified of being the kind of man who picks up the phone and calls the landlord and says, 'I can't pay this month.' Instead you place another fucking bet. You told me stories. Beautiful lies."

"Sarah, remember the life we had? The dresses I bought you, the necklaces, all that fancy shit? Would it be nice to take Henry to Cancún every Christmas? Miami. Belize. Fuckin' Bali! Don't you remember that? And we can still make it to Greece. I know it."

"Fuck off, Jason."

He saw red then, suddenly, the cold burned away in a flush. "So what? You want me to be small? You want me to be a regular nine-to-five? Is that it? Is that where you put me—on the shelf with the rest of the small men?"

Her face changed in a way that pried at him—this wasn't moderation or bargaining; this was pure anger. "I want my husband to stop gambling with our lives. I knew about it. I always knew. But now that we have Henry in our lives. It's different. We have a five-year-old boy. I want my partner to be honest. I want my son to have a father who doesn't teach him that winning at all costs is the same as being a man."

He swallowed. "You can't take him from me."

"You don't get to make this about fear." She walked around him, paced a small arc, and then stopped, so close their shoulders nearly touched. Her hands were trembling but not from cold. "Tomorrow I'm calling a lawyer. I already said it. I meant it."

He laughed, a harsh sound. "Do it. See what happens. I'll die!"

She stared at him, jaw working. Her voice dropped, close as a punch. "I just want you to know: I'm not doing this for you. I'm doing this for me. And for him. I will not stand by and let our *son* grow up thinking men get to gamble away their promises."

He felt himself crumple a little under the weight of it. "So that's it? You're filing papers?"

"Yes. And I want to see you survive without your illusion. Let me see if your manhood is more than a betting slip." Her words were flung wide, like a door thrown open and left there.

He stepped forward, grabbed her arm. "Don't say—don't say things like that."

She wrenched away, furious now, the cold sharpening her, the empty bus stop amplifying the sound of her breath. "I'll say what I need to say to wake you up. You are not a victim here, Jason. You are an addict. Men don't win by lying. They don't win by putting a number in their phone and deciding what everyone else should think. They wake up and do the messy work."

A bus moaned down the avenue but didn't stop. The shelter's fluorescent light flickered once and hummed. Her voice had that hinge—soft with fury, then steady with something like finality. "Tomorrow. You can come with me to the lawyer if you want, but this ends if you don't start."

He felt the street spin a bit, the edges of the shelter closing in.

"You don't understand how much pressure that is," he said, quieter. "To admit you're broken. To walk into a room and say those words. I'd rather die than be the guy who—who says that."

She took a step closer until the smell of her perfume filled his nose and the cold bit the back of his throat. "Then die, Jason. Die inside the man you built on lies. But don't drag the rest of us down with you. You're an asshole, Jason. You are."

The words landed like stones. He looked away because he couldn't fight the shame and the heat at the same time. He felt hollowed, like the bets had been chisels at the inside of him.

There was a long minute of them breathing each other's air, no cars, no people, nothing but the distant wail of a siren and the scrape of metal on metal from a nearby lot. He wanted to make one last argument. He wanted to buy them two weeks, two months. He wanted his dad's voice in his head telling him not to be sentimental, to close with strength. He wanted the market to turn.

He said nothing.

"You teach your son that men are allowed to gamble with the people who love them." Her eyes were wet now. She stepped back, folded her arms, then pulled her scarf up against her face. "I'm not your safety net. I'm not the person who cleans up after you. This is the last time I call it a conversation."

She turned her back on him and began to walk away, her boots thin on the slushy sidewalk.

He felt panic like a physical thing, a pressure in his temples. He ran after her, catching up as she climbed the stoop. "Sarah—please—"

She didn't turn. She put her hand on the door and paused as if to look back. Her profile was a blade. "Come tomorrow," she said. "Or don't. But stop telling me you're going to be something you're not."

He stood on the sidewalk, the bus shelter's light washing him in a harsh square, and watched the snow settle in the street. A taxi splashed by and coated the curb with filth. The city marched on, indifferent. He felt like the last man alive on earth and also like nothing at all.

His phone buzzed in his pocket, a light Morse code. He took it out. Mike, in New York: *Lakers -4.5. Lock. You in?* He read the message, thumb hovering, the same old muscle twitching. He thought of the bus stop's hollow bench, of Sarah's face, of the way she'd said *addict* like a verdict.

He turned the phone off and walked home alone.

IV

The apartment watched him through its thin windows like a thing that might forgive or might not. He pushed open the door and came into the silence. Inside the kitchen the light was pale and the table held cold coffee and a towel left from the morning—evidence of the day's small disasters. He sat, hands on his knees, and finally let himself shake. The shake was quiet, grateful for the privacy of bricks and pipes. The phone buzzed in his pocket one more time. He ignored it. Outside, a car alarm chirped, then stopped. The snow kept coming down.

The fight replayed in his head, looping, sharpening: the wet slap of her words, *You're terrified of 'ordinary.'*

She was right, he thought. The word scared him. Ordinary was death. Ordinary was what came after losing.

He flipped the phone over. The screen lit him up, ghost-white. The betting app was still open. The Penguins were favored by four and a half; the line hadn't moved. His balance blinked, smaller now, ugly. He told himself it was over, he'd called it, he'd meant it. He told himself a lot of things.

He imagined her upstairs in some friend's apartment, maybe already filling out forms, voice calm, pen scratching. He imagined the lawyer's office, the word *petitioner* typed in the top-left corner. He imagined himself across a table trying to explain to a stranger that he wasn't reckless, just brave.

He opened the app again. His thumb hovered. He thought of her standing in that bus shelter, scarf pulled high, eyes full of contempt and something worse—pity. *Then die, Jason.* The words landed again, dull and heavy.

He backed out of the app, set the phone down. Stood up. Walked to the window. The glass was streaked with water and salt, a map of all the nights that had ended like this.

He wanted to hit something, to make noise, to feel control. Instead he whispered, "You win, Sarah." It sounded like surrender and mockery at the same time.

He went back to the table, grabbed the phone, unlocked it again. The line blinked steady—Lakers, -4.5. He stared until the numbers blurred. Then he placed the bet.

A hollow ding confirmed it. *Wager accepted.*

He laughed once, no sound. It was reflex.

He set the phone down, pushed it away. The radiator hissed louder. He leaned back in the chair and stared at the ceiling until his neck hurt. The hum of the building filled his ears.

He thought about her hands, the green dress, the steakhouse, the first lie that had felt like a gift. He thought about the word *ordinary* and realized she was right: he didn't fear losing her as much as he feared being nobody.

The city's noise faded. The rain slowed to a whisper. He sat in the half-dark, the phone between his hands, the screen dimming, then black. He could still see his reflection—just enough to recognize himself before the light disappeared completely.

Brock Eldon *is a Canadian author of fiction, poetry, and essays based, over the years, in South Korea, China, and Vietnam. His work appears in* Salmagundi Magazine *and* The Metropolitan Review, *and is published regularly on Substack through* Null Point *and* The Commonplace Book. *He writes,* "The Line *began as a one-act play during my studies in English Language and Literature at Western University, and gradually transformed into prose over the course of a decade. The story's gambling serves as a displacement— standing in for the various forms of addiction I have witnessed, and at times confronted, in the course of my career in East and Southeast Asia."*

Machete Man

Spencer Oakes

The style of this story is not that of a romance. The love story, however, is inescapable.

I went from the serrated lines in the earth's crust and the shaking air outside Uranium City to gliding above the coast in less than a morning. The plane circled.

The rigger and I sat next to one another through a layover and connecting flights. He talked about his plans to hole up in a friend's apartment over the winter; he wanted to see what would come of it, if anything would happen. Grand plans, he said, grand piano, too. He moved on to jazz records, college, and where he had yet to go to college; the time he played charades with an ex-boss and her ex-husband; they were all naked, he said.

I never worked oil, I told him. Me neither, he said. He told me he wasn't actually a rigger, that he'd been in school during the oil days. The apartment—the one he'd bury himself inside—wouldn't be his until summer ended, one week away. He had some time to kill, even though the days were already shorter than long. That must be the violence of youth talking, I thought, the idea of time to kill.

Our job up in the bush finished early as fires burned more than normal, a new normal, everyone said. I stared at my watch. I nurtured the second hand, saying to myself, there's no need to kill anything, whatever death happens will happen. Another second moved along, and then one more.

"There's some fun to be had in the city." He pushed his hair back out of his eyes to where it held and ordered us more cans of beer from the flight attendant.

"I'm going to stay with family," I said, "get my truck."

The plane fell slow onto the runway.

"I've got friends picking me up from the airport, come with," he said.

"My truck," as the tires touched the tarmac, "I should go get it."

I didn't get my truck. Not then, anyway.

Coming off the plane I had a missed call from my mom. A text, too, saying the truck leaked oil on the driveway. I've been told a mother's love goes without saying. I left the airport with the rigger and his friends who were also younger than me and trembled with life. I thought about my dog, Pinny, waiting for me. I'd paid the kennel through next week.

Someone in the car handed us the capsules and described them to be like mushrooms but better and, also, not really like mushrooms, and then a bottle of tequila appeared. The air conditioning kept us cool. We drove toward the city on a long stretch of concrete, the freeway to town, so long it became hard to imagine that man could have ever made such a thing. Man can do anything. I opened my window and the warm air replaced my head. Then a cigarette replaced the tequila and soon the heavy traffic and highway guard rails fell off. In their place appeared sidewalks and hot suburban streets and towers filled with family, full of business, and before my head came back to me as the rigger put his arm around my shoulders in the back seat, as we smoked and drank, and talked of the wildfires and how we could have burned alive—This feels like killing time! I shouted out the window. And he raised his voice and told everyone else about where we'd just come from, a place called Uranium City, a basin town of plastic blasts and radioactivity. A man-made stop on the search for invaluable yellow dust.

"Isn't that illegal, or banned, or something?" The car had more people in it than I remembered. "Don't uranium mines, like, irreparably damage the environment?"

"What's that old saying, a little risk, a little reward?" Something the rigger would have said on site. "Very few places on the planet take on the risk of mining for uranium, but the high levels of uranium ore in the ground continue to exist, sitting dormant, relatively untouched in the modern era. Experts on TV, leading experts and scientists in the field—the top economists—say it's worth much more than oil. That's important to remember." The rigger, the know-it-all.

"Sounds immoral."

"You just need a more cosmic perspective."

"It's toxic metal." I talked over everyone and out the window, swallowing the hot wind, "In the old days they all got cancer, we probably did, too, all radioactive." The car's energy shifted. Something in me glowed blond and nuclear and my head turned to air if it hadn't already. "So we're all doomed, then." I couldn't catch anyone's eyes. "Doomed and damaged."

"Well," the rigger said, "it's impossible not to come up with at least a little damage." He laughed with me and we shared a cigarette.

The day went on like this. The car drove and drove. The sun dipped. The rigger and I, passengers again, while his friends, brimming with whatever they liked, softened up my old body until I oozed into a new shape, like some fictitious thing that only comes out at night, far from man-made, the way of the rat.

In the morning, my head returned. The rigger and I came to in the back seat, almost baked alive. The car soured overnight. Opening a door didn't help. I found out later that the woman driving the car brought us to her house. She couldn't get us to come inside. She'd left us in the car.

The rigger made arrangements for the two of us to stay there for a couple days. I barely opened my eyes and finally got us from the car to inside the living room to a couch. The rigger laid on his back on the floor and laughed about it all. He said I needed the couch. He laughed until he passed out and I watched him go back to sleep, or black out again, the man with the cosmic perspective.

I lingered on the couch until mid-afternoon, like a kid. No one around. I slept in, touched myself, got bored, slept some more. I thought about visiting my mom. I needed my truck. I missed my dog. I decided I'd go to the kennel later that day to get Pinny.

While the rigger and the woman, Janie, whose house we were in, caught up on the many events that can occur in an absence, I took a spin outside. Hotter than ever. I checked my phone and missed another few calls from mom and when I returned them no one answered. I dialed the kennel, but the phone battery died. The small house sat white with dark-green trim. The house looked out of breath and dirty in its old age. Bamboo in the yard reached for the sky, never going to make it. I got my bag from the car.

"Machete man!"

The rigger popped his head through the clatter of a storm door and tossed a beer. The can slimy in my hand. I liked her house and imagined what my life would be like if I lived there, standing in the yard while Pinny zoomed around. She liked to run figure eights. She liked to tie the world up in knots, my dog.

Inside I ran hot water. The mirror steamed under the hum of the bathroom fan. In the condensation I saw an invisible me, barely a shape. I opened the window. No one seemed to mind me taking my time. Pockets of air came and went. The water turned my skin red and melted away the last several months. I wiped the glass and looked sunburned in the mirror. I'd gotten dark from spending so much time outside. My hair glistened, UV and grey hairs. I'm cooked, I thought. I pushed my wet hair back, the way the rigger would, hand over hand. It looked darker wet. Looking at my reflection, this new, small gut that I swear weighed nothing but a few years, sagged away from my already sagging body. I inflated my chest. I'd been young. The mirror hung on the wall from speckled ceiling to linoleum floor. I let the shower run while I sat on the toilet, dripping wet, shitting, looking at myself. There were no towels. I wiped. I sat there for a while more, in a puddle, running my hands over my head, smoothing down each and every hair.

I sat at the small kitchen table with chrome trim. The chairs matched the table. The rigger took his turn in the bathroom. A slim window over the table had been propped open and a light breeze touched the floral curtain covering it; it moved like it was haunted. The battery in my phone had charged a little, so I phoned the house and no one answered. The kennel hadn't returned my call either. It was the start of the weekend, so they were busy, probably. Pinny's size posed a danger to mom's old and breakable body, otherwise she'd have stayed there. Out of nowhere, she said she'd be unsafe with the dog. I had exhausted the yellow pages to find a kennel on short notice. Summer had just started then, most everywhere booked solid. Whoever answered the kennel's phone spoke another language, but we made it work. I dropped Pinny off. I'd see her again in a few months, when we'd pack up the truck and the truck camper and drive south into warmer weather. The two of us would drive in search of surf breaks. The towns nearby the water were always small and populated with fishermen and carpenters and a different kind of tourist. The people on the edge of a world, looking to escape, to kill some time in the margins. Plus, the surfing. I didn't know how to surf but liked to watch from the beach, from the rain-forest driftwood, from the bull kelp boneyards. Those kids in the water with their hair sun-fried yellow and bodies stringy and sandy and just golden in a way that never seemed to change.

The rigger emerged towel-wrapped from the bathroom, steam following behind him. He talked about how nice it felt to be back in a civilization with hot water and razor blades and the time to make use of the things of that nature. He said, 'of that nature'. He looked even younger standing in the living room, all spick and span, and I could see his ribs under his muscle and skin and beads of water and heat marks. He dropped his towel.

"What's her name again?"

And I told the rigger about my dog. I told him about what they call lurchers, a kind of mutt, that Pinny walked and slept and sprinted like a greyhound. I told him how she came to be my dog after I saw her at a track. The track had been set to close forever, and I heard someone in the crowd say that because they were clos-ing the track the dogs would be put down. This would happen all over. A lot of dogs would die. I never thought about why I went to the races because I just did. I liked the dogs more than the money, or the money at stake, I now realized. I remembered watching Pins & Needles—her racing name—with her long strides and black-hole coat streaking over the red dirt like some otherworldly thing with otherworldly velocity, her lightspeed body held down by the earthly weight of a straw-coloured collar. This dog is going to die, I thought then. I waited around after the race. The owners asked $1,000 for her. I didn't have that much on me, so they drove me to an ATM

and I took out what I had. When we got back to the track I thought
I heard guns going off and dogs barking.

"I hate dogs, would you believe that?"

The rigger put on a collared shirt the colour of the bamboo outside the house. He looked like another version of himself, clean,
taller maybe. I thought back to a few days ago, him and I beginning
work to a sunrise stretching across the camp and above the plains,
him and I helicoptered into unknown territory, him and I wading
through the overgrowth of wheatgrass and jack pines. A life of fires
a world away.

The airport woman walked out from the kitchen. Janie said,
"The weather station says there is going to be a heatwave you
know." She brought out three cans of beer.

I could see the condensation.

Inside the house, all overgrown and wet.

I didn't get my truck or make it to the kennel, and the rigger and I
were in the thick of it by the time the shadows on the ground were
at their longest. Janie drove the three of us to a park with a view of
some water and sunset mountains, a whole thing. He kept fixing his
hair. He did it while introducing me to some people he knew. These
are my friends, he said. Everybody sat in the grass.

I said nice to meet you to the people. Regular people, I think,
not hard to picture, pretty much whoever you're picturing right
now.

Janie, the airport woman, developed from her bag a long bottle
of wine, light in colour, sunlight bouncing through it as if it were a
prism.

"Drink?"

"I drink." I said.

The rigger and I'd already had several bits of bottles of different things back at the house. Shadows turned to night, reaching their final form. He told the group about what we'd been up to for the last few months on those crooked northern plains. Staking out the middle of nowhere, actively searching for uranium deposits in the earth, explaining the work. He looked at me.

"He's my machete man!"

That's what they called me. They'd drop us in the bush, with a satellite phone and these little machetes and saws you could fold up, to clear sites for deposit exploration. I led teams of geos, like the rigger and others like him, through horseflies and thick fields of undergrowth. The search parties rarely found anything, and we spent most of our time, hours of our days, slashing and sawing away to give a helicopter enough clearance to pick us up and return us to camp.

We found success early on. Most nights at camp had been backdropped by explosive sounds only a few kilometers away, the work of a dedicated blast team, working through the night. The inhabitants of the camp *whooped* with optimism.

"Send in the drones!" the company said.

"Boom goes the dynamite!" men would say.

Slowly the earth contorted itself into a stony terrace, similar to the rice fields a world over. Then, wildfires halted blasting for several weeks. The fires were always closing in on us in a way that never seemed real. In anticipation, I requested we raze the wooded area ten feet out from the perimeter of the camp and the nearby lake to limit the fire load. Anything that would catch and light up had to go. Everyone got a machete. Everyone got a saw. We set up industrial sprinklers. Drew up an exit plan for fire day: (1) Remain calm. (2) Meet at the water's edge. (3) Board the pontoon boats and motor to the middle of the lake. (4) Wait for extraction. These dimensions of the work—the blasting, the burning, the planning—kept spirits high. Fire day never came.

A voice from the group. So far away now from extraction.

"Will we ever go back to our regularly scheduled programming?"

The new friends kept asking that. So drunk. It might have been Janie, or a woman who looked like her.

"Now, back to our regularly scheduled programming." She repeated, this time like a news anchor, bored of the rigger, making fun. She even looked like Walter Kronkite, and I said as much. No one knew who that was. The bottle of wine came my way. My head replaced entirely. (5) Extraction complete. This feeling I knew well. I am the Kronkite of my time, I said out loud, an accident, I think, the most trusted man in town.

The rigger swayed back and forth on a wooden bench, and I could see him entering a sweet spot. Then he threw up little splashes into the grass and onto his sneakers, the colour of the pulpy side of a grapefruit. I had to say something, tell him to get a handle.

"There's no apartment," he said, "no grand piano, no jazz, nowhere to go."

At least, that's what I think he said.

"Jesus man, at least make it seem like you have a handle."

I moved closer on the bench and tried to prop him back up, but he fell into my side, head on my shoulder. He tried to speak. I heard something like 'regularly scheduled programming'. Airport woman lay on the grass, the others gone, and I nudged her with my foot to take us somewhere. "Janie," I said.

After the park, hours later, practically morning, the low lights of the house illuminating a humid living room, a couch, and bright TV, I saw the rigger and her pass a glance. She noticed him. He could only see black. He'd drank more than anyone. His head bobbed like a bird's. I found a spot between the two of them on the couch. His bird-head lopped itself back into the wall behind.

The evening matured and felt tapered off and young, while I got older and older. I'd been young before, walked faster then, had been softer in thought and touch, a boy acting out boy-type acts of pleasure and of pain out of that boyish fear I think everyone gets. Not now. These days my body aches, pulls tight and pops. I used to be so slick, a blue pool of joy, emanating. The rigger snored.

"Machete man," she said, so soft-spoken. She looked around like she didn't even live there, not really, and gave off that out-of-place frequency that only others always have. Our hands touched.

And just then something connected, charged protons and electrons, feeling the same kind of way like when a fog lifts after days of being socked in. We closed in on each other and then I held her hand to the bedroom. I walked slow; she moved a little faster. We went at each other in the dark, out of sorts, only seconds, maybe, cutting one another to pieces. I hacked away, looking for whatever I could find, new lands, a sharper blade, familiar territory.

The rigger, my boy, on the couch, yet inter-dimensional.

I'd been right about waking up early, but again it was the sun and its heat that got us up.

He sat on the short stairs outside the front door, shirt off, and when I joined him, he slapped my back.

"Good work," he said, smiling, with an elbow-to-rib combo.

"All I am is work," I said, a serious face, master of deflection, to avoid a replay of the evening, what we'd done, the sex that made me feel sick, toxic waste, to not say how no one moves when they're drunk, that what her and I did had the characteristics of a dream, one of those dreams of frustration, a dream of limits and sweat when your head comes to as a tight ball—there had been no sound in the room and even less air—I kept it all inside.

He smoked. "All I am is work," he repeated. Inside the house we heard footsteps and a door open and close and after a moment the toilet flush, then a door again, feet sounds, heavier than before, door, open, close.

I sensed we'd overstayed our welcome and I could tell the rigger sensed it, too. He passed his cigarette to me.

The smoke went inside me and then outside me. I took off my shirt, too. The earth spun so hot, everything so hot and explosive. Instead of saying anything else, we remained in silence and did damage, this time to our lungs, in the morning light.

A long, silent drive. The rigger dozed. Janie watched the road. It took forever to get to mom's house.

Mom lived on a street of houses identical in build and colour and rundown-ness. It would be a single poplar or the high reaching pampas grass in the front yard that set things apart. That's it. The natural world had always done that, though. Created differences. The whole neighbourhood like that. I thought about how my mom never wanted to move from this place and how I could take it or leave it. Janie pulled up to the curb as I pointed out the house. We got out and she drove away.

I examined the ivy climbing the house and I examined the weeds. I admired the lack of polish and the fact that I lived here once but not now. I phoned mom, to give warning. She still didn't answer.

I remember a basketball net that used to be here. I remember people being around and not around and a fire in the garage when I turned ten—birthday hijinx. And, of course, her garden. Her garden that won awards. She installed mirrors on the insides of the fence which reflected the light, more to look at, her work repeating. I thought back to the cops knocking on the door, praying they weren't looking for me as I watched them from the living room window—mom stomping from kitchen down the hallway to the front door. That was around the time she didn't want me back there anymore. 'What did you do now?', she'd said.

Being a kid doesn't last long.

The place looked ill. Then the rigger threw up on a small bed of wilting spearmint hydrangeas, his puke glowing. The colours accented one another. I walked to the door and knocked. Again, no one answered. I had the keys to the truck and could leave anytime, but it felt right to wait. She may have stepped out, though I knew she never would.

I closed my eyes and let the sun sit on me. The rigger flopped onto the long grass.

"Where are you going to go?" I said to him. "Now that you have nowhere to stay."

"Less is more." The rigger looked up from the hydrangeas. "Do you have gum?"

The heat wave didn't seem so bad.

After almost an hour I started up the truck and let it run for a few minutes, cooling the cabin. The rigger went around back to relieve himself and I'd said to finish off the rest of the hydrangeas. I thought maybe he got lost or needed me to clear a path, for old times' sake, and found him in mom's backyard staring through one of the backside windows that looked into the living room. He didn't say anything and so I looked, too. I saw a familiar set up: the floral sofas and chairs, old wood shelves with glass doors full of china and candle holders, the pristine white carpet and a TV older than me. The TV showed images of dogs and cats and a news reporter interviewing pet owners, always breaking news. The kennel looked familiar. Mom sat upright in a La-Z-Boy chair I didn't recognize. Forest-green leather that could be mistaken for black. Her lips and hands were pale, her body looked like it had been vacuumed of its colour and good light. I recognized the kennel on TV.

I drove as fast as possible. I drove faster than I ever had, pushing the engine to reach its top speed, thinking I'd be able to catch up to her, somewhere out there. I opened the small back window for air. The window led to the truck bed. I had the feeling of being followed. I could see Pinny back there, in the rear-view mirror, just her presence. I sped up. Pinny's perfect black shape unchanged in the mirror, her primitive limbs and crude black body weightless to me, planetary, a shining transmission. Always so fast. I thought to drive as fast as she could run, faster, even. Maybe I'd go back in time. The traffic lights came at me in streaks of green and yellow and red and then, with my eyes shifting from the road to the mirror, I could only look at that beautiful dog floating behind me. The heat wouldn't go away. I rolled down my window. I had to shout into the air, my head gone for good. *Out of the way*, I said. I slammed on the breaks, nearly hitting two men in a convertible. The tires squealed, producing black lines. I kept on. Faster now. I got the feeling of being surrounded, like all the dogs of the world were laying down again. No more machete, no more man. *Take me with you*, I said, I couldn't see straight, *ha ha ha*, take me with you, again and again, *please, girl*, I pleaded and I laughed, the master of deflection—through the windshield the outside world entirely headless and unstable and radioactive.

I arrived at the kennel well after the news vans and reporters and animal activists. I left the rigger in the backyard. Hated dogs, he'd said.

Reporters were multiplying.

"Care to comment on what's happened here?"

I ran from the truck, the engine hummed.

"The dogs were left unattended during a series of rolling black outs. A result of the heat wave. Sir, did you or someone you know have a dog here? I'd love to get a comment for channel six."

There were lots of people on the scene. No police or firefighters, one ambulance and paramedics. A pack of dogs had been drawn to the parking lot from the surrounding neighbourhood, lying in mourning on the steaming asphalt—dogs always knew. Their owners judged from the sidewalk. I couldn't remember if I'd checked my email. Phone had been dead. I pulled it out, read an unread message and let the thing drop to the pavement in pointlessness. I stood in the parking lot beside a massive Newfoundland, brown and panting, stretched out in the heat. The dog stared at the building with its tongue out. It reminded me of Pinny, the way she'd lie around so elegantly, too long and too tall to sit like a normal dog, even goofier looking in the bath, such a small place for her. She wasn't meant to be confined to such small spaces, though I think she liked it, *god*, she was something, my little alien.

I stretched out beside the panting Newfoundland and stared at the sun.

Afterwards, all the rigger said was that he was sorry about my dog. He never found a place to stay, so we made sure we were always on the go. I don't remember telling him to drive south with me, but that's what happened.

On the beaches, there were people and dogs and children playing around. I didn't pay them any mind. Instead, I watched the water come closer on its dark-blue treadmill. The rigger walked the shorelines. When I closed my eyes, blackness folded toward me.

I never could say how I felt.

Spencer Oakes *is a technical writer from Saskatoon. In his free time, he runs* Helmet Books *and plays in the band* PC Dagg. *His fiction has appeared in* Blue Moon *and* Geist. *He's also working on a novel. Of* Machete Man, *he says, "I don't have a dog. I started writing this story by imagining what that might be like."*

To Alex

Antoine Robertson

To Alex,

Today we rode the shuttle together again. The bus jostled, and your hand brushed against my thigh.

To Alex,

Today was the big game against Trinity. You played very well. You got hit really hard during one of the plays, but you got right up. I think later you went to the medic. Whatever it was, you were fine. I asked you if you were hungry after you got home from celebrating with the team. You said you were *good*, in that slurred way you get when you're drunk. You took off your clothes, crawled under the throw blanket my sister gifted me freshman year and went to sleep on the couch.

To Alex,

Today, you wore a pull-over polo shirt, unbuttoned. Tufts of hair on your chest peaked through. We were talking over breakfast, and I purposefully did not look at you. I stared into my bowl of flakes, avoiding getting lost in how amazing I find you. If I had looked up at you, I would not have been able to hide my admiration.

To Alex,

Tonight, we went out to celebrate the end of the semester.

We drank. A lot. You drank more than me. I said something, I don't remember. But whatever it was, you laughed uncontrollably, landing your head in my lap. You didn't move it right away. In fact, for what seemed like time stopping altogether, you let your head rest there while my hand fell over your muscular shoulders. And in that moment—however long it lasted—I could feel you exhale. As if you were breathing for the first time; letting go and giving up. And I was there, catching you. You picked your head up, gave me a hug, and went into your bedroom, closing the door behind you.

We didn't need to say anything, but we both knew: I am your best friend, a safe place. And if you could be weak anywhere, with anyone, it was here with me.

To Alex,

Today, me, you, Candace, and Nichelle took a drive out to the beach house we rented for a couple of days as the summer started. I shared my bed with Nichelle; you and Candace shared the upstairs loft. You might have thought you were being quiet, but we heard you. Every kiss, every giggle, every breath and moan of ecstasy. You might have heard us too though. My Nicey doesn't mind being loud and expressive. But we are all close friends. I met you because of Nichelle and Candace. And now we are all inseparable. I don't mind if you hear me, see me, feel me, understand every minute and intimate detail of my life.

To Alex,

Today, the rain stopped, and it was sunny enough to finally make it onto the beach. You jumped into the slapping embrace of the Atlantic while Candy, Nicey, and I laughed from the shore. We wanted to bathe in the sun, or perhaps in the light of your contagious joy and boyish frivolity. You emerged from the rolling crests like a Greek deity, the sun beams dancing off of your shaved head, droplets of sea water ensnared in the strands of hair mapping your chest and abs, your swimming shorts clinging to the sculpted mass of your thighs like a dramatic flag in raging battle. I was glad for my shades, hiding my stare. I couldn't keep from staring, nor did I want to. The sounds of the ocean quieted, the sweltering heat subsided, and I took in every movement of your body like a slow-moving dance. Unashamed, un-recoiled, I devoured the sight of you like staining a memory into my head I never wanted to discard. My breath slowed, my skin tightened, blood rushed through me like a racing surge. I have felt this feeling before. This satisfying nervousness. This pleasing rise of trembling anticipation. It was the first time we hung out alone. You invited me back to your dorm after class. Because of the all-nighter I had pulled for the day's exam, I collapsed on your cheap department store futon, while you sat at your desk reading. You read and I quickly drifted to sleep. I had never done that before, fallen asleep in someone's room before. There must have been something instantly reassuring me, something allowing me to comfort myself in a strange environment that all pretense and precaution melted away in the resignation of your cool demeanor and confidence. I awoke, perhaps an hour and a half later, with you still at your desk reading. Just as calm, pensive and focused, just as resigned as I had left you before I began dreaming. At that sudden realization of trust and relief, I knew then the only feeling I could ever have for you would sprout from Love.

To Alex,

My therapist thought these series of letters would be of some help, somehow. That articulating my feelings would allow me to understand them better instead of bottling them up and stressing me out. Perhaps these words are meant to embarrass me or show how ridiculous I am being. I feel that too, of course. But the more I get the chance to think about what it is I am actually feeling, the more natural and unrepentant I am. Why can't I love my best friend?

You'll never get to read these words, of course. Or hear them escape from my mouth. These letters are not meant to be sent. Just written, just for me. Maybe God. And He definitely doesn't want you to know how I am feeling. These words, like my feelings, are meant to be expressed here alone, but never shared.

To Alex,

I think it is helping. Writing. I never thought much of myself as a writer. Do you remember the English class we took with Dr. Stockton sophomore year, and the creative writing midterm he thought was supposed to inspire us? It did little else than send me to the infirmary after a scary panic attack. I would have failed that class, lost my scholarship, and had to drop out of college if you hadn't finished my midterm for me. That's who you are to me. That's who you have been and will probably always be.

When everyone else sees me, they think it's all working out, that my life has smoothed out the cracks and nothing bothers me. Nicey once told me "I'm glad I can lean on someone so clear and confident about who they are."

Alex, you're the only one who has seen me pace our apartment floor, worried about getting rent in on time, or how I was going to afford getting back home after my mom got sick. You offered your car and drove with me the eight and half hours to Lake Charles to see her, all the while calling it a "boys' trip" to the girls. I remember that was the first time I sat through a full Jimi Hendrix album, and it was your first time hearing Jill Scott. We went back and forth between Zach Bryan and Musiq Soulchild, Robert Glasper and Bob Dylan. Not even Nicey can match my enthusiasm for music. She finds my taste all over the place, and she only likes the popular stuff. Your talent is appreciating a beautiful sound wherever you may find it.

Mom is doing a lot better by the way, and she always asks about you. "When you talk to Alex, tell him Mom says hi! And that we love him!"

To Alex,

We talked on the phone today. We talk just about every other day. But this time I could hear the excitement in your voice. Summer is coming to an end, school is about to start. Senior year! I am grateful for the break, but I will be glad to be back at school. I will be glad to see you soon. I am not taking as many classes this semester, because I have my internship. Nicey will fill much of my free time. But at least I can make more of your games this year. That is what I am most excited about. See you soon!

To Alex,

I love Nicey! I really do. We've been dating since high school. I remember how shocked I was that the hottest chick in school was hooking up with the school nerd. I didn't think we would last this long, but I can't imagine doing life without her. When we both got into the same college, we thought surely things would change, we would get tired of one another or lose each other in the crowd of horny teens awaiting fresh meat. Her freshman roommate was Candace, a spunky cheerleader from Ohio obsessed with this guy on the rugby team. Nicey at first couldn't stand the guy. He was smug, arrogant, and drank his coffee black, no creamer! "Who does that?! What are we, fifty?" That first semester Nicey would escape to my dorm room every night just to avoid Candace and her boyfriend. Until one day, I came to her dorm, and you were the only one to answer the door. Shirtless, as always, drinking a cup of black coffee.

"Hi, I'm Alex," you introduced yourself.

"Candace's boyfriend?" I asked, quietly laughing to myself, as you fit to the tee Nicey's description of you. My first impression was definitely that you were smug, arrogant, and desperate for admiration. I did not think we would get along. You were the jock from Mississippi who majored in business management, and I was the biomedical engineer student whose last time a ball was in his hand was when I had a presentation on VSEPR theory.

"Nichelle is your girl?" You asked slyly. "Yes," I replied, still reserving my repulsion.

"Lucky bastard!" You shot back. I was struck by my familiar pride of knowing that Nicey was attractive to just about every guy who met her. And though they wanted her, she wanted only me. As well as being equally offended. Who was this guy who would talk about my girlfriend who was his girlfriend's roommate? The balls!

You moved around the dorm room as if it were your personal living room, offering me a place to sit and to pour me a cup of coffee. It was three o'clock in the afternoon. I declined. I didn't notice then, but I can recall Chris Stapleton playing in the background.

You break the silence with, "Candace is probably on her way back from class. I don't know where Michelle is." Of course you wouldn't, she's *my* girlfriend.

"Nichelle." I correct you.

"My bad," you shrug.

I sat both awkward and irritated for what felt like an hour, as you swayed across the room, your veiny feet seemed to float about the floor in effortless strides. I looked at you like I would a graph or chart, decimating your frame and structure with skepticism and inquiry. The muscles in your back revealed curves and formations I had never known were anatomically possible for a guy my own age. Your calves and thighs were like etched marble. It wasn't attraction then. It was pure curiosity. I had to genuinely ask myself: "What made this guy so special?"

Then something happened. It was quick, fleeting. In the moment I did not understand the significance, but it was the one movement that took me off guard, eased my suspicions, and is perhaps what opened the floodgate to the whirlwind which has been our friendship ever since. You noticed my scrutinizing you, and you turned your head to meet my inspecting gaze. For that brief moment I met the depth of your blue eyes, drowned in whatever false bravado you had conjured for the less concentrated observer. And then you smiled, a slow turn of the corners of your lips, into a self-pleased and relieved expression.

"We're gonna see a lot of each other," you divined.

I laughed aloud. Perhaps nervously, perhaps knowingly. But something in the way you looked at me and the way I laughed relaxed us both. We began talking. The usual freshman questions: "Where are you from? What's your major? What dorm do you stay in?" We learned very quickly that we were from very different worlds.

"How did you get into rugby?"

"I got into it quickly once I found out there were no more football scholarships. I like it. They call me 'the Bulldozer'," you flex. I was impressed and recognized quickly as much as there was brawns, you also had brains. And big heart, though perhaps misunderstood.

That has been the stay of our friendship. In a world that tries to contain us and define us, I have been the only person to see you for all your sides, and you see me for all of mine. Even more than our girlfriends, there is something unique about the way we talk to one another, as if we have existed on another plane from another time with a language entirely our own. We couldn't have planned this or manufactured what would come from that first meeting. And ever since our closeness has been as natural as the rising sun or the change of the seasons.

To Alex,

I thought this would help. I thought putting these feelings down I could make sense of them and walk away with the words locked away in this unassuming composition book I keep wedged between my physics books. But it isn't. I see you now with frustrated anticipation. Wanting to reach out to touch you or hold a second longer when we hug. Your scent stays in my nose long after you have left a room, and your blue eyes haunt my dreams. Being your friend was once a comfort. Now, it is a torment.

To Alex,

We drank too much last night. You won your match, and I aced my electrophysiology exam. We were a week out from homecoming and decided to get an early start on the fun. I still wonder if it was the worst mistake we could have made… or the best.

Nichelle and Candace came over first to the apartment with the drinks. We took a couple of shots of tequila while blasting Doechii and Kendrick Lamar. The girls tossed their hair wildly in the winds of the music, while we laughed and reclined against the kitchen counter, watching them adoringly. I could catch you from the corner of my eye looking at me while you smiled.

"These are the best days of our lives!" you said.

"Oh gawd, you're so dramatic," I laugh.

"No really, this is what I came to college for. To have fun with people that I love and who love me. I don't think we'll have days like this again. And that's ok, because right now this is perfect. You're perfect. And I'm glad we will look back on these days and remember them together." You sounded like lyrics to a country song. I take a huge gulp of whatever concoction was in my red cup, nudge you, and then grab Nicey by the waist to dance.

People quickly filed in. Friends, classmates, some people we didn't even like, and even a handful of folks we didn't even know. We didn't care. We were all having a good time and our night was not to be disturbed by pettiness.

The night seemed to go on for hours, as if days had come and gone and we were all still in our apartment imbibing on our evanescent youth. We drank more, definitely. But I remember everything. And what I remember most was how my courage and anxiety clashed within me like raging waves on a shore of sharp rocks.

You found me in the bathroom staring at my reflection angrily. "Yo! What's wrong?" you asked, alarmed. "Nothing," I said.

"Are you sure? Is it your mom? Do we need to drive down again? I can clear everyone out, make some coffee to sober up. We can be on the road in thirty minutes tops." You spoke sternly, strongly, as if you were on a pitch organizing your teammates.

"I'm fine, bro," I insisted. You grabbed me by the shoulders and turned my face to look at yours. Then you smiled.

"You're drunk," you laughed. You bring me closer to embrace. "You're gonna be ok. I was worried for a minute though."

I melt in your arms, nestle my face in your neck, and I am sure I let out a single tear in that moment that felt like a lifetime.

"I think I want to talk to you about something, when we get a chance," I say, half muffled in the muscle of your neck.

You peel me off of you and again become serious. Looking me deep into my eyes again, you understood I was serious too and replied simply, "Ok." You give another hug and reassuring pat on the back and then walk out of the bathroom.

The rest of the night seemed to quickly come to a quiet. One by one, two by two, our guests waved their goodbyes and stumbled out of the door. Then by threes, and then the larger groups were the last to gather their belongings and exit. Leaving the original four hosts to look one to the other with satisfied exhaustion. Nicey at once undid her bra and allowed her breasts to bounce freely underneath her shirt. She took the hair tie from around her wrist and put her hair in a ponytail. She kissed me on her way to the kitchen to grab herself a drink of water before kissing me again on her way to the bedroom and whispering in my ear, "let's go to bed." I smile at her lovingly. Both with wantonness and sorrow, as if we were about to say our own goodbyes and walk into a night of unhappy endings.

Candy simply stood in the doorway of your room and winked at you, signaling you to follow her. You grin and say, "Tony and I are gonna clean up a little first." You look back at me assuring me that you have not forgotten the last thing I had said only about an hour or so ago. The ladies close the doors behind them, leaving you and me and a tide of red solo cups on the living room floor.

I go sit down on the couch. You remain planted, towering above me. "What's up?" you say softly. You are serious, attentive, and concerned. As if the guy taking body shots only some time ago had walked out with the rest of the rowdy rabble and standing before me was the friend that I knew would always find the right mind to come to my defense. "I won't try to guess what this is all about. But I can tell it's been bothering you for a while now. I've noticed. I didn't want to say anything, but I have definitely noticed."

In the silence you come and find a seat close to mine on the couch, patiently waiting for my response. I close my eyes and feel myself cowering behind the well of emotions I feel might swallow me like the whale did Jonah. You do not break your concentration, or the intensity of your concern. Just waiting.

I let out a sigh, "Bro… I love you."

"I love you too," you smile. But my silence confuses you, and you return to being concerned again.

"No, I love you," I corrected. "Like, I love you. Like in a way I'm not supposed to love you."

"Oh," you say in return. And then turn away. Perhaps to think about what I just said. Maybe how you want to tell me to find another roommate. Or maybe replaying our entire friendship in your head weirded out by how indistinguishably close we have become.

Maybe thinking about the time the heater broke in your room the first semester we had gotten the apartment and we had to share a bed for two months. Or the many times I have walked in the bathroom while you were in the shower. And junior year when we travelled to DC for student government and chose to share a hotel room and you masturbated in the bed next to mine while we talked about girls we both wanted to hook-up with. I masturbated too. We were best friends and that type of stuff didn't freak us out. But perhaps this will.

I know you must have been thinking about all those things, because over the past few months that's what I have been thinking about. Wondering if our entire friendship has been based on some sick obsession I have had for a guy I just wanted to spend my entire life loving.

The silence choked me like a thick ring of smoke. I could hear Nicey rustling beneath the sheets in the next room, like a rat in the walls searching in the blind night for scraps of food. I didn't dare break your concentration. I wouldn't rob you of whatever you felt was necessary to say, or do. I even braced myself for impact. In that moment I felt like the most deceptive person in the world, and I deserved for you to hit me.

You looked up at me with a confused look on your face, about to say something, but then you stopped yourself and sighed. I could see the water welling in the lids of your eyes. Not quite tears, but something was moving in you and you were trying to make peace with it.

"I love you too," you said in an almost inaudible tone. But I understood clearly because I stared as your mouth shaped the words I could not believe you were making. I sat like a gargoyle atop an abbey gateway, transfixed by fear and disorientation. You tried to say it again, but the look I gave you assured you that I heard you clearly the first time and didn't need you to repeat it.

"I don't know what this means," you admit, as you move closer.

"Neither do I," I say.

You look over your shoulder, making sure the door to your bedroom is closed. And then to my bedroom door, making sure we were in fact completely alone. You place your hand on my thigh, unlike the times on the bus, or in class. This time deliberately, gently. I move closer, never breaking eye contact from those two orbs of wintery blue.

I remember what your chest felt like against mine as your lips pressed against mine. I remember the bread-y taste of beer on your breath. I remember you closed your eyes while I peaked through mine to make sure I wasn't fantasizing again. I remember feeling the scratchy stubble of your chin as we pulled apart. I had thought about this moment for some time- how it might feel, how I might feel. I have woken up in puddles of my own making dreaming about what one kiss from you could do to me.

What would happen next? Would everything begin to make sense instantly? Would we pledge ourselves to one another and plan a world tour of Pride parades during the month of June? What would happen to me and Nichelle? What would happen to Nichelle?

What I thought would feel like relief turned to instantaneous grief. Sensing my angst you held me tightly. You rested your

244

forehead against mine, closed your eyes, got up, and went into your room.

To Alex,

I have not seen your face in a full week. Which is pretty impressive, considering we are roommates. Mornings, you are gone before I can make it to the kitchen. Around campus I capture glimpses of your dashing from one end of the quad to the next, entering buildings you never have before, talking to classmates you'd usually rather ignore. At night, I don't even wait up. I know you'll keep yourself well passed rugby practice, and clomp into the apartment after 1am.

I'm sorry. I just couldn't hold it in any longer. I just couldn't keep this secret to myself anymore. I see now I was only being selfish by passing my burden on to you instead.

I told Nicey that I needed some time to focus on grad school applications, and we haven't seen each other in the same amount of time that you have been avoiding me.

I'm sorry.

To Alex,

We talked today. You found me at home in the early part of the evening, when I thought I would have the apartment to myself while you were at practice. You found me wiping away tears with my textbooks pushed away from me. How can I study when there is still so much on my mind, and no friend to talk to me about it. You found me smoking marijuana while listening to Donny Hathaway.

You politely close the door behind yourself, and calmly place your book-bag by the coat closet. "We should talk." It was like hearing the crisp opening of an ice-cold beer bottle. I wiped my face, put out my joint, and lazily walked into the room where the crime we committed took place. I made sure not to sit in the same place, but instead in the place you had been while you found your seat in the place I had been.

This time you did not let silence dominate the conversation.

"I'm sorry," you begin

"I'm sorry too!" I jutted out loudly.

"Wait," you say gently, "I'm sorry. I should not have kissed you. Not that I didn't want to, I think it's not who I am. It's not who we are. I'm your friend, and you're my best friend. And I want to make the world the best for you. I wanted to be whatever you needed me to be, because I do love you. I just don't love you in the same way."

I don't take long to respond, because I know exactly how I feel. "I want you in my life for as long as I have a life. I want to experience every great thing with you by my side, and all the not so great things with you by my side. You are my best friend, and any way you love me is the best way."

I don't remember what else we could have said to each other. I don't think it made any difference. I didn't need my friend to be anything but my friend, and so long as we could be that for each other, I was satisfied.

At some point we ordered a pizza and watched tv. We laughed and clowned each other and gossiped about the party as if nothing had happened before, as if that terrible week was just one of a bunch of misunderstandings that we would eventually iron out along the way.

I guess that's the way it is with guy friends sometimes: so long as we know we are each other's friend, the other stuff isn't as important. It'll work itself out. In the meantime, we will be okay.

We laugh well pass midnight, flipping through channels, talking over our favorite shows about music. At one point you look over to me with a wide smile and say,

"I will forever be your friend."

To Alex,

I haven't written one of these letters in four years now. Today is my wedding day. Nicey is walking down the aisle, and I can't help but let a few tears douse my face. She told me only two weeks ago that she is pregnant. And I am the happiest man alive! Our relationship wasn't always easy. My first year of grad school we even broke up for a couple of months. But I knew, as confidently as I know anything else, she's the one I want to be my wife.

You are standing beside me. My Best Man. You pat me on the back as I place the wedding band on her finger. I understand now what you meant back in college. I get to do life with the people that I love and who love me.

If the baby is a boy, Nichelle and I have agreed we will name him Anthony Alexander.

And there it is, my present and my past coming together, awaiting whatever the future may hold. And whatever the future holds, I know, as confidently as I know anything else, you will be my friend.

Love Always,
Tony

Antoine Robertson *is the proud son of Jamaican and Scottish immigrants born and raised in Nashville, Tn. Robertson has only recently followed his passion for creative writing with his first published work here in this anthology. A graduate of the University of Georgia, he now lives in the Atlanta metro area and splits his time between reading J.R.R. Tolkein, spending time with family and friends, and nature walks. Of* To Alex *he writes, "I wanted to write a story I would want to read about the varying depths of male friendship."*

Running

Simon Johnson

In January, Nick's brother crashed his car and put himself in the hospital. Simple. Either of us could have predicted it would happen. That's just the way Nick's brother was. Inevitable. Nick and I stopped driving together for a while afterwards. Both of us got nervous. I became caught up in work and school, making excuses so that I did not have to mention what had happened, not capable of betraying feelings so cryptic and raw. We were the castaways and stray survivors of a tarred and metallic storm. With us came the flotsam of guilt.

Both of us worked office jobs. I managed mine between classes, and every day I sorted papers, blending white on white and filing yellow sheets littered with black marks I was not allowed to read. I lived downtown in a small apartment two floors above the office I worked in. I did not pay for heating or cooling and I bore the seasonal extremities with veiled stoicism. I told myself that this was the process of character. I said I was partaking in the Buddhist tradition of suffering to achieve growth. I sustained myself with intellectual farces. I was miserable at my home and job. My mind atrophied until I could no longer stand the mire of town. Then I would leave to drive backroads alone and empty. Wondering what it would be like to lose control as Nick's brother had. To crash into the locust or sycamore trees at sixty miles an hour. Wondering if it would matter.

I think Nick felt alone, too. Through the winter and spring he visited his brother in the hospital and worked and fixed his truck. He spent every Wednesday and Sunday evening at church, his knees folded against the cold, rigid pews. Still, there was a staleness of living. A terrifying stagnation into routine. Between us was the crash, a bothersome haze of uncertainty. And so we drove, the two of us separated by fear and by change. We drove fast and hard. We did not think about school or work or life or death—we drove.

The summer that year was hot in the way all Eastern Oregon summers are hot. It was hot enough to cause mirages on the road that weaved and shimmered like boiling engine coolant. It was hot enough to melt the creosote between the asphalt and make it gum up and stick to your shoes. The carcasses of roadkill cooked and festered on the sides of the road, laced with flies and maggots, drying into leather tack boards patchy with fur.

I was driving, taking recourse from the acrid heat, the nihilism of office hours and directionless classes. I whipped my pickup through open fields and collections of homes clotted together at the base of the mountains. Passing silver grain silos and stark farmhouses, the rusted frames of derelict combines and skeletal wheat conveyors, thickets of tangled blackberries and the creek beds where no animal dared stir in the onslaught heat of noon. It was a place where nothing happened.

I found the old Miata on a washboard road that led to nowhere. Abandoned at the boundary of loose gravel and packed dirt beside an old hoarder's property. The Miata sat immobilized, the lifeless effigy of a vehicle. The tires sank flat into the thistle patches and torrents of desert sun had baked and split the soft top until it would not close properly. The oil leaked and caked up on the engine block like burnt gruel, the gravel below glistening in rainbow polychrome and the dirt gumming into a bog of tar. Once-black paint had faded into sunbursts of gray. Rust pierced the body and the metal sheath of the car could be dissected into each ferrous layer. The car was being sold for cheap.

I drove back down to the highway and called Nick. It was the type of car that I thought he would like, sporty and iconic, something he could throw around without worrying about. I knew Nick would still be cagey about cars, cagey about me maybe, but he picked up.

"I found a Miata. It's for sale cheap on Sumac Road. You should buy it."

"Why don't you buy it?" Nick asked.

"Because you have the money."

Nick thought.

"Let me take a look."

Nick bought it the next week. He trailered it to his garage and it clattered to the ground when we let loose the chains. It was a piece of shit and we loved it. We put on new tires, the cheapest performance tires that Nick could find. He bought a fresh soft top and the two of us cranked on it, bending it to our vision. We changed old bolts and we greased spinning parts. We ran the engine, making sure that the motor would turn over and the pistons would fire without exploding us. I put my ear to the hood and absorbed the car. I closed my eyes and let the engine rattle me, listening for imperfections in combustion. Letting the spirit of the engine strangle my own and force the whole rest of the world to disappear.

The car started to look alive again. I was ready to drive it, I told Nick.

"I drove it the other day," he said. "It's a little shaky, but it feels balanced."

"Without me?" I asked him. Then, "do you think you can track it?"

"I wouldn't." He walked to the other side of the garage and sorted the tools. "I still don't trust it. Maybe after looking through the engine, replacing the brakes and suspension. But I don't know."

We took the Miata out that evening and we rumbled through the wheat fields with the car clamoring and just holding together between the faded paint and rust and the places where the body was corroded away.

Driving was an old tradition between Nick and I. We drove together once after the crash. On an overcast day in March we took Nick's truck to the mountains, driving through the snow of late winter and the runoff creeks of early spring. Our conversation was broken, the tires whirred across the wet roads and the wind buffeted over the grille, neither of us quite sure what to say or how to speak. I was at the wheel.

"I think I'll move next fall," he told me as I turned onto an old highway. "I visited a school on the east coast last month. I'm applying."

The road was drying from rain and as we drove steam lifted from it in the rare winter sun. In places the road was a makeshift waterway where the plowed snow banks melted and ran. The vapor and water danced in front of us and parted, lifted, as the truck swept past.

"Shit, Nick. What are you studying?"

"It's a seminary. I'll be a priest."

I adjusted past the intestines of a dead squirrel that had been scattered across the road.

"You, a priest?"

"I thought you might not take it seriously."

"No, no. Seminary sounds like a good place for you. Enlightening."

"I think so. The people there were smart and sophisticated. They talked philosophy. They all read a bunch."

Nick and the academics. I found myself irritated by the notion, frustrated by the idea that he could substitute the presence of others for mine. Their intelligence became an abstract threat to my own. I was an asshole that way.

"I'm sure they're smart enough," I told Nick. "But when you get to the truth of it, no one knows anything, really. College students especially think that they do, but no. Take me for example. I'm a charlatan. Everyone's a charlatan."

The mist of the road contorted all around us. I ran over a flattened pine bough that had fallen inside the white line.

"Think about morality. Everyone has their little take on it, but no one is right," I kept postulating. "Nobody *lives* their morals anymore."

I missed the downshift into a corner and braked too late. I barely carried us out of the curve and hit the gas again. Nick held on and squinted. He didn't say anything about the poor driving.

"I'm Catholic," said Nick. "You know that, and I see people living good, moral lives every day. You sound jaded. Nihilistic. I guess that tracks from an atheist."

I laughed. "Don't accuse me of nihilism. Anything but! I'm a moralist."

"So, sorry," said Nick, "and you live your morality?"

I didn't know where I was taking us. I kept hammering through the turns, sinking the tires into the cambered asphalt, wheels like the hooves of a thoroughbred. The next junction was still miles ahead and I did not think about it or prepare for the decision. I just drove.

"The East Coast is awfully far away," I said.

Nick buying the Miata was a release for both of us that summer. It gave us a focus, a bond. One last thing to create. We spent our nights in the garage doing maintenance on the car. We tuned the engine and we replaced broken parts, greasing our hands and blackening our shirts and emerging late in the night, dirty and tired and joyous.

I asked Nick how his brother was as he grabbed cans of soda out of the garage fridge.

"He's better. His leg is healing, I think he'll be up and about soon."

"Good. It was bound to happen though, with how he drives. So reckless, the dumbass."

Nick traced his thumb around the rim of his can and took one cold drink, then another.

"You don't really understand," he said.

"There isn't much to understand," I said. "He was going too fast and he crashed."

"But in what world do you get to criticize someone's driving? You don't even know where you're going half the time. You're a reactive. Never have I met someone with less initiative."

"Look, I tried to help, okay."

Nick picked up an empty parts box and began bifurcating its seams. He discarded the packing and sliced at the tape with his nails. "You didn't see him. You didn't even call."

He flattened the box and let it fall.

I walked to the sink and washed my hands, thinking that perhaps the soap would lift more than just the grease from my skin.

The old plumbing gurgled and coughed. At the level of my head and lungs, the infumed atmosphere of the shop curdled, sour and acrid like a musty liquor. I turned to the open bay of the garage with my towel and stood in the foyer of space between the empty night and the car. The two of us drank, hesitant to say anything more in the confines of our shame. The light of the moon shriveled over us and space constricted into discomfort.

Nick spoke first. "Have you ever had a thought that you can stand behind?" he asked. "Something without the slightest trace of hypocrisy? Something that encapsulates the entire rest of your life? Because the most important fucking thing in the world could come to you, and you have to do it. It's imperative! I guess you've never felt responsibility like that, though."

"I'm not sure what you mean."

"It doesn't matter. You didn't even visit." His words fizzed in the aspic air of the shop.

"Nick, I know. I've thought about him, though. And I haven't stopped thinking about it. The reasons for it. Why he put himself in the hospital just by driving down a backroad. Can you explain that?" I asked. "Tell me."

Nick paced between the car and the garage door. His feet fell quietly on the brushed concrete. He said, "I guess I drive because I need to. Something about the power, the control. The freedom, maybe."

I tossed my towel into a heap on the garage floor and smelled my hands, still seeped in oil and grease.

"It's been on my mind, but I can't find an answer. I'm driving and I'm burning the shit out of the atmosphere. I'm murdering trees and the noise of the car is probably fucking with the birds, but I love it. It's terrible."

"I don't think love necessitates goodness," said the future priest. "But I don't know. Like you say, I don't know anything. Nobody knows anything. I just get a sense that sometimes what we need, or feel we need, can conflict with what we feel is right. I could be way off, but there's a balance to it."

He looked down and crumpled his can. We stood there, the two of us watching out over the rolling hills in the night and the nocturnal animals and insects croaking, but we did not share anything more. We watched as the horizon grew into black and shuttered us from the world. The only light left was that of the garage and the moths filed toward it and fluttered hopelessly.

"You know," Nick spoke. "I'm going to have to sell the Miata before I leave."

"That'll be a shame. It's a good car, for what it is."

"It's been good to us, but it's just a Miata."

It was just a Miata, a car. And cars rust. The iron of their chassis a testament to their impermanence. The burning oil and fuel a reflection of decay and degradation. The miles under their wheels, translated to analog on the odometer, like the hours logged on paychecks. Never enough, always too small, too fleeting. All of these things an entropy of place. It was July and the days were hot and long. We worked and we reposed into dour habit. In the evenings we drove the Miata with the top down and still the heat baked us. We escaped our homes, our town. We lost ourselves in the speed of grain fields and rolling hills and under the lifeless towers of windmills. Together, we drove.

One time after the crash, deep in February, I went with Nick to see his brother in the hospital. It was snowing without wind, and the flakes thickened the air and held it together like starch in water. Through the blizzard, the red luminescence of the emergency sign became dull and effete. We drove into the parking lot and my mind was so lost in the storm that I killed the engine. The engine reignited with a damp sputter and we sat there, the two of us, a veneer of idling exhaust coating us in the cab like a soft weighted blanket, laden with apathy. And for a moment, in the warmth of the cab between the snow, I thought that I may never have to confront another thing in my entire life. But Nick opened his door and the cold buffeted me. The snow fell into the cab, melting before it could reach me, evaporating into thin air. When Nick left for the hospital I did not follow. I sat at the wheel of the idle truck and refused to believe that past or future existed. They became entwined in a cosmic field of bleary hallucination and they faded into indistinction and then nothingness. I refused to believe in anything except for the present moment. I was incapable of decision and motion. And, alone in the truck and trembling for the cold, I became fearful. The snow fell across the windows and I became afraid, desperately afraid over things that I had yet to encounter or even know.

And then, before either of us are able to stabilize ourselves in the world well enough to gain bearing, it is the end of August and we are driving before it is dark and the light has been stripped away.

Nick and I are side by side, driving in that old Miata with the black paint all chipped and the loose shift stick that keeps unscrewing and the interior that may fall apart at the next bump, but we are unbothered with these things. We are unbothered with the world right now, and perhaps we are incapable of caring about anything at all in this moment except for the car and the road and the setting sun. We both know that Nick will sell the car soon. That he has to. He will consign it to the rust of scrap yards and the battery of the sun. The pistons will decay as the tires char and crack and even the windshield will be shattered. But Nick is smiling and for now the engine is strong and it is clean and other than the lifter tick that takes off at three and a half thousand rpm nothing is wrong in the universe.

This road winds and Nick takes each corner confidently and he is fast. The creek is below us. It cuts its way through settled loess and loose soil. Everything in these rolling hills is held together by the roots of sagebrush and tall hemlock weeds and xeric locust. The dry dirt held together out of necessity and belief, and the hills do not slump or landslide. There is no water in the creek, not even for the deer or the pheasant, and the ponds are full of algae and scum and this is August. The hills to the driver's side are ripe with wheat and I look for deer coming out with the dusk but I do not see anything. The driver is considering the road and he is smiling as the yellow stripes flash below the old car. We share forced grins and show each other that we have forgotten all outside circumstance, careful to avoid talking because to talk would be to admit a future, to expose vulnerability.

Nick takes every corner fast and I hold on. I reach for the handle and I pray because if we flip or careen or ramrod into the hillside, that's it. The top is down and the breeze is life sustaining, but there is not a thing between our upturned heads and the road. When the car flips there will not be a thought behind it. Just a pair of ink stains on the road, meaningless as the twitching corpse of a gray squirrel or possum, bodies drying into leather tack boards on the road. But Nick holds the steering wheel with an arrogant nonchalance and he does not seem to mind or even think about those things. We never slow down.

Perhaps it is because we are too brave. We are brave and we are youthful, but we are also good and we know the road. Know it so well that we brake late into each turn and we cross the double yellow without a thought. Everything is calculated. Brake late, heel-toe, throttle, throttle. There are no other cars on the road and for a moment we achieve true freedom, and there never has been any-thing like that in history, not for Alexander nor Khan nor Musa. Nothing so powerful and so unrestricted. Nothing so pure.

Nick takes all of the turns fast but he brakes too late into the sharpest corner and the wheels slip and I know that that is it. Nick's hands tighten and each muscle in his arms tenses. He makes micro adjustments on the wheel and his focus elevates and the wheels have slipped. Nick's mouth is tight, his eyes sharp, and I can see the creek bed below us and it is coming toward us fast. The breeze is washing sideways over our heads and the black locust trees along the creek are grasping at us with their crooked branches and the wheels have slipped. But Nick has talent. He's better than me and he saves it like nothing at all and he keeps driving, faster and faster.

Even then, I do not panic. There is a faith between us and it goes unspoken. It is a different sort of faith, not the type that you pray for, and it is not clear either. This faith of old friends is like the Columbia River. Dark and silty. Rotten basalt cliffs on either side, choppy white waves abounding. Lumbering below the surface, persistent and strong. We do not mention it.

The sun is setting over the wheat and the hills and it is almost time to light the pop-up headlights but we savor the dying sun. Quail flush in the draw below us. A pheasant croaks but our ears have been conquered by the engine and we do not hear it. The sagebrush and the willows and the tall prairie grasses settle from the day. We do not talk and the sky is alpine blue trending bloodstained violet. We are driving toward the river and toward its lifeless cliffs, all desolate and proud and mournful. It will be dark when we get there and we are fine with that because at these speeds everything means nothing. We are beyond even relativity now and we know that the light will find us instead.

Nick downshifts just to hear the sound and I grin when the engine laughs in the innocent way only a Miata can. We are really going now. A hundred miles an hour. Not a soul within fifteen miles. Nick is relaxed. I grip and hang on to the car as we take the corners twice the posted speed and it really does feel like flying but the tires stay true to the road. It is just the two of us and the car and the setting sun and we drive to the big river as the moths come out and the bats alight in the high beams and we drive toward the dusk, everything passing us by so fast, everything coming toward us.

We find the river in darkness and the world is black save the dim lights of power outposts reflecting between the shores. The car is singing over the road and the wind is cool and Nick is smiling for it. The wheels twirl and the car and the road and the two of us are all hopelessly entwined and it is like we are dancing. A swing and a pavane. Partners being exchanged and lost and found again. Nick is enamored with the road in the night, and I feel that he has forgotten that the day must come. Forgotten that over and over the day will fire upon this scene where nothing changes and nothing happens. Even after Nick sells the car and leaves, the day will come. But the road curves away from the big river long before then and we leave it behind, still yearning for something, and we drive. Faster and faster, no end in mind.

God do we drive.

Simon Johnson *is a student from Eastern Oregon. In his free time, he skis, rock climbs, and reads. He likes adventuring and getting lost in Oregon's mountains. His work has appeared in* Oregon East. *He writes* The Effusion *on Substack (@simonljohnson). Of* Running, *he writes, "Unsurprisingly, I've spent lots of time driving a Miata around Eastern Oregon, and that acted as a conduit to explore the challenges faced by these boys during their coming-of-age."*

Daiquiri

R. A. Hinkle

"I'll have a daiquiri. Two of them," I tell him.

"Frozen?" The bartender asks.

"Jesus Christ, man. No." I say, "The way Hemingway drank them. Double rum, no sugar. And I want the freshly squeezed lime puck tossed in there. Not a wedge."

I stumbled through the sand. A daiquiri in each hand. The sweating plastic cups fighting my grip.

"Can you believe this place? Hemingway's home and they can't make a proper daiquiri on the whole island." I sat by Loon, who was thinking he should be out on that boat, sails up, catching the wind. "We'd be men like him killing safari animals if we didn't have microplastics in our balls."

"Yeah." Loon sipped through the slim cocktail straw. His face puckered.

"Don't you think? Doesn't he make you want to go to Africa and kill something monstrous?"

"Monstrous? No. Makes me sad to think about it."

"What does?" I took a big swig of my drink. It hit me like a wave. Too much lime. That bartender was an amateur. I was getting to muttering this to Loon, but I guess he was answering my question.

"Killing those animals. I'd catch a big fish." He paused. "I feel like an animal sometimes when I'm driving down the road alone."

"What other animal you know drives a car?"

"That's the ridiculous part. Not that animals don't drive cars, but that we do."

He was always saying weird shit like that. "You know what's sad?" I asked.

"What's that?"

"Hemingway offed himself before the Camaro came out."

"If I had all the money I could need, I'd have a '68 Camaro. Black with white stripes, and it would be loud. That's a manly car."

"That's right." I nodded and took a small sip of my drink.

"They say the Mustang is going electric soon. Hybrid, too, but nothing fully combusted. Those batteries are destroying the planet."

"Who says?"

"You haven't heard about the batteries? The mines? The waste? Christ, man!"

"Not the batteries—the Mustang. Who said that?"

"Just something I heard."

"It's the plastic that bothers me. Even the steering wheels and brakes. All in the air. Right in your balls, too."

"Yeah."

Loon downed the rest of his daiquiri. I followed. The baking sun had done its work on the drink. It sat on my stomach like swamp water. I muscled to keep it down.

Loon's beach chair creaked beside me. He leaned on his elbow and looked me over.

"You're looking a little burnt, Monty."

"No. I forgot to take my blood pressure pill is all. I'll be tan tomorrow."

"And wrinkly." He leaned back in his chair, chest wide and open and covered in monochrome hair.

I watched the sailboat for a bit, but it soon disappeared beyond the horizon. A warmth bore inside me that outmatched the sun. Heavy drops of sweat gathered on my upper lip; I could feel it as a sheen across my forehead.

This was it, my origin story. I lifted my hand and saw how the perspiration glistened as it built. Sweat-Man. What a hero I would be.

I felt drunk for the first time in a long time. Alcohol made me tired these days. I didn't know why I drank anymore. But I felt good. Dizzy, almost. An elated loopiness.

Loon was a good pal. He was always there. The boat was gone and the sun would be setting, but Loon was there. I realized then that I loved that man. I looked at him. He had a stupid grin on his face. The homo must love me back. Marriage finally made sense. And I knew also why friends had no need for marriage. Not to one another. Friendship was too sacred.

"You want another daiquiri, Loon?"

"Yessir."

"What kind?"

"Strawberry."

"Frozen?"

"Yeah. Frozen."

R. A. Hinkle *is a truck driver from Middle Georgia. In his free time, he rides motorcycles and officiates weddings. He is the author of* Reason to Be, *a novel. Currently he writes his 'Trucker's Journal' on Substack (@treyhinkle). Of* Daiquiri, *he says, "I wrote this story to explore the intimacy of two old friends watching the world they knew pass away."*

Thank you to the writers who made this book possible.

**BAD CLOWN
BOOKS**

Bad Clown Books is an independent publisher of cool books, new and old. Check out what we are publishing next on our socials:

Substack: @badclownbooks

Instagram: @badclownbooks

badclownbooks.com

www.ingramcontent.com/pod-product-compliance
Lightning Source LLC
Chambersburg PA
CBHW032009150726
47990CB00005B/1900